SOMETHING EXPLODED IN THE SKY . . .

. . . something metallic, something swirling, something from Hell. Four dark beasts filled the southeastern horizon like the lions of the Apocalypse. The reflection of morning light off the sand splayed like blood across their wings . . .

Startled from the half-daze of the monotonous watch, the sentry grabbed his rifle and flung himself against the sand-filled bags at the front of the trench. It took a moment for his brain to register the fact that the planes were coming from the south and not the north—they were friends, not foes. The thick canisters of death slung beneath their wings were not meant for him.

"What the hell are those?" he asked his companion as the planes roared over their positions.

The other soldier laughed. "You never saw A-10 Warthogs before?"

"They're on our side?"

"You better pray to God they are."

═ H O G S ═

GOING DEEP

JAMES FERRO

BERKLEY BOOKS, NEW YORK

HOGS: GOING DEEP

A Berkley Book / published by arrangement with
the author

PRINTING HISTORY
Berkley edition / May 1999

The Penguin Putnam Inc. World Wide Web site address is
http://www.penguinputnam.com

ISBN: 0-425-16856-5

BERKLEY®
Berkley Books are published by The Berkley Publishing Group,
a division of Penguin Putnam Inc.,
375 Hudson Street, New York, New York 10014.
BERKLEY and the "B" logo
are trademarks belonging to Penguin Putnam Inc.

PRINTED IN THE UNITED STATES OF AMERICA

10 9 8 7 6 5 4 3 2 1

Prologue

The desert stretched without borders, without anything but heat and pink light. It lay as it had lain for thousands of years: silent, undisturbed, impenetrable.

And then came the roar.

It started as the somber rattle from the back of a dying man's throat. The next second a hurricane pounded the air, whipping sand and stone in fury.

Then something infinitely worse exploded in the sky, something metallic, something swirling, something from Hell. Four dark beasts filled the southeastern horizon like the lions of the Apocalypse. The reflection of morning light off the sand splayed like blood across their wings, vengeance glistening against their seething muscles. Their stiff, muscular bodies profaned the pink flesh of the horizon, bringing fire and damnation.

Startled from the half-daze of a monotonous watch, the sentry grabbed his rifle and flung himself against the sand-filled bags at the front of the trench. It took a moment for his brain to register the fact that the planes were coming from the south and not the north—they were friends, not foes. The thick canisters of death slung beneath their wings were not meant for him.

"What the hell are those?" he asked his companion as the planes roared over their positions.

The other soldier laughed. "You never saw A-10 Warthogs before?"

"They're on our side?"

"You better pray to God they are."

PART ONE

THE LUCKIEST DEAD MAN

1

"Get into the damn cursor now!" Doberman shouted at the fuzzy shadow in the corner of his infrared targeting screen. He pushed all of his 120 pounds against the A-10A's seat harness, as if his body's momentum might somehow improve his aim—or help hold the target steady. But the huge dish of the Iraqi ground intercept radar station continued to slosh around in the screen, refusing to lock. Doberman blamed the wind and clouds, cursed his adrenaline, and kept his hands glued to the controls as he pushed below twelve thousand feet, his only aim in life to blow a good hunk of Iraqi early-warning hardware to Hell where it belonged.

Outside the bubble cockpit, Devil Two's straight, stubby wings cut through the thick air, balanced perfectly by several thousand pounds of ordnance. The Hog's twin GE TF34 turbofans, mounted above the fuselage like Flash Gordon's rocketpack, pushed the nose of the dark green warplane faster and faster toward the gristly sand of the desert.

From a distance, the A-10A looked a bit like a winged pickup truck headed for disaster.

Up close, it looked like a weathered two-by-four loaded for bear.

Inside the cockpit, Doberman narrowed his eyes until he saw only the television screen in the top right-hand corner of his instrument panel. Slaved to the infrared seeking device in the nose of his air-to-ground Maverick AGM-65G missile, the display provided the pilot with a heat picture of the ground below him. Finally, it glowed radar dish; he locked, drew a half-breath, and clicked the trigger. Devil Two kicked slightly as the missile whipped out and up from beneath her wing. The pilot caught a glimpse of the Maverick's exhaust and stared at it, momentarily entranced by his first launch in combat. He snapped back to attention, thumbed another missile up, and pointed the A-10A's nose in the direction of what ought to be a long metal trailer jammed with radar equipment. He launched, then rolled up another one.

No matter how much you trained for combat, no matter how refined the lines and arrows on the maps, real life blurred past you like a freight train flinging itself down a ravine. Doberman barely realized what he was doing, pushing buttons and talking to himself, searching his front windscreen for his next target. Forever and forever passed. Every curse known to man failed to get the stinking thing to show up. Altitude kept bleeding away. Captain Thomas "Doberman" Glenon mashed his teeth together, his face gnarling into the unflattering pose that had helped earn him his nickname. He was ready to concede he'd lost his way when something clicked in his head; without conscious thought he pulled the trigger. In the next moment the Maverick went whoosh-bam-thank-you-ma'am, flinging its three hundred pounds of high explosive toward an Iraqi radar trailer.

Less than a minute had passed since he had begun his bombing run, but it had seemed like a lifetime. The plane was already low enough to draw serious antiair fire. He kicked his head back and got ready to take some Gs.

Flying in Devil Four, Lieutenant William James "BJ" Dixon was late eyeballing his target area, late putting his eyes over to the Maverick screen. Everything was coming at him twenty times faster than it should. The fact that he'd practiced this attack several times over the past few days didn't matter, and the abilities that had helped him rate among the best pilots at every stage of his training seemed to have deserted him. His head felt like a hand grenade with the pin removed. His arms and legs moved in heavy oil. The Hog growled at him, yelling at the pilot to get his shit together. No drill instructor had a meaner snarl.

Dixon glanced down at his hand, aware that he was squeezing the control stick hard enough to bend metal. He couldn't unclench. The plane jerked toward the ground, propelled by the tension in his arms and legs.

His main target was a tropo-scatter communications tower not far from the radar dish his flight leader had hit. His eyes darted from the windscreen to the television, back and forth, waiting for the shadowy finger to appear. Finally, he saw something in the tube and pushed the trigger to lock and fire in practically the same motion. As the missile burst away, he worried that he hadn't locked up on the right target—the screen had been a blur and he'd only picked the biggest shadow. Quickly, he put another Maverick on line, yelling at himself to study the screen more carefully, trying to narrow the world down to the small tube and its depiction of the target area. But too much was happening—he'd drifted off course and now overcorrected, and if the tower was still there it wouldn't appear anywhere in the screen. Finally, he saw a squat shadow he recognized as a radar van, slid the cursor in for a lock, and fired.

Glancing up at his windscreen, he realized he had gone lower than planned—a hell of a lot lower.

The altimeter read two thousand feet.

Dixon yanked the stick back, jerked it for dear life, his whole body trembling with panic.

Doberman returned to twelve thousand feet, reorienting himself to continue the attack. While he'd practiced mid-altitude bombing a lot in the last few weeks, he still felt vaguely uneasy attacking at this altitude. Nor was he used to going after something so placid, though well protected, as a radar installation—officially an "early warning ground control intercept station," GCI for short. The Hog's "normal" mission was close-in troop support and tank busting, and if it had been all the same to Doberman, he would have spent this first day of the air war against Iraq cruising about fifty feet off the ground and blowing up recycled Russian armor near the Saudi border. But the GCI stations located deep within Iraq were an important part of the enemy air defenses; taking them out was critical to the success of the allied air plan. The fact that such an important job had been given to Hogs meant that the Air Force brass in Riyadh had finally realized how capable the slow but steady low-altitude attack planes really were.

That, or they were desperate.

On the bright side, the mission planners had given them pictures and everything, as if they were Stealth fighters. And as his friend Shotgun had said yesterday: Draw a little snout on a trailer and it practically looks like a tank, so what's the big deal?

Keying the mike to ask his wingman, Lieutenant Dixon, how his Maverick run had gone, Doberman spotted a command building through the broken layer of clouds below. It was the last of his primary targets, and too fat and juicy to pass up. He glanced quickly to the Maverick targeting screen, found the building, locked it tight, and kissed it good-bye. As the missile clunked off the wing rail, the pilot put his eyes back to the windscreen and spotted two trailers within a few hundred feet of each other, looking for all the world like the photo he'd memorized before the mission. With his Mavericks gone, he was down to the dumb stuff—six cluster bombs sat beneath his wings, clamoring to be dropped. Doberman tucked the Hog toward the ground, rolling the big plane over his shoulder like a black belt karate instructor tossing an opponent to the mat.

As the attack jet headed downward in a steep dive, the Hog's leading edges grabbed at the air as eagerly as the pilot himself. Unlike a swept-wing, pointy-nose fighter, the A-10A Thunderbolt II had been designed to go relatively slow, an important attribute when you were trying to plink tin cans a few feet off the deck. Even so, with all the stops out and the plane growling for blood as she plummeted toward the yellow Iraqi dirt, she felt incredibly fast. The Gs collected around

Doberman's face, tugging at his narrow cheeks and unshaven morning stubble.

This was the part of flying he loved—the burning rush that made you feel hotter than a bullet rifled out of a flaming barrel. His scalp tingled beneath its razor cut, and his oversized ears—the only parts of his compact body that might be called large—vibrated with adrenaline.

But this was more than a rush, more than fun and games. He wasn't flying a training gig, and the gray blotches and boxes below hadn't been plopped there by overworked airmen anxious for a weekend pass. White cotton balls appeared all around him. They puffed and curled as he flew, inside-out tennis balls that frittered into thin air as he approached.

The innocent puffs were shells, exploding just out of reach.

Okay, Doberman thought, they're shooting at me. Fair's fair; I hit them first.

He continued onward, flexing his fingers in his gloves as he held the stick, telling himself not to overdo it. Even a blue-collar dirt mover like the Hog was designed to be flown, not muscled.

You stay loose, you stay in control.

The cluster bombs vibrated on their pylons, demanding to be fired. Each bomb was actually a dump truck for smaller bombs; once dropped, it would dispense a deadly shower of hundreds of bomblets for maximum damage.

Doberman was all eyes. His eyelashes blinked the flak away, blinked aside the other trailers, found the one that had been waiting for him, the one right in the middle, dug into the side of a sand dune months before in preparation for this exact moment.

Two CBUs fell from his wings. Doberman rocked in his seat, dodging the Hog to the left. He saw the dark shadow of another set of trailers slide into the middle of his windscreen as he jinked; he eased back, angling to get it into his sweet spot. Finally it slid in like a curveball finding the strike zone; he held it for the umpire and pickled two more of his bombs.

He was low now, below five thousand feet, lower than he'd been ordered to fly and nearly too low to drop any more cluster bombs effectively because of their preset fuses. His head buzzed with blood and the exploding 23mm antiaircraft shells the Iraqis were firing at him. There was so much flak in the air, Doberman could get out and walk across it.

That was probably a bad sign.

On the other hand, a lot of stuff was burning. That was good.

Gunning his A-10 off east of the target area, Doberman turned his neck in ways it had never gone before, looking for Dixon. His wingman didn't answer the radio calls, but that wasn't necessarily surprising—just before the attack the kid had been so nervous that he had obviously forgotten to key the mike before talking.

Two other members of the 535th Tactical Fighter Squadron (Provisional), Devils One and Three, had been assigned to hit a second GCI complex about ten miles to the east. Doberman thought he saw a finger of smoke rising from where it should be. He and Dixon were due to head south and join up with the other Hogs in a little over ten minutes. From there they would head toward a forward air base in northern Saudi, rearm, and fly back north for a second round of shoot-'em-up.

Then they'd head home to bootleg beer, real long showers, and a few good hands of poker. Doberman had lost over five hundred dollars the night before, the latest and by far the worst in a series of shellackings he'd taken since landing in Saudi Arabia. The pilot was determined to make at least half of that back tonight.

No way his luck could stay as bad as it was last night. He'd bitten off some of the worst hands of his life. And even when he'd had a good hand, inevitably someone else was fatter.

Doberman had held aces over eights in a full house on the last hand, hunkered down in front of a pot that held at least three hundred bucks. And damned if Shotgun, of all people, hadn't been holding four aces.

"Dead man's hand," said the other pilot, pointing to the cards on the table as he raked the chips in. "Doc Holliday drew that the day he was killed. Never bet on that. Can't win."

Shotgun's grin floated in front of Doberman's face as he

scanned the sky for Dixon. He saw a dark shadow rising through the clouds a good distance behind him. He lost it, saw it, lost it. "You got a little low, kid," he told his wingman. "Get up over the flak." Then he turned his attention back to the ground, looking for a place to put his last two bombs.

There was an Iraqi gun battery just off his right wing. The Hog seemed to growl at him when he spotted it through the clouds—as if she wanted a chance to kick a little dirt in the eyes of the people who'd been firing at her all morning.

Didn't Doberman owe her that chance?

He banked sharply, hunkering down in the thick titanium bucket that protected the cockpit. As soon as he pickled the two cluster bombs, he knew he'd missed his target; the plane ran into a good hunk of wind and he hadn't compensated for it. Angry at himself, he slammed the Hog around and worked into position for a run with his cannon. The plane screamed as she bled speed and energy, then whistled as the pilot edged her into a dive. The safe tactics of middle-altitude bombing were shelved—Doberman hunkered in for the kill, sliding down from five thousand feet.

The four-barrel Iraqi peashooter desperately spun around to face him. As its slugs spat past him, Doberman gave the Hog's cannon a full five-second burst, then jinked left as the flak-shooter burst into a magnificent collection of red, orange, and yellow flames.

Climbing once again, Doberman caught the muzzle flash of a second gun as it tried tracking him through the sky. Something snapped inside his chest, and the methodical Air Force pilot was replaced by a seething werewolf screaming for vengeance. He tucked the Hog around for another attack. Just as he fell into the dive, he caught a dot of a shadow out of the corner of his eye, well behind him.

"About time you caught up, Lieutenant," he said.

There was no answer.

"You have to press the little doohickey to get the radio to work," he said sarcastically. Doberman pushed his Hog earthwards, deciding in mid-plunge to leave the gun in favor of a building slightly to the south. It hadn't been tasked, but what the hell, a building was a building.

"Seriously, Dixon, let's see if that cannon of yours works," Doberman called as he lined up on the building. "Get yourself oriented and trail on this pass, Okay? Then we'll head for SierraMax."

Still no acknowledgment. Doberman felt a twinge of anger at his wingmate; he liked the kid but he'd be damned if he wiped the young newbie's ass for him.

Doberman bored in, unconsciously sinking lower and lower in the well-protected cockpit. He worked the building dead into his sights, then felt the stutter-stutter-stutter of the Hog as it grinned bullets from its nose. The top of the structure blew apart, bits of stone, roof tar, and machinery cascading upwards—followed by a spectacularly showy explosion.

One of his shells had ignited a gas line.

Doberman winged through a fireball, shouting like a cowboy busting a favored steer at a rodeo. Banking and climbing away for all he was worth, he congratulated himself for expending ammunition in an extremely expeditious manner. The Hog swaggered a bit—not so much out of pride but because it had taken a few bullets in the stabilizer—but in general he was in fine shape for the return run home.

Doberman pointed himself toward the rendezvous point, then craned his neck to see if Dixon had followed in on the cannon run.

It was then that he realized why the young lieutenant hadn't acknowledged his instructions.

The plane behind him wasn't an A-10A. It was a Mirage F-1. And it wasn't a French jet that had strayed over the lines either. The dull green and brown camo on her wing was punctuated by a bright red streak of Iraqi lightning, and had Doberman had the time or inclination, he would have had no trouble picking out the three stars sandwiched between the red and green fields in the Iraqi flag on her tail.

2

At roughly the same moment that Doberman discovered Dixon wasn't on his tail, the young lieutenant was staring into the blankness of the sky in front of him, slowly realizing that he was lost.

Completely and utterly lost somewhere deep inside Iraq, without the vaguest notion of which direction he had to head in.

A compass sat directly in front of his face, and the instrument panel across from his chest was dominated by an INS navigational system. While not without its problems, the unit could nonetheless be counted on to give at least a semiaccurate location. But at the moment it was about as useful to him as a map of Wisconsin.

Climbing after firing his Mavericks, Dixon had run into an aerial minefield. Antiair shells exploded in every direction, the Hog bucking and shaking like a car with three flat tires on a washboard highway. Miraculously, none of the shells did any damage, or at least not enough to affect the plane. Dixon climbed and climbed, his heart skipping as his lungs gulped in rapid staccato. Finally clear of the exploding black bursts, he kept going—to nearly twenty thousand feet, which took forever in a loaded Hog. It wasn't what he had planned to do, and certainly not what he had rehearsed for days. Still, he got the plane's nose angled down and prepared for a second run with the Mavericks; he was still in control.

Dixon had been a quarterback in college—Division II—and he gave himself one of his old pep talks, as if he were clearing his head after a particularly vicious blitz. When Doberman failed to respond to his radio call he felt a twinge of anxiety, but pushed it away, hoping his flight leader was just too busy to respond.

He had flown wider than planned, and further north—and lost his leader, at least momentarily—but as he peered through the broken cloud layer he could feel his confidence returning. He pushed downward, searching both the air ahead for Doberman and the ground below for his briefed targets. The clouds made both tasks difficult; he willed them away, sliding toward the Iraqi complex in a shallow dive. Suddenly the radar dish Doberman had targeted snapped into view.

Dixon was surprised to see it still intact.

Okay, he told himself, I have a target. He steepened the dive, confidence beginning to build.

Then clouds filled the windscreen. He turned quickly to the video monitor. A blur fell into the crosshairs and he pushed the trigger on his AGM, locking not on a dish but a building. He fired anyway, continuing downward into clear sky.

But now the site was jumbled around, different from the satellite pictures and maps he'd studied. Doberman's dish was gone; the trailers were laid out in a different pattern. He shot his eyes back and forth, trying to orient himself. The muscles in his throat closed, desperately trying to keep his stomach acid from erupting in his mouth. Black bursts were exploding in front of him; there was fire and smoke on the ground. Finally, he saw a grouping of trailers he thought he recognized, locked on the middle one, and fired. The Maverick clunked away as the plane followed the motion of his arm, stiffly pulling to the left in a long descending bank as his eyes remained glued on the television display, now completely blank.

More than thirty seconds passed before he pulled his head upright. By then the Hog had flown beyond the target area. There was nothing on the desert floor in front of him.

In that moment, Lieutenant William Dixon—star athlete, star student, prized recruit, a young man headed toward a top F-15 assignment until his mother's failing health had complicated his career priorities—forgot how to fly. His arms and legs moved independently of his head. With his left hand he reached for the stick when he meant to adjust the throttle; with his right he tuned the radio when he meant to check the INS settings.

A voice in his head yelled that he wasn't breathing right. He'd been hyperventilating probably since takeoff, and the voice knew that a good part of his problem was physical. But Dixon couldn't get the voice to do anything but yell impotently. The A-10, confused by its pilot's commands, started heading toward the ground.

Doberman smashed the throttle and threw the Hog into a tight turn, trying to get inside the Mirage and set up an overshoot—putting the faster but less maneuverable plane ahead of him, a classic turn-the-tables air-combat ploy. The Mirage pilot anticipated the move, and traded some of his altitude for speed, breaking off in a diving straight line away. The tactic would have meant death for the Iraqi if Doberman had been able to complete his turn; even with the widening range and the lost energy, his Sidewinders probably could have caught the Mirage.

But Doberman didn't have a prayer of turning in time, much less firing his heat-seekers; in fact, he didn't dare complete his turn. The bogey had tossed off two heat-seekers just as the Hog started away. One shot off wild, sucking the fire off one of the diversionary flares the Hog driver kicked out.

The other sniffed the air and caught a faint whiff of Hog turbofan dead ahead.

Dixon blinked his eyes, focusing not on the windscreen but the horizon indicator below it. He had to get it level. That was his first job, before all others.

The round sphere spun madly, whirling with no discernible axis. It fluttered and waved and shook without any pattern. It refused to be controlled, refused to assume any direction other than its own.

The pilot reached out and grabbed it, sparks flying from his hands. The sparks ignited his flight suit, burning his safety harness away, setting his arms and chest on fire.

He held on. His breath roared in his ears, as rapid as the rod on a locomotive's wheels. His entire body was on fire, but he held the sphere tight.

It stopped spinning. The cowl around his head lifted ever so slightly. He had both hands on the stick, and he had control of the bomb-laden Hog.

"The plane is level," he heard himself say. Next step, climb to a safe altitude.

How do you climb? You put the nose toward the stars, you pull your arm gently back, you feel your chest relax. . . .

Slowly, his eyes rose with the nose of the plane. The pilot found himself staring into the muddled gray of the Iraqi dawn.

But where there should be clouds, he saw flowers—hundreds and hundreds of grayish-white lilies. Their mouths turned toward him, delicate satin tongues that brushed gently against the hard surface of the warplane's fuselage. Dixon and his Hog were surrounded, folded in an endless blanket of beautiful flowers.

It was the most wondrous thing he'd ever seen. And then he realized that he had seen these flowers before.

At his mother's funeral three months ago.

3

Several miles to the east, Devil One and Devil Three were mopping up their attack on a similar set of dishes and trailers. Flown by two of the most experienced pilots in the squadron, the Hogs had made a serious dent in the Iraqi air defense system. They might have looked more like bathtubs with wings than attack planes, but together the two Hogs had done enough damage to impress even a snot-nose Strike Eagle commander.

And with a lot less fuss than a sissy-ass state-of-the-art F-15E required, thought the pilot of Devil Three, Captain Thomas Peter "Shotgun" O'Rourke. Like a lot of other committed A-10A drivers, Shotgun had nothing but disdain for the pointy-nose fast-jet community. Unlike most other Hog drivers, he expressed it at every opportunity.

Just now, his audience was an Iraqi radar trailer. In all likelihood, its crewmen didn't hear a word he was saying, even though he was shouting at the top of his lungs.

They'd get the message soon enough. He held his Hog's stick tight between his knees as he squeezed the trigger at the top of the handle. Dust erupted from the building, metal evaporating under the ferocious onslaught of cannon shells. The pilot stopped yelling and stared at the windscreen in front of him, pushing the trigger an extra second to complete the destruction. Then he pulled up, feeling the rubber of his mask and the tight fit of the helmet around his pudgy head as the Gs hit home. He could taste metal in his mouth, and felt the steady rush of his breath down his throat into his lungs.

Shotgun put the Hog on its wingtip, scanning ahead for the flight leader, Major James "Mongoose" Johnson. A greenish-black hulk was climbing maybe a quarter of a mile off to his left. Shotgun checked his fuel and did a quick scan of his instruments and warning indicators. Clean, he pitched the Hog more or less level.

"Devil One to Three. Shotgun, you back there?"

"I got your butt in my pocket," Shotgun replied.

"Let's dance down to SierraMax and pick up Doberman and his pup," said Lead.

"Gotcha."

Mongoose could be a hard-ass—a lot of the maintenance people hid when he came around the hangars—but he and Shotgun went back a ways. Shotgun had seen him pull strings to keep a fellow pilot from going to jail in Germany for a minor brawl; in his opinion that was as true a test of desirable character as any known to man.

The two jets climbed as they flew south. Without the weight and drag of the bombs, the ride to twenty thousand—practically outer space to a Hog pilot—wasn't nearly as hard as it had been when they set out from their home base at King Fahd Air Base a million hours ago. But they took their time about it, careful to keep parading their eyes through the sky around them in case an intruder somehow managed to sneak nearby.

They were still climbing as they approached the checkpoint set for the rendezvous with their two mates. Devil One angled toward an easy orbit; Devil Three fell in behind. They were about sixty seconds early—an eternity for the notoriously punctual Doberman, who was leading the second two-ship element.

Shotgun eased himself in his harness, loosening not only his restraints but his mask and helmet. Steadying the Hog with his left hand, he reached his right hand down to a custom-sewn pouch on the leg of his flight suit. There he removed a small titanium thermos—bulletproof naturally—

notched the cap to the open position with his thumb, and began sipping.

His radio crackled in mid-swallow.

"Shotgun, you want to look me over for damage while we're waiting?" asked Mongoose.

"Be with you in a minute," he grunted back.

Mongoose guessed what Shotgun was up to. Few if any other Hog pilots would drink coffee on such a long mission—hell, on any mission. And at twenty thousand feet! If the sheer logistics didn't get you, the piddlepack would. But that was one of the many wondrous things about Shotgun—he never seemed to have to pee. And no obstacle, whether it was gravity, an enemy missile, or a general out for his carcass, ever stopped him from an objective.

Which made him the perfect wingman.

Mongoose shook his head, then rechecked their position for the third time. After they picked up Doberman and Dixon, they would fly back across the border to Al Jouf, a spit of a strip in northwestern Saudi Arabia. There they would be refueled and rearmed. After that, they were supposed to cross back north and put some dents in Iraqi tanks—child's play after this mission, though as far as he could tell things had gone pretty damn well so far.

Assuming Doberman and the kid showed up soon. They hadn't answered his radio check.

Thinking about anything too much made you worry about it, but sometimes it was impossible to clear your head. As flight leader and the squadron director of operations or DO, Major Johnson felt enormously responsible not just for the mission but for the men flying it. And that made him think a lot. He thought about Doberman and Dixon, willing the two Hogs to appear. The cloud cover had continued to thicken; he worried that the second half of the mission would be grounded. He wondered about the other members of the 535th who had been assigned to fly with other squadrons for the opening-day festivities.

Mongoose took another gander at his fuel, then glanced back at his watch. Doberman was now a full three minutes late. He didn't know him very well—the entire squadron had been patched together for deployment only a few weeks before—but it seemed uncharacteristic of the captain, who could be anal-retentive when it came to planning and poker. He was the kind of guy who not only stacked his chips according to color, but made sure they were all facing the same direction.

Which meant you always knew how much you'd won from him. The guy had the worst luck on the base.

Shotgun replaced the thermos, then ran his hand into another pocket in his flight suit. "Born in the USA" blared from two small but powerful speakers carefully sewn behind mesh patches near his knees. He was thinking he might change the CD—he was in kind of a "Greetings from Asbury Park" mood—when Mongoose reminded him he was supposed to be checking for flak damage.

"You still with me or what?" barked the major, the radio barely audible over Springsteen.

Shotgun closed in on Devil One and eyeballed the aluminum. The green camo looked completely unblemished.

"Gees, Goose, if I didn't know better, I'd swear you had that sucker washed and waxed."

"What the hell are you eating?"

"Twinkie. Want one?"

"Christ. How the hell do you do it?"

"Do what?" By now Shotgun had passed slowly under Devil One and was surveying the other side. "Cleaner than the day you drove it out of the showroom," added the pilot.

"Let's see how you made out," said the flight leader, winging back to inspect Shotgun's A-10A.

"I thought I heard something hit my left wing," said Shotgun. "But it feels okay."

"What the hell is that racket in the background?"

"RWR's giving me trouble. Just checking the settings," answered Shotgun.

"I didn't realize your threat indicator played guitar."

"Shit, you wouldn't believe the things Clyston's techies

can do with a pair of pliers," said the pilot. "This sucker's better tuned than a Spark Vark."

"Uh-huh. Maybe we should just have you fly over the missile batteries and knock out the radar for us."

"That wouldn't be any fun. Ahmed has to have something to play with."

A "Spark Vark" was an F-111 fighter-bomber outfitted with special gear to detect and jam enemy radars. The RWRs in the A-10A were based on technology that dated from Vietnam; while they could detect a variety of radars—usually—they couldn't jam them.

Or play guitar.

Jamming was left to a countermeasures pod carried on the right wing of the plane. The needle-shaped enclosure and its electronic guts were many years old and about two generations behind the times. The ECMs worked well against the radars they were designed to work well against, but the Iraqis had plenty of sophisticated defense systems beyond their reach. Devil Squadron hadn't won whatever lottery had been held for the few more advanced versions that had been shipped to the desert. And even those were considered a bit behind the curve.

But hell, a Hog with advanced ECMs? Kind of against the point, in Shotgun's opinion.

He held steady while the other Hog came in for an inspection. Shotgun waved at Mongoose, then glanced at his watch again. Devils Two and Four were now more than five minutes late, an eternity in a war zone. And Doberman hadn't answered Mongoose's two radio hails.

If it were up to him, he'd head north and find them. But it wasn't his call.

Mongoose swung under the other plane, consciously trying to take his time and focus on the job in front of him. Doberman could take care of himself.

Shotgun's Hog was unblemished. They'd anticipated heavy antiair, but the truth was, they'd encountered only sporadic fire, most of it unaimed. Still, all it took was one lucky shot to ruin your day.

Just as he was about to tell Shotgun he was clean, Mongoose heard a hail over the radio from their E-3 Sentry AWACS controller. "Cougar" was flying back behind the border, helping coordinate the air war in this sector. The airborne situation room functioned like the coaching staff in a stadium skybox, calling in plays and alerting the pilots to blitzes and stunts.

"Go ahead, Cougar," said Mongoose, expecting to be asked why they were playing ring-around-the-rosy in the middle of the desert.

"We're tracking two Fulcrums headed toward SierraMax. Are you in contact with Devil Two?"

"That's a negative." Mongoose felt his voice start to crack, despite his straining effort to keep it level.

"He had an F-1 in pursuit when we lost him on radar. We haven't been able to reach him on any frequency. Is his radio operating?"

Shit. Shit. Shit. Shit. "Copy. Vector me in."

"That is a negative. Repeat. Negative. You are to proceed according to your frag. Confirm."

There were very few times in his life that Mongoose wished he flew a pointy nose, fast-moving fighter, but this was definitely one of them. He gunned the large turbofan engines that sat behind the cockpit, turning the plane north-wards in what he hoped was Doberman's direction.

He knew Shotgun would follow, so he didn't bother keying the mike to tell him.

There was no sense answering the E-3. All he'd end up doing was cluttering the airwaves with four-letter words.

4

Doberman could practically feel the heat seeking missile boring in on him as he flicked out more flares. Jinking toward the ground, he rolled the Hog's engines away from the Iraqi missile, trying to present as cold a target as possible to the enemy. He couldn't see what was happening behind him; it was all touch-and-feel, bred by hundreds of drills and simulations. The Hog's GE power plants were cool for jet engines, and the primitive seeker in the Iraqi air-to-air missile sniffed the air for the plane in vain. It missed the flare as well, continuing harmlessly into the desert—though Doberman had no way of knowing that as he skimmed down as close to the ground as he could get.

Above him, the Mirage pilot gathered his senses and energy for another try. When Doberman realized he was free and began turning to climb off the deck, he found the F-1 diving for him from about five thousand feet in a head-on attack.

The French had built the Dassault-Breguet Mirage F-1 during the 1960s. It was a reasonable effort, capable of Mach performance and a variety of roles, with a single engine and a pair of 30mm machine guns under the fuselage. Its wing area was better suited for low-altitude flight than some of Dassault's other efforts, and perhaps on paper, the plane ought to outmatch an A-10A any day.

But they weren't flying on paper. Doberman kept on trucking, determined to stuff his nose into the Iraqi's face. In a close-quarters attack, it was cannon versus cannon—and there the Hog had the advantage.

The Mirage driver poured on the speed, coming at him like a bat out of hell. Suddenly, the underside of his plane began to sparkle. Doberman resisted the impulse to return fire, realizing it was a waste of bullets from this distance. Instead, he bored in, expecting the F-1 to turn in an attempt to swoop behind the Hog to finish him off. Sure enough, the Iraqi began angling away to the left, no doubt confident that he could outrun the strange and slow American machine.

Doberman executed his own turn into the Iraqi and lit the cannon. It was a textbook maneuver, the angle of separation nearly nonexistent, the Hog right on the Mirage's rear end.

But he missed. The F-1 jinked to the left, then slid quickly into a scissors, and for all his maneuverability Doberman couldn't quite get him locked in his sights. By the time he decided to fire the Sidewinders, it was too late; though he had a lock signal, both heat-seekers rode wide as the Iraqi put out flares and accelerated clear.

Doberman watched his adversary disappear into the distance. Part of him was relieved—and another part was pissed, since he had blown an opportunity to make history by shooting down another plane in an A-10A. He pulled the Hog into a lazy turn south, once again looking for his wingmate.

He was beginning to wonder why no one answered his radio calls when a dark shadow in the top corner of his eye warned him he had taken the Iraqi much too lightly. Only an extreme, gut-wrenching pull to the right that shook every bolt in the Hog's body saved him from being perforated by the diving fighter's guns. Even so, he caught some lead in the rear fuselage; the Warthog grunted and hissed at the flesh wound.

Cursing himself, Doberman flattened his jet out less than a hundred feet off the sand.

The Iraqi pilot was obviously out of missiles. But he had learned from the first head-on-head attack. He sat high above, staying south, obviously waiting for Doberman to run for it. He looked like a cat eyeing a can of tuna.

What a cat wouldn't do for a can opener the size of those DEFA guns the Mirage carried.

Not that Doberman was worried. He knew he would come up with something. Hog drivers always did. He just didn't know what that something was yet.

Better to let the Mirage commit itself, he decided. Cannon versus cannon head-on, I like the odds. I can still make history. I just have to make it quick while I still have enough fuel to get home.

He tried contacting Dixon again; then called to his other squadron mates.

No response. What the hell was going on with them? Dixon should have been over his shoulder, warning him about the Mirage.

Unless the Iraqi had gotten him first.

The F-1 snapped out of a turn and accelerated in his direction. Once again the Mirage pilot had made his move too soon, though he had more altitude and speed this time; he would hold the advantage when they finally closed.

Doberman drew a deep breath, then tapped the throttle bar for good luck. If he chose to, he might be able to break off now and run away to the west, slide back, and escape. It would strain his fuel reserves to the max, maybe beyond, but it would keep him in one piece.

But where was the fun in that?

He was just moving his stick to angle for another head-to-head encounter when a white light seemed to shine on the F-1 from above the clouds. In the next second, the enemy plane disappeared, replaced by a burst of frothing white vapor.

5

Pedals to the metal on as they flew toward the GCI site their two wingmates had been tasked to hit, Shotgun and Mongoose heard the AWACS vectoring a pair of F-15 interceptors to nail the Iraqi fighter. The MiGs had changed course, but both the Mirage and the A-10A had gotten up off the deck and reappeared on the Sentry's scope. The distance and effects of ground clutter interfered somewhat with the Sentry's ability to track the planes, but considering that the control crew was two hundred miles away and keeping track of several million other things, they did a hell of a job. The radio exchange crackled over the airwaves like an old-time radio drama.

"Turbo Three, contact fifteen east SierraSierra, five thousand," called the lead F-15 pilot. He was telling his wingmate and the AWACS controller that he had the Mirage on his radar.

"Don't hit the friendly," answered his wingmate.

"Sorted. Aw, shit. Clean now. Fuck me."

Shotgun echoed the Eagle pilot's curse. The fighter had lost the Mirage. Shotgun leaned forward in his seat, trying to urge a few more miles per hour out of the Hog. He and Mongoose had all the stops out, but were still at least two minutes away.

"Clean high," said one of the F-15 pilots. It wasn't clear which one.

"Contact. Five thousand. At twelve, eleven east, uh—"

"Screw the numbers, just do it!" screamed Shotgun.

His mike wasn't open, but as if in answer to his urging, the Eagle pilot called a missile shot—"Fox One," the time-honored signal that a Sparrow air-to-air radar missile had been launched.

"Fifteen, fifteen, turn right," said the second Eagle pilot, the rest of the transmission scorching into unintelligibility.

Did they get the Mirage?

Static filled Shotgun's ears.

It was like listening to the final seconds of a basketball championship on a malfunctioning AM radio. Except that a lot more than bragging rights were at stake.

Cursing, he slapped the com panel, as if that might somehow clear the reception.

Wow, thought Doberman as his adversary turned into a silver-black glow. I'm having a religious experience.

That or my oxygen hose is kinked all to hell.

In the next second, he realized that something physical, as opposed to angelic, had taken out the Mirage.

Something American, he hoped. F-15's flying combat air patrol out of the south, most likely. But why hadn't he heard them on the radio? Why hadn't he heard anything on his radio?

Doberman, turning the Hog southwest, flipped through nearly every frequency before realizing, duh, that his com-munications gear had given up the ghost.

No wonder he'd lost Dixon. And the rest of his flight.

Damn, they were probably halfway back to Al Jouf by now.

Hell, he'd better watch for the Eagles, in case they decided to take him out for acting snotty and not answering their hails.

The pilot searched the skies in vain for his benefactors. They had to be F-15's, firing Sparrows from beyond visual range; anything else would be doing victory rolls in front of him. Maybe they'd gone on to put out some other fire.

Doberman's relief mixed with disappointment as he checked his course toward SierraMax, the squadron rendezvous point.

He'd been robbed of his shot at the scumbag. Instead, he was going to have to buy some stinking pointy-nose jock a round of drinks.

Would he have beaten the Mirage?

Shit, yeah. Damn straight. Cannon versus cannon, nothing could take the Hog. He was just lining up when those guys broke up the party.

Hell, even Dixon would have wiped the Iraqi's ass for him. Where was that boy anyway? He should have been over Doberman's back; would have gotten the damn Iraqi before he launched the missiles.

Maybe he'd make the nugget stand for the F-15er's beer.

Mongoose heard the Eagle pilot call "Hotel Sierra" as the Iraqi jet turned into instant scrap metal.

Hot shit. Got that son of a bitch right between the eyes.

Mongoose and Shotgun were still a good ninety seconds south of Doberman. Meanwhile, the two Eagles kicked toward the east, backing up another pair of F-15's that had been sent after the Fulcrums Cougar had first warned them about.

"Devil One, this is Cougar. We have you headed north. Please advise."

Well, at least the controller was being polite, Mongoose thought to himself. He waited for the second call before answering. When he did, he asked a question of his own.

"We're short one Hog," he told the Sentry. "You see him anywhere?"

The overworked controller was temporarily stumped. Mongoose spotted Doberman's plane—at least he assumed it was Devil Two. The Hog was heading south about two miles away.

"I'm on him," responded Shotgun before he could finish pointing him out.

"Copy that," Mongoose told his wingman after the plane failed to respond on any frequency. "Take him back to Al Jouf."

"Where are you going?"

"I've got to find Junior."

"Say, Goose, you looked at your fuel gauge lately? It's that big dial on the right side of cockpit, right near the handle you have to pull if the tanks run dry."

Damn Shotgun. Always a wise ass.

"Yeah, just take Doberman home," he snapped. He glanced at the map folded out on his lap, calculating that he had just enough in his tanks for a pass back over the GCI site before running home.

Assuming he found a tail wind.

"Goose?"

"Go. That's an order."

"Aye, aye, Captain Bligh."

6

It took forever for Dixon to realize the lilies were just the clouds playing tricks on his eyes. He passed through them, climbing high above the earth where he could clear his head.

There was something wrong with his oxygen supply. At least that's what he blamed the hallucinations on. He was incapable of such extreme panic; it had to be something physical, something tangible, something that could be fixed by turning a dial or adjusting a switch. He moved his hands deliberately around the cockpit, putting everything in order.

Slowly, the lieutenant regained control of himself and his plane. He began by breathing deeply. At first his lungs rebelled, aching with the effort. Then he felt his shoulders starting to sag, the muscle spasms finally giving way. He rocked his head to the left and then the right, his spinal cord cracking as the tension was released. Dixon was a long way from relaxed, but at least he could fly the plane.

He still had six iron bombs attached to the hard points beneath his wings. They were slowing him down, robbing not just airspeed but precious fuel.

One by one, he let them go. The Hog seemed to buck slightly with each release, as if she were protesting that they had not been used on the enemy.

For all he knew, they might be dropping on one of Saddam's palaces.

Dixon glanced at his watch, saw it was past time for him and Doberman to be hooking up with the others at the point they called SierraMax.

Where in God's name was that? Where was he?

He worked at the map, and realized he was now about twenty-five miles west and maybe fifteen south of the GCI site.

Not horribly off course, all things considered. But he was alone. Had the others tried to contact him? He hadn't heard their calls. Had they been shot down?

It didn't make sense to go to the checkpoint. His best bet was to head straight to the airfield at Al Jouf.

He'd screwed up the mission big-time. But his job now was getting to the air base in one piece.

Strange things happened in combat all the time, confusing things, bizarre things. There were excuses, not necessarily bad ones either—the fog of war and all that.

He'd gotten turned around, lost track of his leader, lost track of himself. But it had been his first time in combat.

The fog of war.

No, it was something more than that. You didn't know who you were until you stared down the barrel of a gun. Life was one big question mark until then.

If that were true, William James Dixon didn't like what the answer had turned out to be.

7

The smoke curled in a thin line from the desert, as if fueled by the final embers of a spent cigar. It was about five miles south and three due east of the GCI site—exactly where a damaged Hog might crash after the attack.

Grimly, Mongoose altered course and continued lowering his altitude. He made double sure his radio was tuned to Guard—the band a downed flier would use to call for help.

The twisted wreckage in the distance could be a Hog. Then again, it could be a truck, smoked by somebody returning home with some bombs or bullets to spare. Mongoose was by it too fast and too high to tell.

The radio stayed silent. A good or bad sign, depending on how he cared to interpret it.

Mongoose whirled his head around, making damn sure he was alone in this corner of the sky, then cranked the Hog back for another pass. This time he slowed the big plane down to a crawl; any slower and he'd be going backwards.

The major berated himself for picking Dixon for the mission. He liked the kid, but hell, Dixon had been in the cockpit barely long enough to qualify for a learner's permit.

True, Dixon had fighter jock written all over him. Easy-going bravado, spit-in-your eye aggressiveness, and just the right touches of intelligence, insubordination, and selfless dedication to remind any older pilot of his early years—accurately or not. Lean and, at six-four, on the tall side for a pilot, he had an upper body toned by the squadron weight machines and a daily run. Dixon was a recruiting poster come to life.

Or maybe death. Mongoose pushed himself high in the seat as he walked the plane across the desert, his eyes sorting through the wreckage for anything that would mark it as a Hog—a flat stubby tailfin or a thick round engine among the most obvious.

But no. He saw a wheel and a body and then another body. Some sort of truck, definitely.

He couldn't help feeling relieved, even though he was looking at corpses.

Enemy corpses, but he shuddered a little.

Mongoose cast a wary eye at his fuel gauge—not great, though he still had a little to play with. He angled the jet toward the GCI site, marked out in the distance by a thick plume of black smoke. From here it was difficult to tell if the smoke was coming from one source or many.

Mongoose continued to monitor the rescue band as he headed north. Part of him hoped to hear the telltale chirp of an emergency survival beacon activated by ejection; part of him was relieved that he didn't. He expected the gunners at the GCI site to start firing at him any minute. Sure enough, gray fingers began raking the sky ahead. The rattle wasn't particularly threatening yet, falling far short of the Hog, but it distracted him all to hell. He had to stay low to see the ground clearly, which would mean running through the top of the triple-A in about ten seconds.

"Devil One, this is Cougar," snapped the AWACS. "Are you reading me?"

"Go ahead, Cougar."

"We're showing a flight headed south we think is your boy. You copy?"

"Who does he say he is?" Mongoose asked.

"Not responding at the moment. We're a bit busy here," added the controller, a not-too-subtle hint.

"Yeah, right, I copy. Heading back," said Mongoose. He pulled a U-turn and gave the ground batteries a good view of his twin rudders as he slid onto coordinates that would get him back to Al Jouf with three minutes of fuel to spare.

Assuming he coasted halfway.

8

His domain had come down to this: a single pad of lined white paper in the exact middle of a plain steel desk, a thin, dented silver Cross pen he'd once thought of as lucky, and a telephone.

Colonel Michael Knowlington continued outlining the large triangle he'd drawn around the phone number on the top of the page, his eyes lost somewhere between the thick line and the memory of many other triangles, drawn on many other sheets under many other circumstances.

Nostalgia was not useful. But it was difficult to push it completely away. Much earlier this morning, when the first group of "his" Hogs took off on their long mission to bomb radar sites in Iraq, Knowlington felt as if he were standing at an airline terminal, killing time before a flight. And then, just as he turned to walk back through the hangar area, he somehow remembered watching an RC-135 take off in Alaska a million years ago.

For a moment, the white-haired, balding colonel thought his mind had thrown up a completely irrelevant memory. Then he remembered he'd watched that particular flight not with detachment but a premonition of doom; the plane had later gone down in a thunderstorm, all personnel lost.

It was at that moment that he admitted to himself how

much he dreaded this afternoon. Knowlington felt—knew—
he'd lose at least one pilot, maybe two or three, of the twelve
he was responsible for. He was especially worried about the
four-plane group led by the squadron DO, Major Johnson. In
his opinion, they'd been assigned to do something well
beyond the Warthog's capabilities, flying hundreds of miles
to bomb sites that were part of sophisticated antiair systems.
Going deep was not exactly the job the A-10A was designed
to do.

But his opinion didn't count. His being here in Hog Heaven
was only a freak of war, someone else's unlucky throw of the
dice. A few weeks before, these planes had been headed for
the scrap heap, and he'd been given "command" of them to
make sure they got there. Then General Schwarzkopf himself
had decided there should be more Hogs in theater, and that
was that.

Real War Rule Number One: Things change. Rarely for the
better.

What really bothered Knowlington watching the Warthogs
take off wasn't a premonition or pessimism, but a realization
that for the first time in his life he didn't care to have his
fanny in the cockpit. He didn't care, really, to be here at all.

What he did care for, what he wanted more than anything
else, was a drink. But instead, Colonel Michael Knowlington,
paper commander of the 535th Tactical Fighter Squadron
(Provisional) of the 99th Air Wing (Temporary), picked up
the phone and asked for help connecting to the stateside
number. Yes, he told the communications expert on the other
end, he was well aware of the time back in D.C. And yes, it
was a private number. This was Colonel Knowlington on the
line.

He waited. The metal building rattled as a misplaced
Hercules crossed overhead.

The phone was answered on the fourth ring, just as he
worried that the answering machine would take it and he'd
have to try again later.

A sleepy voice asked, rather than said, hello.

"I'm looking for Nitro," Knowlington said.

"What?"

"Hey, Nitro. This is Skull. How the hell are you?"

"Mikey?"

"One and the same." Knowlington slipped back in the stiff desk chair, relaxing a little, picturing his old wingman asleep in his pajamas.

"Jesus, Mike—where the hell are you? You in trouble?"

"Not exactly. Well, sure, I guess I'm always in some sort of trouble." The phone line wasn't secure. "You probably can figure out where I'm at," he added. "It's pretty warm, but I'm not getting a tan."

"Jesus, Mike. You know what time it is back here?"

"I need an important favor. Today if possible."

"I'm listening."

Knowlington smiled, remembering another time Nitro—Captain Grenshaw at the time—had used that exact phrase. It was over a UHF radio as Knowlington—he hadn't earned the Skull handle yet—tried to help vector in a Jolly Green to pick up the downed pilot.

"This is going to sound really, really dumb," the colonel told his old friend, "but my chief needs a manual for something you guys make."

"You're shitting me, right?"

Knowlington laughed. He'd had the same response himself when the chief of his maintenance section—actually, his capo di capo, Chief Master Sergeant Alan Clyston—told him two days ago that the Air Force had somehow neglected to supply anyone in Saudi Arabia with a manual for the AGM-65G Maverick missile.

Something of an oversight, considering they were being used today. Everybody said they worked the same as the other models, except for the fact that they had bigger warheads, were a lot heavier, and used infrared instead of video when they guided themselves to a target.

Same thing, except different.

"I wish I were kidding," Knowlington told Grenshaw. "My guys claim they've figured them out, but I want to make sure, you know?"

"Some things never change. Shit."

While Knowlington doubted Saddam was listening in, he

was squeamish about giving out too much information over an open line. But he had to make sure Grenshaw knew what he was talking about. "It's a G," he hinted. "Does that make any sense to you?"

His friend had to think for a second or two. "We're talking about something we first used back in our war, right?"

"Well, you might have used it there," said Knowlington, "I dropped strictly iron potatoes."

"It was a piece of shit in those days, right?" asked Grenshaw.

"I was hoping your joining the company would make it work a lot better."

"Fuck you. Yeah, I know what you're talking about. It works great now. I can't believe you don't have the manual."

"Can you do it?"

"Of course. I'll get you a dozen."

"There's a friend of ours who can get them over quick, Bozzone—"

"That old phony is still in uniform?"

"Tucks his shirt in and everything."

"Damn. I would have thought they'd kicked him out years ago."

Bozzone was younger than Knowlington, but Grenshaw didn't realize the irony.

"I think they tried, but he wouldn't go," said Knowlington. "Billy's a general now."

"Yeah, I heard. I thought they gave him the star to get rid of him."

"Didn't take the hint."

"You know what, Mikey, I can get them there faster."

"Really?"

"One of our congressmen is going over on a fact-finding tour. He'll be leaving in a few hours, as a matter of fact. I can make some calls. It's done."

Our congressmen. Knowlington shook his head, but said nothing.

"Listen, you want some steaks?" added Grenshaw. "We'll get you a crate. You still drinking Jack Daniels?"

His men would love the steaks. But the colonel declined. "Just the manuals," he said.

"I'm not trying to bribe you," Grenshaw said with a laugh.

"No, we're fine out here. Got more of that sort of thing than you'd think. It's the manuals I need."

The voice on the other end of the line changed. "How you doing, Mike?"

"I'm hanging in there. Have my own wing."

"Your own wing?"

"Yup." Knowlington didn't bother explaining the paper-work, much less the fact that most of his meager supply of Hogs were under de facto control of other commanders here. Nor did he say that he had ceded much of his actual responsibilities to Johnson.

Maybe he didn't have to. Maybe it was common knowl-edge that he was played out. Because Grenshaw immediately asked if he was being screwed.

"Nah."

"You know, I can help if you need it," said Grenshaw. "Shit, we can use somebody with your background our-selves."

"Maybe after all this is over," said Knowlington.

"Honor and country, huh?"

"Something like that."

"Don't go punching out again. Leave that to the younger guys."

"Don't worry."

"It's been great talking to you, Mikey. We have to get together next time you're in town. Dissect a few old mis-sions."

"Sure thing."

"Fly straight," said Grenshaw, his voice nearly thirty years younger as he recalled the first half of their personal motto.

"And get shot down," answered Knowlington, hanging up.

9

It began as a wobble so slight Doberman didn't even realize the plane was shaking. But by the time he was ready to line up for his landing at Al Jouf behind Shotgun, the A-10A was bucking sideways worse than an out-of-balance washing machine about to explode. Nothing he did seemed to calm it.

The funny thing was, the instruments were at spec and the wobble didn't seem to affect the plane's ability to fly. It was like driving a race car with one wheel out of alignment on an empty track—it might whack the hell out of your perception, to say nothing of your body, but you were never in any danger of crashing.

At least, the pilot hoped that was the case. The plane didn't seem to want to go down, or spin in, or implode—just to slide back and forth a lot. It tried to move left, then right, then left and left, and then right. Doberman wasn't entirely sure what would happen if he let it. And he didn't intend to find out. He corrected constantly with the rudder and stick, eyeing the engine gauges carefully to make sure they were running precisely in parallel. No amount of adjustment or cursing cured the problem.

At least it took his mind off the Mirage. He was still pissed off that he'd lost his chance at shooting it down. He'd decided now that he definitely would have creamed the SOB if the F-15's hadn't gotten in the way.

The scratch of concrete spreading out in his windshield was the centerpiece of a forward air base. It had been carved out in the middle of the wastelands only as a staging area for some Special Forces units and Hogs, but Doberman saw all sorts of planes lining up in landing patterns. The sharp, businesslike commands of the tower personnel were punctuated by even sharper gasps for air; they were doing a brisk business in emergency landings.

But hell, there weren't any wrecks that he could see. Things must be going reasonably well.

Doberman did a last-second check of his instruments as the Hog's wheels snapped into position beneath the fuselage, helped by the jet's slipstream. Nosing toward the concrete, the plane finally shook off her shudder. Doberman felt a shock of relief run through his body as he pushed her onto the ground.

He felt another kind of shock a few minutes later, surveying the rear of the plane from the ground. The back third of the A-10A looked as if it had been used as a backstop for a platoon's machine-gun practice. Foot-long pieces of the interior were exposed, wires and fried metal falling through the jagged gaps. The engine cowling was nicked in a star-burst pattern, and it looked as if someone had tried to write his name on the rear stabilizer. The radar warning antennas, light, and most of the rest of the center part of the tail section had been ground into chewing gum. The fuselage in front of the twin tailfin was creased, spindled, and corroded. Bits and pieces of the baglike fuel tank were exposed; it looked slightly singed.

Shotgun whistled, shaking his head as he trotted over. "Jesus, Doberman, the assholes who shot at you would have taken off your tail if you'd been going any faster," he said. "Here's why your radio was out. You lost the antenna."

The pilot pointed toward the top of the fuselage. Somehow, the UHF/TACAN fin on the very top of the plane directly behind the cockpit had been blown clear away.

"Damn," said Doberman. The fin was only a few inches from his seat. Why the hell hadn't he heard—or felt—what hit it?

"Put a new one in, Dog Man, and you'll be set," said Shotgun. "Hell, this is nothing. Hog eats this kind of stuff up. Shit, it likes taking flak. That's what I'm talking about."

"I guess so. Looks bad, though."

"Nah. This is all sheet metal. It's like on a car. Hell, they just take out a screw here, screw there, bam, you're back to normal."

A technician who had been listening to the conversation rolled his eyes, then left to get his chief so they could decide what to do. His guess was, put a bullet through the A-10A's nose and call it a day.

"The plane shook a little when I was landing," said Doberman. "But the instruments said I was fine."

"That's what I'm talking about." Shotgun held out his arms as if he had had to explain the facts of life to a raw recruit. "This fucking plane was made to get hit. Not like those sissy pointy-noses. Now, you're flying an F-16, right? You couldn't have ejected fast enough. F-15? Man, Saddam's serving you lunch right now. But this—God, all you need's a new paint job and you're outta here."

"I don't see any bullet holes in your stinking plane."

"Hey, that's not my fault," said Shotgun. He turned his head back toward the runway. "What do you think Dixon's plane'll look like?"

"I don't know. The flak was pretty bad when I lost him."

"He wasn't too talkative on the radio coming in," said Shotgun. "I think he got rattled. First day and all."

"He'll be okay," said Doberman. It was a reflex, as if he were sticking up for his kid brother.

"Shit, I didn't say he wouldn't be, did I?" Shotgun pointed to a Hog steadying itself for a landing at the far end of the strip. "Maybe that's him. We ought to start a pool on the number of bullet holes. Whoever gets the most wins."

"Wins what?"

"I don't know. A case of homemade beer."

"Gee, there's a prize," said Doberman. "And how the hell would you count them on my plane?"

"Good point."

The hot Saudi air whipped into Dixon's face like a blast from an afterburner. He caught his balance against the fairing strip of the cockpit's windshield, checked to make sure the ladder had scrolled itself downwards, then hoisted his long legs around and over the Hog's front end. The uncontrollable urge to get his feet onto the pavement kept him from noticing the shake in his thighs, kept him from noticing anything until he was down, leaning against the darkened green camo of the A-10A's body, leaning and then sinking. Dixon had never puked from flying before, not even the first time he'd pulled negative Gs, but he lost his cookies now, guts erupting in a bilious flow that spread out below the big jet like oil from a ruptured tanker. He puked and puked, stomach and chest exploding as if they had just invented the phenomenon. His mind flew out with the fluids, evaporating on the tarmac.

Exhausted, still shaking, the lieutenant found himself on his hands and knees beneath the jet's wing. He was soaked, though thankfully, from sweat, not puke. Carefully, his stomach still turning, he backed out from under the plane. Still bent over, he found himself face-to-face with Doberman.

"Yo, Lieutenant, where the hell have you been?"

Dixon fell back, startled, his heart stoking up as if he'd been caught off guard in an alley by a couple of thugs. He fell against the hard metal of the airplane, trapped there.

"Lost your breakfast, huh?" Shotgun said with a laugh, standing behind Doberman. "They teach you that in F-15 school? Oh, that's right—you never matriculated, right?"

"Ease off, Shotgun," said Doberman.

"Hey, I didn't mean anything," said the pilot. "You okay, kid? You look a little, you know, loose in the head."

"I'm okay." Dixon heard his voice crack, as if he were nine years old. He pushed himself off the plane, standing on his own two feet. He towered over Doberman, who was short even for a pilot.

"What happened?" demanded Doberman. "Did the Mirage jump you too?"

Dixon shook his head. "I lost you somewhere in the flak."

"My radio went out," the captain added. "Is that why you lost me?"

"Yeah, I guess."

"What happened?"

What had happened? Dixon started to tell him everything—how the plane and world had started moving at warp speed, how he'd lost track of where he was and fired his Mavericks poorly, how he'd risen through the flak and gotten rattled—how panic had flooded his bloodstream.

Something stopped him. Whether it was ego or Shotgun's grin or the look on Doberman's face—a look that expected a right-stuff playback—Dixon couldn't find the words to tell the truth with.

"Uh, I don't know exactly," was the best he could manage.

Shotgun laughed. "What do you mean, you don't know?"

"After I called the antiair battery when you started lining up your Mavericks, I thought we were breaking the figure-eight," said Dixon.

"I didn't hear the call," said Doberman. "My radio must have been gone already." He nodded. "Did your Mavericks hit?"

Dixon shrugged.

"Did you get the tower?" Doberman asked.

"I don't think so."

"No?"

"I don't know. I thought I locked at first, but then I realized it wasn't it."

"You get anything?"

"A van. I can't even remember."

Shotgun was scouting around the plane. "Jesus, you're not even scratched," he said. "You're a lucky son of a bitch. You should have seen what happened to Doberman's plane. Chewed up and spit out."

"You all right, kid?" Doberman put his hand on Dixon's bicep. Though the captain was half his size, his grip hurt.

"Yeah, I'm fine."

"I'm sorry I lost you," said Doberman.

Dixon knew he was the one who ought to be apologizing, and more, but he kept his mouth shut.

Maybe it was the hard light of the desert, but to Doberman the kid looked like a teenager, and a scared one at that. His clouded blue eyes and fuzzy red cheeks seemed to belong to a thirteen-year-old, not a towering, overachieving, aw-shucks fighter jock. Dixon had All-American good looks to go with a tall, athletic frame, but he suddenly seemed stooped over and frail. It could've been the aftereffects of the vomiting spell, but damned if the kid didn't look a lot like he was going to cry.

Doberman had opened his mouth to say something encouraging—he wasn't sure what the hell that might be—when a damaged F-16 careened in for a landing on the runway not far away. The yelping roar of the plane's engine took the words away; he settled for a punch to the shoulder.

They didn't teach that in leadership training, but it was the best he could manage at the moment. Someone on the maintenance crew was shouting at him; there were a thousand things to get squared away before they took off again. Until Mongoose came in, he was in charge of the group.

A black master sergeant nearly as fat as Shotgun pulled him by the shoulder and shouted in his ear. "Hey, you Glenon?"

"Yeah. Who are you?"

"Call me Jimbo. I'm running this crew here," he said, gesturing indiscriminately toward the swarm of maintenance people. The sergeant, well into his forties, had a confident, easygoing crease in the corner of his eyes, put there by a lifetime of squinting at airplane parts. "We were hustled out here at the last minute on loan so we're making do. What else is new, right?" The chief stopped and pointed at Doberman's plane. "That your Hog?"

Doberman nodded, then followed as Jimbo began walking toward it. The sergeant nodded his head as he went, as if carrying on an imaginary conversation. Finally, he turned and smiled. His cheeks puffed out as if he were blowing into a tuba. "You took some beating, huh?"

"I didn't even realize I was hit."

"No shit." The sergeant uttered the phrase without the slightest hint of amazement. Once again he began walking; the nods took up where they had left off.

"We got one more plane in our group. The Devils. Major Johnson. He's running a little late," said Doberman. "He was just clearing the border when we landed."

"I'm sure he'll be here," said Jimbo. "We're getting a hell of a lot more action here than they thought. A lot of guys short on fuel."

"We're supposed to be back up in an hour," said Doberman. "What do you think?"

"You're not going to make it in an hour."

They had arrived at the rear of Doberman's Hog. Three airmen stood staring at different sections of the plane, a little like gawkers at a museum.

Or a traffic accident.

"We got a mission," said Doberman, feeling that he ought to exert a little authority. Some of the older NCOs thought they ran the show.

They did, but you didn't want to admit that to them.

"Don't we have priority?" the pilot added when the sergeant didn't comment.

"Oh, your planes have priority," said Jimbo. "That's no sweat. We'll have the others shaved and perfumed before the puke dries on the lieutenant's uniform. But you need a radio before you fly again, doncha think?"

"So plop one in."

The sergeant gave Doberman a world-class NCO-to-officer smile. "Well, sir, as soon as we get one here with an antenna and all, we'll do some plopping. We're kind of triage, me and my guys; colonel just got us out here to keep the strip clear. Still, we can handle the sheet metal. Meantime, don't you think you should be rubbin' a rabbit's foot or something?"

"Why?"

"You fucking Hog pilots are all alike." Jimbo's cheeks worked like a set of bellows as his head bobbed back and forth, smiling, shaking his head, frowning, all at the same time. Finally, he ran his thick fingers through his thicker brush of hair and smiled again. "Sir—no offense, no disrespect, all right? But whack me at night if you're not the luckiest dead man this side of Baghdad, all right?"

"It flew okay," Doberman protested, defending the plane. "Except towards the landing. Then it shook a bit."

"Sir. No disrespect. Here, come with me, all right?" Jimbo clamped Doberman's forearm and pulled it toward the fuselage. "See this? Half an inch over, you got no more tail. No, seriously, sir. This? A little deeper, the cable's gone. No disrespect but your hydraulic line was missed by what, the length of a thumb? Sure you got backup, but look at this—what'd it miss by, two inches? And here? Oh, maybe a quarter of an inch, that's gone, some of our Special Forces guys are looking to sweep you up and bring the parts back in a body bag."

The sergeant continued around the plane, pointing out a dozen places where, had the shell landed an inch to the right or left, backwards or forwards, Doberman would have been fried to, as Jimbo put it, crispy critters with extra sugar frosting.

"I got a guy who'll patch up the worst of it so you can take it on back to King Fahd," concluded Jimbo. "A couple of hours, tops, assuming we get that radio. It won't look extra pretty but hell, we don't have the car wash working today." He winked. "Mechanically, you pulled a miracle, getting hit like this without going down. I mean hell, it's a tough plane and all, but this much flak, the odds are something would go. Like I say, sir, no disrespect and I admire your balls, but whack me at night if you aren't the damn luckiest son of a bitch dead man on this planet right now."

10

Once Mongoose told the controller how low on fuel he was, he got pushed to the head of the line, right behind a Phantom Wild Weasel that had sucked an assortment of scrap metal into one of its engines. He had to sweat the last few miles to the field; the fuel dial increased its downward spiral quicker than the altimeter and the turbofans started to complain. Finally he said screw it, concentrated on the blur of tarmac, and put the A-10 down with a spoonful of petro to spare.

From the air, Al Jouf looked like sand punctuated by airplanes and dust storms; on the ground, the dust storms turned into people and the rest turned to chaos. As Mongoose trundled to the end of the runway, an Army corporal appeared from nowhere and began directing him toward the edge of the desert; for a moment the pilot wondered if the guy was an Iraqi infiltrator, trying to sabotage the plane by sinking it into a sand dune. But as he turned he spotted a long row of boxes on low-slung sleds, parked behind another Hog. Next to them was a dragon, the wheeled machine used to load the A-10A's GAU-8/A "Avenger" Gatling cannon.

The ground crew pitting the planes wanted him as far to the right as possible, so they could fit others into the small space they'd been allotted. Mongoose pushed along as best he could. Not only was he wary about running off into the sand, but he had to take a fairly severe leak; he nearly always did at the end of a flight.

Meanwhile, men were running all around without paying any particular attention to the moving aircraft. Barely missing a Special Forces sergeant with his left wing, he decided he'd gone as far as possible. He practically flew out of the seat and onto the desert, relieving himself directly into the Saudi soil.

Few pees felt as sweet.

"Hundred-mile piss, huh?" said a familiar voice behind him.

"Five hundred miles, more like it," he told Shotgun.

"Ought to use your piddlepack," said the other pilot, grinning into his face.

"Can't a guy get some privacy?"

"Sorry." Dressed in his flight gear, Shotgun managed somehow to look totally disheveled and completely comfortable at the same time. He'd customized the gear so thoroughly Mongoose half suspected he had an onboard climate-control unit.

"Did Doberman make it?"

"Ah, no sweat." Shotgun reached into one of the myriad of pockets and pulled out a thick cigar in a protective metal tube. "Want one? Clyston got me a bunch. Says they're from Cuba."

"No, thanks. How about Dixon?"

"Not even a scratch on his fucking plane," said Shotgun, puffing the cigar into flame. "He looks like he was in a parade."

"They do BDA yet?" asked Mongoose. Bomb damage assessment was especially critical, since their targets were part of the Iraqi air defense system.

"They're running a little behind," said Shotgun. "A few more people decided to stop by than they planned, I think. Man, this is good." He paused and spit out a wad of chewing gum. "Sure you don't want one?"

Mongoose shook his head. "We have to be back in the air in a half hour."

"Yeah. Just enough time to find some coffee," said the other pilot, starting away.

"Hey, Shotgun, hold on—where are Dixon and Glenon?"

"Up ahead, near their planes I think," said Shotgun, pointing. "Say, Goose—better zip up, huh? You're a little out of uniform."

Mongoose found Dixon sitting beneath the wing of his Hog, next to the wheel, legs crossed beneath him.

"Yo, Lieutenant, what the hell are you doing down here?"

Dixon gave him a blank look, said nothing.

"Doberman tells me his radio went out before you fired your Mavericks. What happened?"

He continued to stare.

"Did you lose him before or after you fired your Mavericks?"

"I think it was after. He didn't break the way I thought he would."

"Did you try and find him?"

Dixon nodded.

"Did you have trouble reading the AWACS when they first contacted you?"

This time Dixon shrugged.

"Cat got your tongue?"

"No, sir."

"Did you hit the tower?"

"I don't think so."

"Lieutenant, get the fuck out here and tell me what the hell happened."

The six-foot-four Dixon crawled out on his hands and knees like a kindergartner.

"Something wrong with you?" said Mongoose.

"No," said the young pilot, getting to his feet. His thick, close-cropped blond hair was crusted with muddy sweat. "I need a drink of water or something. I'm thirsty. Maybe I'm dehydrated. After I fired the Mavericks, I spun around and went after a couple of trailers with my CBUs."

"They hit?"

"No. I mean, I don't think so. I was too high."

"How come you didn't take any flak?"

"I'm supposed to apologize because I didn't get shot down?"

Mongoose, pissed that he'd nearly run dry searching for someone who didn't need to be searched for, rubbed the bridge of his nose and squeezed his eyes down with his fingers. "What about the AWACS call?"

"I acknowledged when I heard it."

"Why didn't you try contacting them sooner? Or me?" he added pointedly.

"I thought I did. Maybe I selected the wrong frequency."

Mongoose frowned. That wasn't unheard of, especially when things got hairy, but it wasn't necessarily something to hand out a medal for. On the other hand, there had been a lot of traffic, and there were plenty of non-screwup explanations for missing a radio call.

"See if you can find somebody to check the radio out, just in case," Mongoose told him.

Dixon nodded.

"Hey, you okay, kid?" the major asked, making his voice as calm as possible.

"I'm fine," snapped Dixon. "I just need some water, that's all. When are we taking off again?"

"The triple-A was heavier than hell," said Doberman. "It started before we even got in the clouds and followed us right down. I'm not surprised he's rattled."

"He's more than rattled," said Mongoose. "He couldn't give me a straight answer on why he didn't go to SierraMax."

"We got separated. I think he got lost when he came out of the bombing run."

"Yeah."

"His Mavericks hit. I went over and checked it myself with the intelligence guys," said Doberman. He was sitting on a pile of iron bombs waiting to be loaded beneath Mongoose's Hog. "He probably scored with the CBUs too. They screwed up half his video with their equipment. Watch they don't do the same to yours."

"So why didn't he tell me that?"

"He ducked under the wing and took a nap or something."

Doberman shrugged. "Everybody reacts to stress different. I think he's just being cautious about taking credit. Kid's never been in the frying pan before."

Mongoose didn't bother answering. He'd made a mistake, picking Dixon for this mission. The kid was too green. He saw it in his eyes.

"You mad because he lost me?" Doberman asked. "My radio was out. Could've happened to anyone in that flak. Check his INS—ten bucks says it gave him the wrong coordinate and he got confused. He just doesn't want to admit it."

"It's more than ego," said Mongoose.

Why the hell had he missed it back at King Fahd? Why hadn't he realized it when he was slotting the pilots for the missions? Dixon was the only lieutenant he'd had fly the first day.

Hell, there probably weren't more than a dozen lieutenants flying missions in A-10's today. Going deep, right into the heart of Iraq—shit, what was I thinking?

He was a hell of a pilot, though. He had the stuff.

No, he had moves, but not the stuff. His eyes were empty. He was a liability in combat.

I made a mistake once; I can fix it now, Mongoose decided. I have to.

"I want you to trade planes," he told Doberman. "You take Dixon's north with us. He can hang out until yours is fixed enough to fly home."

"Gees, Major, don't you think you're being kind of hard on him? I mean—"

"It's an order," snapped Mongoose. "No discussion." He turned before Doberman could react, and went off to see how much longer it would be before the planes were ready to go.

11

He was a failure. He'd frozen and puked under fire.

Worse, he'd just lied about it. Now he was trapped and ashamed.

But God, he'd never felt so scared in his life.

12

The way Shotgun figured it, any base that had more than a pup tent to it ought to have at least a dozen coffeemakers going at any given moment. All he had to do was find one.

True, this was a bare-bones, front-line operation, but that was no reason to skimp. He figured the maintenance monkeys were just holding out on him when they answered his questions about scoffing some Joe with cross-eyed stares.

You'd think he asked for tea or something.

A Special Forces unit had taken over a good portion of Al Jouf, adding homey touches like sandbags and trenches. Shotgun figured his best bet lay in that direction. He soon found himself staring into the business end of a highly modified Squad Automatic Weapon.

"Nice laser sight you got there," he told the gun's owner, pushing the barrel away. "You got any coffee?"

"Excuse me, sir," spat the man, a sergeant who spoke with a very pronounced Texas drawl. "This here area's off limits."

Shotgun smiled into the sergeant's face. The thicker the accent, the further north they were born. "So you got any coffee?"

The soldier scowled. Shotgun was at a slight disadvantage; he'd already decided he wanted to save his other cigar, and so had nothing to barter. His only option was flattery.

Fortunately, he had an easy subject.

"You do the work on that gun yourself, Sarge?" he asked.

"This is a standard piece of machinery."

"Shit. Besides the sight, the barrel's reworked, and if that's a stock trigger I'm Buck Rogers."

The sergeant's lip upturned ever so slightly, but his expression could not be considered a smile. "Jealous, Buck?"

"Nope. I'm just trying to figure a way to get my parachute rigger to fit a holster for one on my vest here."

"You probably have enough trouble not shooting yourself with that Beretta in your pocket. Sir."

Shotgun smiled. "Pick out a target."

"Excuse me?"

"Pick out a target. You hit it first, I go away. I hit it, you point me toward some coffee."

"Just go away."

Shotgun unsnapped the top of his holster—not on the Beretta, but on his personal weapon, tucked into the opposite corner of his belt.

"Sir—"

"Don't think you can outshoot a pilot?" said Shotgun with a grin.

The sergeant's face balled up in anger, but he got only halfway into his crouch before the discarded bottle he'd eyed forty yards away exploded in dust. He looked up at Shotgun in disbelief.

"At least, I figure that's what you were aiming at," said the pilot, pushing the custom-built 1911 A2 Colt back into its pouch. "I don't bring the good sight with me because you have to conserve weight and all. With the plane."

"You a gun nut?" asked the sergeant.

"Nah. I just like coffee. What do you say? Hate to kill Iraqis without a good shot of Joe going through my veins, you know what I'm talking about?"

The sergeant grunted, frowned, then pointed toward a pair of general-purpose tents a few yards off. "Coffee's in there. Anyone barks at you, tell 'em Rusty sent you."

"Thanks, Rusty."

"Don't push it, sir," said the sergeant, lumbering away.

• • •

Doberman found a corner of the desert near some bomb skids and resituated himself. He took out his anger at the way Mongoose had treated him on his equipment snaps, adjusting and readjusting his anti-G pants and the rest of his gear.

He was mad at Mongoose, but the sergeant—Jimbo—had shaken him with all his talk about dead men and luck.

Luck was a strange thing. It could easily run out.

Hell, he wasn't lucky. His skill had gotten him here. He was a kick-ass pilot, one of the best in the squadron. Everybody knew that. You relied on luck, they brought you home in a bag.

Doberman looked up and saw Shotgun ambling over, a Styrofoam cup hanging out of his mouth.

"Want some coffee?" Shotgun asked.

"Are you out of your mind?"

"Hey, relax, Dog Man. It's too early for a beer, right? Besides, we got more work to do." He reached into one of his pockets and pulled out a small cupcake. "Want a Twinkie?"

"That's not a Twinkie. Twinkies are rectangular. That's round."

"No shit?" said Shotgun, examining it. "All of them?"

"Yup."

"How about that. Guy told me it was a Twinkie."

"Where'd you get it?"

"Special Forces." He thumbed back in their direction. "Tell them Rusty sent you."

"I don't have time. Neither do you."

"Shit, you're going to be here all day. Guy told me it'd be a miracle to have that plane back in the air by dark. Guess they lost their manuals or something."

"No, I'm going up with you and Johnson. I'm flying Dixon's plane."

"Really? How come?"

"Because the major told me to, that's why. And he had a rake up his butt when he did it."

"What happened to Dixon?"

Doberman shrugged. "Johnson thinks he screwed up."

"Did he?"

"No way," said Doberman. He wasn't sure why he felt so protective of the younger pilot all of a sudden—today had been only the third or fourth time they'd flown together. "The kid got turned around after dropping his bombs and didn't hear the AWACS calling, that's all. I think he was looking for me and just ignored them so he could stay up there a while longer. Hell, that's what I would do."

Shotgun nodded. Any self-respecting wingman would ignore his own skin to save a buddy.

"Johnson got righteous about it," Doberman added. "He shoves his hand in my face and says, no discussion."

This was a difficult concept for Shotgun to fathom. He blinked his eyes trying to process it, then pushed the cupcake into his mouth and gulped down the rest of the coffee. A full third of what was in the cup splashed across his face and onto his suit, where it joined a well-established montage.

"He acts like he's got a stick up his ass sometimes," Doberman said. "A fucking rake. He just about told me I screwed up by getting my plane hit."

"Ah, you're exaggerating."

"Listen, I heard a lot of stuff from guys who served in Germany with him. He's probably frustrated because he's not head of the squadron."

"That's not Mongoose. He's a good guy. He knows his stuff and he sticks by you. What the hell else do you want?"

Doberman realized he was being harsh. It made sense to put your best pilots in the planes that were going to the dance; he would have done the same thing.

It was just the way the major had gone about it that had burned him. He could have been, well, more diplomatic.

"He could have asked me if I wanted to bump the kid," said Doberman.

"Yeah, and what would you have said?"

"Well, I would have told him shit yeah. But that's not the point." Doberman shrugged. "He could at least have been more diplomatic."

"There's a fucking war on," argued Shotgun. "How diplomatic do you expect him to be?"

"I don't know," Doberman conceded.

"How'd the kid take it?"

"I don't know. I wasn't there."

"See? You don't even know if he was diplomatic or not."

"I meant with me."

"Oh, fuck yourself. Nobody has to be diplomatic with you. You're the Dog Man. And a goddamn Hog driver, for christsake. Diplomatic. Give me a break."

"Hey, where are you going? The planes are this way, remember?"

"I'm thinking refill before we take off," said Shotgun. "There's time."

"No, there isn't."

"Shit, I can make it."

"Hey, Shotgun, hold up a second." Doberman jogged the few steps toward his friend. "You think I'm lucky?"

"How's that?"

"Lucky. You know."

Shotgun laughed. "You? You're the least lucky person I know. Why the hell do you think we let you play poker with us?"

"Yeah, that's what I thought."

"Sure you don't want no coffee?"

Doberman shook his head, and watched as Shotgun ambled off in search of more caffeine.

Not having to take a leak while you were flying—now that was luck, especially after twenty cups of coffee.

What Doberman had was skill.

Mostly.

13

Mongoose walked him off into the sand, trying for a little privacy. A big MH-53J Pave Low helicopter idled a short distance away, its throaty whine filling the air with anxious energy. The big special ops chopper sounded like it wanted to fly all the way to Baghdad and personally take out Saddam.

"Listen, kid, I'm putting Doberman in your plane for the rest of the day. I want you to baby-sit his Hog until it's patched together well enough to get back to King Fahd. They may have to scrounge around for some parts, but the chief swears he'll have it back well enough for you to fly. Jimbo's a good guy; he crewed for me a couple of years ago. But listen, you look at it real careful and you think it won't fly, that's your call. Then you stay here, all right? I don't want you taking any chances. I've talked to the commander and I sent word back to Hog Heaven about what's up. You got it? You all right, Dixon?"

"I'm fine."

"This isn't a grounding or anything. You don't have to get pissed off or anything." Mongoose had to tilt his head upwards to look into Dixon's face. None of the emotions he'd expected—anger, resignation—showed through the dazed stare. "I just want the most experienced guys in the cockpit today. All right?"

Dixon shrugged.

Really, what more did he expect? What would he have done in his situation?

"You got something you want to talk to me about?" Mongoose asked.

"Should I?"

Yeah, thought Mongoose. You ought to fight me on this. If you're smart, you'll tell me to go to Hell. You'll tell me I'm out of my mind to keep you from going up. You'll tell me you're the best goddamn pilot in the Air Force, anything to keep flying.

Because if you don't, if you just keep standing here with a look that's only half angry, I'm going to think you screwed up big-time back there.

For no reason but my gut.

"I just think there's something on your mind," Mongoose offered. "You feel bad about losing Doberman when things got tight?"

"I guess."

"The Mavericks look like they all hit. You got the tower. It's on the tape."

Dixon nodded.

"You weren't sure?"

"Things were moving so fast. The images weren't sharp."

"Well this isn't training. What about the CBUs? You saw them hit?"

Dixon hesitated. "I think I was too high."

"You sure?"

He shrugged. "Pretty sure."

"Did you have your targets in the sight, or what?"

"Yeah. Gees."

Mongoose couldn't tell whether the kid was being overly conservative. Hell, the kid might not even know.

No use belaboring this.

"All right. Hang in there," said Mongoose. "I got to get going."

Dixon watched Major Johnson walk back toward the planes. He felt the wind grip the sides of his face, rubbing sand against his cheeks.

Guys like Johnson and Glenon, it was easy for them. They didn't think about what they were doing. They just went up and punched buttons, held on for dear life. Pilots like Shotgun—shit, he was oblivious to half the world. He flew by the seat of his sticky pants.

BJ Dixon was different. He thought about things. Maybe he thought too much, but that was the way it was.

A fatal, deadly flaw.

14

"This is CNN."

James Earl Jones's voice shook the walls of Cineplex. The network's logo spun around and filled the immense television screen that had not only given the Devils' squadron room its unofficial nickname but had made it a very popular hangout.

Especially now. Off-duty pilots and most of the intelligence officers who shared the Devils' Hog Heaven trailer complex crowded the room, watching as the TV flashed a picture of the night sky over Baghdad, shot from a downtown hotel room. One second, the night was dark, blank, peaceful. The next second, more triple-A than Skull had seen over Hanoi during the Linebacker raids filled the heavens.

Knowlington listened in fascination as one of the television correspondents described what it was like to watch an air raid outside your window. He'd never been on that end of it.

On screen, the sky erupted with flash after flash, reflections of explosions on the ground. The F-117As were hitting their targets.

"Take that, you goddamn son of a bitch!" said someone in the room.

And with that, Cineplex erupted in a cheer.

•   •   •   •

Colonel Knowlington was still standing by the door, eyes glued to the television, when someone grabbed his sleeve fifteen minutes later.

He turned and looked into the well-creased face of Chief Master Sergeant Alan Clyston. Clyston had started as an airman crewing Knowlington's Thud three decades before; since then he'd been associated with most of the colonel's various commands and assignments, while working his own way through the ranks. When Knowlington was told he was going to Saudi Arabia, the colonel had shanghaied him to serve as the squadron's chief NCO, in charge of everything from paper clips to cluster bombs. Knowlington called him capo di capo; the people who worked for him just said "Sarge"—and genuflected. Pudgy, with a lot of gray in his thick, bushy hair, the man could still strip and reassemble an engine blindfolded faster than anyone on the base. He was a walking encyclopedia on everything the Air Force flew, but what Clyston was really an expert on was people. Anybody who crewed for him would march barefoot to Baghdad if he asked.

And any officer who crossed him would wish he'd done that instead.

"'Scuse me, sir," said Clyston. "Can I catch you outside a minute?"

"You remember that guy on TV doing the commentary?" the colonel asked him in the hallway. "He flew F-4's."

"Didn't catch him," said Clyston.

"Shot me down in a training exercise once." Knowlington led Clyston down to his office. "Your manuals on the Maverick are on the way," he added. "A congressman is hand delivering them."

"Really? Gees, sir, good work."

Knowlington laughed. He half suspected that tracking down the manuals had been something of a test; Clyston seemed able to locate and appropriate anything he really wanted.

Like the TV and the trailers.

"I got good news and I got bad news," said Clyston inside Knowlington's spartan office.

"Bad news first."

"They're connected. Major Johnson's group got their target, all planes back to Al Jouf intact."

"That's the bad news?"

"One of them got chewed up pretty bad. I talked to Major Johnson and then a buddy of mine who was rustled out that way to make sure the planes are patched together. Jimbo. Remember him?"

"Round black guy, always nods to himself?"

"That's him. He'll get it back together as quick as any one I know." Clyston tried to make himself comfortable on the small steel folding chair, an exact mate to the colonel's. He had offered to find the colonel better furniture several times, but Knowlington—who could have a leather-clad suite airlifted through his own connections if he chose—had declined.

"They're scrounging for parts," added the sergeant. "One of the things they can't seem to find is a radio. Johnson's got fried."

"That's the bad news?"

"I'm getting there. I was thinking I would put somebody onto a Herc that's heading in that direction. I could have them on the ground in two hours tops."

"So do it."

"I had to use your name a little to get space on the plane," said the sergeant.

Knowlington shrugged. Usually he could figure out where Clyston was going, but this time the sergeant had him flummoxed. He only beat around the bush like this if it had to do with personnel.

Damn.

The colonel realized what it was as the name formed on Clyston's lips.

"Probably going to have to be Technical Sergeant Rosen," said Clyston.

"Oh, Jesus, Alan. For cryin' out loud. Not her."

"Whatever it is, she can have the plane back here tonight. If I was positive it was just plopping a radio in and out, I could send half a dozen other guys. But Jimbo didn't exactly have time to do an X-ray, you know what I mean?"

"Damn."

"It's got to be her if you want that plane back tonight. Otherwise, there's no guarantees."

"Tell her I'll cut her fucking tongue out if there's another incident like General Smith."

"You know, she wasn't totally unjustified—"

Knowlington's eyebrows ended the conversation.

"You keep your F-ing mouth shut the whole flight, you keep it shut at the base, you come back here and you report to me. You got it?"

"Yes, Sergeant," Rebecca Rosen told Clyston twenty minutes later as she stood waiting for the C-130 crew to finish loading their gear.

"They'll throw you the F off the plane if you act up. And at the base—you say nothing. F nothing. It's a special ops base. They'll bury you in the sand, we'll never find a body."

"Yeah, yeah."

"Don't yeah-yeah me, Rosen." Clyston shook his head, and once again considered sending someone else out to Al Jouf.

"Look, Sergeant, I'm not a total asshole." She stuck her nose up in the air like she was a stinking English princess. Five foot two, a hundred and ten pounds when wet, and she thought she was a stinking Amazon. "I just don't suffer fools gladly."

Clyston rolled his eyes. "Your problem is that you never met another member of the Air Force who you don't think is a fool."

"I don't think you're a fool, Sergeant," Rosen told him.

"Get the F out of here, Rosen. I want to see that airplane in my hangar by 1800. No, 1700. It has a date with Saddam tomorrow. You got it?"

"I'll have it here if I have to fly it myself."

Clyston would bet money she would. Better than most pilots.

Colonel Knowlington glanced at his watch. It was nearly ten A.M.

Where the hell had the time gone? He hadn't done a damn thing all morning.

Not true. But he hadn't done anything useful. He'd become one of those red-tape idiots he used to rail against.

Hell, that had happened long ago.

Knowlington slid his notes about the next day's ATO into the drawer and locked it. Standing, he recentered his pad on the desktop, then went to the four-drawer file cabinet and made sure it too was locked. The uncluttered order of the room reassured him somehow, the blank walls a comfortable contrast to the thoughts that jumbled and raced through his mind.

Down the hall, Cineplex was filled to overflowing. Most if not all of the people watching CNN knew more about what had happened than all of the broadcasters and studio analysts put together; still, there was an undeniable fascination to the reports, especially the video of Baghdad being bombed.

Walking toward the chaplain's tent, the colonel wondered about the coverage. Would it provoke sympathy for Iraq? Did Saddam now look like the victim?

Vietnam had been like that. You couldn't blame everything on the media, sure, but they had to shoulder a shitload.

The worst stuff maybe. People applauding—applauding!—when a pilot was captured.

Knowlington had argued with his two sisters only once about the war. He'd known it would be useless before he even opened his mouth. Something—booze probably, but maybe his love for them, too—had made him try.

No way. They knew the truth—they had seen it on TV and in the papers.

Colonel Knowlington found the chaplain's tent. There were a few people standing around a coffee machine at the back. He walked over silently, nodding to an officer from one of the transport units he knew vaguely. Nice guy. Young. Most of the other people who came to these meetings were enlisted. There were no ranks here.

Today was a busy day, and there wasn't likely to be a crowd. The colonel had barely filled his cup when the informal leader of the group, known as "Stores," cleared his throat near the small wooden podium at the front of the tent.

"We ought to try and keep things quick today, since there's a lot going on," said the man, who was a logistics sergeant. The others began sifting among the chairs, everyone sitting near the front, but not in the front row itself. No one was next to anyone else. "We'll just be ad hoc for the next few days; catch as catch can, etcetera. Anyone who has to leave, you know, ought to go when they have to. Okay—anyone have anything to say?"

Knowlington glanced around. When no one else spoke, he rose slowly to his feet.

"My name is Michael and I'm an alcoholic. I've been sober now thirteen days, going on fourteen. I thought it would be easier here, but it turns out it's probably a bit worse. Too much Listerine."

Everybody laughed.

15

In theory, every A-10A had been stamped from the same sheet metal. The parts were completely interchangeable; weapons, performance, characteristics precisely the same. The bare-bones design and facilitated production lines were supposed to churn out the Air Force equivalent of a model T, available in any color as long as it was muted green. Unlike most other military jets, there weren't even different versions or model numbers to complicate matters—an OA-10A was just an A-10A on a target-spotting mission. The only thing different was the mix of bullets in its gun.

In reality, each Hog had its own quirks and characteristics. The one Doberman was driving, for instance, seemed to pull ever so slightly to its left, a bit like a motor boat with a barely loose rudder. After taking off, the pilot triple-checked his flap setting and instruments. Eventually, he decided the problem was with the engines, even though the gauges said the two GEs were operating in precise unison.

His stomach said screw the gauges. One fan had just a little more bite than the other, was a little more aggressive spinning around its axle. No amount of fine-tuning the throttle evened it out either. The solution was all in the stick and rudder, all in Doberman's attitude as he flew. He tensed his muscles a different way to fly Dixon's plane; that was what it came down to.

Another thing—the ACES-2 ejector seat felt different. Totally impossible, but absolutely true. Kid's fanny must've bent it special.

Doberman noticed the rear end of Shotgun's plane had risen a bit high in his windshield; he tilted his nose up a tad more to correct. They were flying a loose trail formation north, climbing to twenty thousand as they ran over the berm marking the border between Saudi Arabia and its aggressive neighbor. A number of tanks were waiting to get their turrets blown off about a hundred miles away.

Luckiest dead man alive, huh? What the hell did Jimbo mean by that?

A quarter inch one way or another.

Yeah, right. A quarter of an inch one way or another and the damn shell would have missed completely.

Doberman snorted into his oxygen mask. He'd been unlucky as hell ever since he got here, and not just at poker.

Another way to look at what had happened to his Hog was the opposite of luck. Hell, nothing had hit Dixon's plane— nothing—and he'd flown through the same shit Doberman had. Now that was luck.

Kid had probably sucked what little luck Doberman had right out of him. Some guys were like that. Luck magnets.

A couple of days ago Doberman had blown a tire landing. That was unlucky as hell. Hogs never blew tires. Never.

It wasn't luck that had kept the plane from becoming a pile of junk that afternoon.

It was kick-ass piloting.

Hey, you want to call that luck? Okay. Maybe to a grizzled old sergeant who had been there when Orville and Wilbur traded in their bicycles, it was luck.

To Doberman, it was skill.

And the hell with anyone who said he was conceited about that.

Doberman peered out the side canopy, staring through the protective glass toward the desolate undulations of yellow below. The sand and grit hardly seemed worth fighting over; maybe staring at it all day made you crazy.

Sure, but so did thinking about the oil beneath it. Obviously Saddam's problem.

"Yo, Doberman, buddy, how's our six?"

Doberman snapped to attention at Shotgun's call. He craned his neck around, making sure his back—or "six," for six o'clock on the imaginary clock face of their location—was clean. As he pushed his eyes toward the front windscreen, he realized that Shotgun had actually made the call to subtly remind him to keep his separation—he was off Devil Three by less than a quarter mile, and closing.

Subtle.

"Nothing behind us but a lot of dirt and open sky, thank you very much, old buddy," he said.

"Don't mention it."

"We're flying silent com," barked Mongoose.

"Fuck you," said Doberman—without, of course, keying the microphone.

He hadn't been paying enough attention, and now as he dropped back, he realized he was also muscling the stick. So he had to wake up and relax at the same time. Doberman blew a long breath, letting the Hog ease under him like a calm horse out on a Sunday walk. His tendency to overmanage the plane was a symptom of fatigue; they'd been flying since nearly three this morning and his butt was starting to drag lower than the wheels.

Mongoose had volunteered them for this stinking BAI hop, another reason to be pissed off at him. The original frag—the fragment or portion of the air tasking order that pertained to them—had them just sitting on alert at Al Jouf before going home.

Yeah, but could you blame him? Who wanted to hang out while there were things to blow up?

They were about three minutes from the assigned kill box when a familiar call sign crackled over the radio.

"Cougar to Devil Leader. Devils, stand by for tasking."

Tasking?

Doberman slipped up the volume on the radio, even though the E-3 controller's voice had been loud and clear.

"We need you to head east pronto," explained the AWACS. "One of our Weasels spotted a shipment of Scuds on the highway."

16

Dixon found himself wearing a rut in the sand at the edge of the runway, unable to tear his eyes away from the stricken planes straggling into the base. Every beat-up F-16, every flamed-out Tornado seemed to criticize him: If its jock could take it, why couldn't he?

Finally, he couldn't stand it anymore. Unwilling to go near anyone whose questions would inevitably lead to more lies, the young pilot collapsed butt-first into the sand, covering his face against the gritty wind. His mind blanked, his brain fogging nearly as badly as it had up north.

He'd sat there for nearly fifteen minutes when he felt a tug on his arm.

"Excuse me—you Lieutenant Dixon?"

Dixon looked up and found an Air Force special ops first lieutenant with a greasy pad of legal-sized paper staring down at him.

"Yeah?"

"Two things. The maintenance people say the parts they don't have are en route; ought to be here in an hour or less. Plane looked worse than it was, or they kicked butt; Jimbo says take your pick. If it's fixed before tonight you can go back to Fahd. If not, we get you a bunk. Check the sheets before you turn in; most of the guys around here are ball-busters."

Dixon shrugged. The prognosis on the parts sounded hopelessly optimistic, given the chaos on the field in front of him, but he wasn't about to argue with anything that even pretended to be good news.

"Second thing, my colonel wants to know if you can help out the intelligence guys. They're, uh, kind of overworked."

"Okay," said Dixon. "What do I do?"

"Find a Major Bauer," said the lieutenant, flipping through the pad to see what his next errand was. He'd already mentally crossed Dixon off the list. "Uh, he'll give you the rundown. Your stuff stowed with your Hog, right?"

Dixon nodded. He rose, surprising the officer with his height. "Where is Bauer?"

"Got me," said the officer, trotting back toward the tower area.

Dixon asked half a dozen people if they'd seen Bauer without getting a positive response. Finally he flagged down a Marine captain with a clipboard who was trotting toward a British plane. Jet engines were roaring all around and he had to practically tackle the officer, shouting directly into his ear.

"I'm looking for Major Bauer."

"Why?"

"I'm supposed to help debrief pilots."

"Here you go," said the captain, handing over the clipboard and ear protection.

"You're Bauer?"

"No. But my plane's ready and I got to get back to my unit. Bauer's up there—there's a communications set in the Humvee. See it?"

He didn't, but the Marine—obviously shanghaied into the job earlier—disappeared before he could ask for more directions.

The clipboard had a thick sheaf of unlined, completely blank paper. There was a pen—which turned out not to work—beneath the clip.

While he recognized the type of plane before him—it was a two-place Tornado, one of the most common British types in the Gulf—he wasn't precisely sure what kind of mission it would typically be tasked with.

It had a hell of a drawing on the nose, though. A woman who was primarily boobs was getting a missile right where it counted.

"Like the tart?" the pilot yelled down from the fuselage.

"Excuse me?" Dixon yelled back.

"The drawing. It's m'wife." He laughed. "It's the backseater's wife actually." He laughed again.

Between the roar of incoming jets and the subdued whine of the Tornado—not to mention the pilot's accent—Dixon caught maybe a third of any given sentence.

"I'm supposed to debrief you," he shouted.

"What?"

"What was your mission?" yelled Dixon.

"My mission? Talmud."

"Tail what?"

"Talldaul Air Base."

"Did you hit it?"

"Of course."

"How bad?"

"Bad."

"Like?"

"Like what?"

"How bad did you hit it?"

"Well, I didn't have a bloody chance to land there and find out, now did I?"

"Was it, uh, destroyed?"

"What, the runway?"

"Damage?"

"Like a tart's face."

"Tart?"

"Prostitute, son. How bloody old are you?"

"Can you spell it?"

"Tart?"

The lieutenant took out his own pen and scribbled something he hoped approximated the shouted information. Meanwhile, airmen were waving the Tornado pilot forward, urging him toward a tank truck. Dixon got the man's unit, his call sign, and the fact that he had nearly "gone empty" before the surrounding confusion and revving Turbo-Unions over-

whelmed the conversation. Giving up, Dixon took a few steps
back—and nearly got run over by a taxiing Hornet.

"Okay, that would be *Tallil*. So did they hit the field?"

"Yup."

"How bad?"

"Like a prostitute's face, if that means anything."

"Did he get both JP 233's on it, or just one?"

"I don't know."

"JP 233's—the things they use to muck up the runway.
The Brits like that word. Did he say 'muck'? The JP 233's?"

"I know what you're talking about. He said it was as
cratered as a prostitute's face."

Bauer crossed his eyes, then sighed. Though he was
wearing an Air Force uniform, he had found or appropriated
an Army sergeant's helmet. He was serious about it too—the
chin strap was synched so tight he could barely move his jaw.
"All the prostitutes I know have smooth faces."

"He claimed he hit it."

"Don't worry about it. Listen, there's an F-16 on the
ground somewhere that went north with a package to Taqaddum."

"Uh-huh."

"Yeah, but I don't need to know about that; he's already
been debriefed. On his way back they were flying right over
a factory at the edge of a lake. Ask him if it was on fire or
not."

"Seriously?"

"Yeah. I think the guy's name was Franco, or something
with a couple of vowels in it. It's in the sheets somewhere but
it'll take me an hour to find it. He's with that Guard unit out
of New York."

Dixon wondered what the F-16 pilot—who he figured
would have been in a very big hurry and flying no lower than
twenty thousand feet—could possibly have seen with all the
cloud cover, even if he happened to be looking in the exact
spot the intelligence officer mentioned. But what the hell. It
wasn't like he had anything better to do at the moment.

17

Even when they were on top of the coordinates the AWACS had sent them to, they had trouble raising the Phantom, possibly because there was so much damn radio traffic. It seemed like every aircraft in the theater was talking on the same frequency. Hell, Doberman thought without too much exaggeration, there were probably a few guys using it to call home.

Finally, a chopped transmission staggered through that included their call sign.

"All right, everybody but Sharp Eyes shut the hell up," Doberman heard Mongoose bark. "We got a situation here."

The Phantom pilot told them a pair of carriers with Scuds had parked about fifty yards from a water tower in what looked like an industrial park. It was ten miles northeast of the way marker they were sitting on. He had also spotted a number of military trucks, including two troop carriers on the road headed in the same direction.

"I'm out of iron or I would have taken them myself," said the F-4 pilot. He sounded younger than his plane, though that wasn't a particularly difficult accomplishment. "I'm also about two ounces of fuel from bingo."

"We'll take it from here," Mongoose told him. Doberman spotted the Phantom's smoky tail at about ten o'clock due north. It seemed to wag a bit as it turned the target over to the Hogs.

Doberman felt his heart starting to pump as they swung down and began looking for the water tower, an easy marker. Shotgun was ahead of his left wing a few hundred yards, Mongoose beyond that. The Hog snorted as its nose got closer to the dirt; the pig loved scraping along in the sand.

Suddenly he spotted a cloud of dust kicking across the sandpapery terrain to his right.

The two trucks, most likely.

"Devil One, this is Two," Doberman told Mongoose. "I got the dust bunny to the north there."

"Roger that," said Mongoose. "Shotgun and I will head for the tower."

Doberman angled his Hog toward the dust cloud, pouring on the gas. The cloud soon separated into the two troop trucks; they'd left the highway, though if they thought that was going to help them, they were sadly mistaken.

The Hog's cannon began to bellow as he put the plane into a shallow dive and hit the trigger, perforating the path of the lead vehicle but missing the truck itself. He gave the Hog a bit of rudder, pushing her nose to the left and getting off a long four-second burst.

Points for concept, but none for execution—he'd killed a lot of sand blowing a double air ball and was now beyond the rug rats. More than a little pissed at himself, Doberman yanked his nose up and dragged the A-10A back over and under like a gymnast doing a flip. The heavy drag of the bombs beneath his wing—in his excitement and fatigue he had actually forgotten he was carrying a full load of iron—screwed up his sense of balance; the plane flailed wildly toward the ground, angry at his hotdogging and inattention.

For a second he thought he had lost it. As he wrestled the plane back to level flight and got her off the deck, he realized it wasn't quite as bad as he'd thought, though he deserved a serious kick in the butt for getting stupid.

The trucks continued to the west as he attempted to put a choke hold on his adrenaline and take things a step at a time. Gearing around for a cannon run, he saw that the trucks were now separated from each other by a good distance. Choosing the one on the left as his first target, Doberman picked up his wing and drove the Hog toward the left rear quarter panel of the fleeing Iraqi. He started firing his cannon perhaps a second too soon; the plane lost a bit of momentum as the powerful Gatling fired, but this time the pilot had the green canvas locked in the crosshairs. The shells rippled in a tight line through the back of the truck. It looked like a zipper coming undone, the two halves peeling apart in a jagged twist of black and blue smoke, then fire, then more smoke, then a melange of colors and death.

The guys in the other truck must have seen what had happened to their friends, for by the time Doberman had the A-10 pointed in its direction, the drably colored Toyota—it wasn't a Toyota at all, but somehow it was more fun to plink if he thought of it as one of the rice burners his brother-in-law sold—was wailing down a sandbank without anyone at the wheel. Doberman lit the cannon and waxed the cab three rounds into his burst.

The gray tower hulked over a trio of wedge-shaped shadows ahead. Mongoose decided the shadows must be buildings, and that the Scuds would be on the other side of the tower. "Swing with me to the east. We're going to turn tight and come in low for a look," he told Shotgun. "Expect ground fire."

"What, you think these guys have slingshots?"

Mongoose was too busy concentrating on the ground to answer. He'd seen photos of Scuds, but never the real thing. Now he wasn't totally sure he'd recognize one.

Not that it would matter. Anything down there was going bye-bye.

"There's a good-sized gun on the roof of that building," squawked Shotgun.

Too late to do anything about it. Mongoose felt himself hunkering down into the titanium bathtub that protected the cockpit as he slammed the Hog forward, still trying to get a look at the parking area behind the water tower. Two long trucks sat nose-to-rear on a narrow driveway. They looked like oil trucks, except that the front of their tanks had cone-heads.

There was more ground fire, but it was fairly light; it wouldn't do much damage unless the Hog stayed in one place for a long time. And he wasn't about to do that.

"They're right behind the water tank," Mongoose told Shotgun. "They have some heavy machine guns and maybe light antiair."

"Yeah. I'm past 'em."

"Come around with me and let's take them out." He noted several trucks and smaller buildings nearby, and a fair-sized revetment with maybe a half-dozen khaki-covered vehicles a quarter of a mile directly north of the Scuds.

"You take the Scuds and I'll get the guys on the roof," said Shotgun. "Shit, Goose, there's a battery of something in that half-donut north of the parking lot. Bitch fuck, these guys got peashooters all over the place."

"You'd think they lived here or something," said Mongoose, pushing the Hog into position to make a decent bomb run.

Doberman's arms felt like lead as he pulled off the remains of the second truck. He heard Mongoose call out the location of the two Scud carriers, and swung back in their direction.

A quick scan of the instruments showed everything running at spec. The slight pull to the left was still there, but the engines pegged in perfect parallel on the gauge. Plenty of gas, he told himself; plenty of explosives sitting under the wings to eliminate as many Scuds as they could find.

He was still looking for the other Hogs when the terrain ahead erupted with a thick black explosion. Shotgun was yelling, "Hot shit!" Doberman pulled his right wing up and pushed straight for the thunderclap of ex-Scud, aiming to mop up what was left. He caught a glimpse of a Hog orbiting back in his direction, off at two o'clock.

"Doberman, there's a flatbed with two guns at least to the west of the tank. Take it out," said Mongoose.

"No, I got it," said Shotgun.

"Where the fuck are you?" Doberman asked.

"Right here," said Shotgun, pulling his A-10 through the smoke cloud. He was well off to Doberman's right, but the roiling dust was so thick Doberman broke off, unable to get a target and not wanting to screw up what was obviously a turkey shoot. He gathered his wits for a better run once Shotgun cleared.

"What else is down there?" he asked Shotgun, his back momentarily turned to the action.

Shotgun's response was garbled. Someone else jumped on the frequency, and Doberman heard an F-16 flight ask if the Hogs needed help.

Meanwhile, Mongoose put himself in a low orbit and played quarterback. He had Shotgun hold off while he directed Doberman in to drop his bombs on a truck parked north of the now-demolished Scuds.

The haze made it tough to settle his target in the HUD, and as he glared into the screen Doberman realized the enthusiasm he'd felt this morning—hell, the giddiness, there wasn't another word—was slipping away. Even the energy he'd just had smoking the trucks was gone. His arms throbbed as he worked the stick, his legs jittered—time to get rid of the stinking bombs and head home. A thick shadow finally loomed in the center of his HUD, smack dab in the dead zone. He went for the trigger, pickling his bombs and arcing back toward the sky, looking for his second wind.

"One of us ought to take out that water tank," said Shotgun. "Discourage them from coming back."

"Yeah," said Mongoose. "Who's closest?"

"I am," said Doberman.

"You got bombs?"

"Negative. Cannon's ready, though."

"Okay. I don't see any more ground fire," added Mongoose. "You?"

"They ought to be out of ammo by now. Stinking machine-gun bullets won't do much anyway."

"Yeah, don't get too cocky," said Mongoose. "All it takes is one."

"I think anyone still alive down there's hiding in the sand," said Shotgun. "They got a bad case of Hog-itis."

Doberman pushed his Hog around and double-checked his cannon. "A good burst ought to nail it. Unless it's filled with gasoline. Then one'll do."

"If you wait a minute, I'll come in behind you."

"I'm lined up now," said Doberman, rushing a bit, as if getting the tower was somehow a competitive event.

"Doberman, take it out," said Mongoose. "Then we go home."

18

Hakim Ibn Lufti was not religious by nature, but he prayed to Allah nonetheless as he snaked his way onto the catwalk surrounding the water tower. The American invaders were all around him; though he had lived in the desert his entire life, he had never felt more alone. The green-black planes had destroyed the missiles and all of his comrades; as far as he knew, he was the only one left alive.

Yesterday, Private Hakim had confided to another man that if the Americans came, he would most likely surrender; this was Saddam's war, and he felt no particular fondness for the head of his country. But the man Hakim had told that to lay in the sand several hundred yards away; he'd caught a fist-sized piece of metal in his chest when the planes began dropping their bombs. Hakim's ambitions had accordingly changed; he wanted nothing more than to extract some revenge on the invaders.

He had carried a missile launcher to the tower to help him do so. He wasn't entirely sure how to use the weapon, however. It was a new model, an SA-16, and though he had heard others say it was considerably better than the SA-7, in fact he had never been trained to use either. He knew how to push a trigger, however, and had some hope that if the weapon were pointed in more or less the right direction, it could take care of the rest.

Hakim had almost fired at one of the jets zooming at him when he was distracted by a billow of thick smoke. He began to choke. By the time he recovered, the warplane was veering away.

Hakim cursed, and pushed the trigger anyway.

Doberman cursed as he watched his cannon shot spitting wide right, a bad putt on an uneven green. The first two slugs punctured the side of the tower, but the plane's pull and maybe the wind threw him off. He had too sharp an angle, and then the smoke got in the way and he decided to slide off and try for a better pass.

Damn it, I have to give myself more room this time, he told himself. I may be tired but I can still hit a fucking water tower.

I'll never hear the end of it if I miss.

It took a second for Hakim to realize why the weapon had not fired. The missile had a prime button that kept it from being accidentally launched.

Tears came to his eyes as he realized his error. Cursing himself, cursing his God, he unsafed the weapon and punched its stock against the steel rail in anger. The jet was far away now, and getting further.

And then, God brought it back. It was as if His hand took its nose, drew it up in the sky, and yanked it backwards. Its strange, stubby wings straightened as it angled around and flew directly toward him.

Fire erupted from its mouth. The tower shuddered, crumpling above him. Hakim cringed, held his breath, waited for death to come. He felt the grating below him start to give away. He held the missile launcher up, falling as the plane flashed overhead. He pressed the trigger as his life evaporated in a steam of metal and fire.

19

Shotgun saw the flash from the tower, saw the rocket shoot out wide, and saw the tower disintegrate, all at the same time. He barked a warning to Doberman and pounded his own plane hard left, shooting flares and giving it gas and pushing his body to the side, trying to add mustard to the evasive maneuvers. Doberman jinked ahead, twisting, diving, and climbing behind a shower of flares.

The missile had shot straight out from the tower, perpendicular to the Hog's flight path. An ordinary SA-7, if it happened to catch a whiff of the exhaust, would choke out its engine swinging back and fall harmlessly away.

This one didn't. This one came around in a tight arc, snorting for Doberman's turbofan.

"It's still on you," yelled Shotgun.

Doberman sensed the missile before Shotgun warned him it had been launched. Something had moved on the tower as he closed in; a sixth sense told him there was a suicidal maniac on the rail with a shoulder-missile. The pilot pushed the Warthog hard in the direction of the launch as he flew past, tossing flares and jinking as wildly as he could. His cannon burst had slowed his momentum, and there wasn't a huge amount of altitude left to use gathering speed. He danced and shook, shoved the forked tail of the Hog in a wild streak across the desert, riding a roller coaster of angles and flares. His stomach rolled into a pea as G forces slammed against his body in every direction. The pilot felt the flesh on his cheeks peeling under the sudden weight of the oxygen mask, plunging itself into his face. But it was a good feeling, blood running away from his head despite the best efforts of his suit—the heady, floating weightlessness told him he was alive.

Doberman had practiced this sort of escape at least a hundred times. He realized he should be clear now, a few miles and a dozen hard turns from the missile. The Russian-made SA-7 was a good weapon, but couldn't hang with you on a serious G turn. He kept going a few more seconds just to be sure, pulled one more turn with more flares, being extra cautious, then turned around, looking for his buddies. His eyes shot over to the altimeter ladder on the HUD, focusing on the white numbers as he reoriented himself, banking hard to the south to snap onto a course toward the others.

In that second, a sledgehammer hit his right wing.

20

The next five seconds defied all known physical laws of time and space. Simultaneously, the universe moved at infinite speed and stood completely still. Doberman was paralyzed beyond comprehension.

Hit a bit beyond midway on its right wing, the Hog slumped in the air. Small bits of the wing were sucked into the turbofan. The GE groaned, its fire quenched by the in-rushing rain of debris.

The engine munched the shrapnel, spat it out, and then, helped by the momentum of the air rushing through the blades as the plane hurtled downwards, kicked itself back to life. Doberman felt the surge in his arms as he coaxed just enough speed to stay airborne; stutter-stepping off the ugly brown earth, he managed to hold the plane in a slow but steady climb. He was even going in the right direction, southwest—though he couldn't for the life of him figure out how he got that way.

Once the plane was stable, the pilot pitched his head back to look out the right side of the cockpit, back at the wing. The missile had gone straight through, blowing a fair-sized hole en route. A bit of the aileron had been taken away; he couldn't quite bend his body around far enough to see how much or what other damage had been done.

On the bright side, the missile had missed the fuel tank.

That, or angels really did drive Hogs in heaven.

Shotgun waited for the canopy to blow, then worried that Doberman had been hit too low, too fast, too hard to save himself. The distance between the two planes closed as quickly as the bile rose in his throat and he felt the empty sickness of seeing a buddy go down.

"Dog Man, get out," he shouted again and again. "Eject. Eject."

"Now what the fuck am I going to eject for?" growled Doberman. "Shotgun, would you shut the hell up so I can think?"

Suddenly, the nose of Doberman's Hog changed direction. The plane began lifting itself off the deck.

A hand reaching down from above wouldn't have shocked Shotgun more.

"Jesus Christ," he yelped. "You are one lucky motherfucker."

"Yeah, right. You're going to explain your reasoning as soon as we put down."

Adjusting his speed, Shotgun pulled almost directly over the damaged Hog. The wing had a gaping hole, exposing organs and underwear, not to mention the ribs that held it together. But it was intact.

Just another day in the life of a Hog driver, thought Shotgun. Damn, I love these planes.

The first thing Mongoose did when he realized Doberman was still alive was curse himself for not taking out the water tank first thing with bombs. Better, he shouldn't even have bothered. The Scuds were the priority, and they were gone. Getting greedy was a good way to get killed.

It was one thing to put himself in danger, and a hell of a different thing to put his guys there. His job was to get them home. Period. Everything else was way second.

Fucking water tower.

"I have a question for you I need a real honest answer on," he told Doberman as soon as the pilot had the damaged Hog headed toward the border.

"Shoot."

"How far you think you can fly that thing?"

"Me? Hell, I'll fly around the world if you want."

Mongoose took a second before responding. His own arms and legs were tired as hell; Doberman's must be aching even more. The control surfaces on the right side of the stricken Hog's wing were shot to hell. Doberman's fuel situation was strong enough to get him back to Al Jouf with only a little sweat, assuming he didn't spring a leak. But that meant sailing through bad-guy country just about the whole flight.

They could turn and fly directly south, safer if he had to punch out, but that made Al Jouf a stretch. King Khalid, another FOL the Hogs had used this morning to refuel, was even further.

And what did he do once he got there?

Mongoose took another glance at Doberman's plane. How long could it stay airborne with a football-sized hole in the wing?

But he couldn't just tell him to bail.

"Do you think you could tank?" Mongoose finally asked.

"If I have to. Why?"

"What I'm thinking is the tough thing for that Hog is going to be landing. Your flap's probably not going to set right, and I'll be honest with you, it'll be a miracle if your landing gear works right."

There was silence from the other plane.

"You can go ahead and respond," he told Doberman.

"You want me to bail out."

"Not necessarily. But that may end up the only option."

"You're also thinking we shouldn't go straight back to Al Jouf because you think I'm going to have to bail before I get there."

"I didn't say that."

"You're thinking that."

"Yeah," Mongoose admitted. "If we try to get back to the base we'll be over Iraq most of the way."

"You ain't going to jinx it by admitting it," said Doberman. "Be straight with me."

"I'm trying."

"If we refuel maybe you can coax it all the way back to Hog Heaven," said Shotgun. "Bail out on the roof and climb down for a shower."

"I'm not bailing out," snapped Doberman. "Period."

Mongoose worked his lips together, not sure what to say. He would feel the same way. But feelings were irrelevant. What had to be done had to be done.

If it came down to it, would he order Doberman to jump out of the plane? Was it his job to do that?

Absolutely.

Not that ejecting was risk-free. The seat manufacturer put survivability at eighty percent.

And they bragged about that.

The flight leader checked his own gauges, calculating distances and plotting a course in his head. There was no sense answering Doberman's declaration that he wouldn't pull the eject handle. What could he say? I'm in charge here?

"Yeah, okay," Doberman said finally, breaking the uneasy silence. Mongoose couldn't tell if he was disgusted, or just tired. "Let's try for a tanker and then on to King Fahd. Line it up."

21

Dixon couldn't find the F-16 pilot, if he existed. There were two F-16's at the base, one of which had been pushed off the side of the runway and left for scrap metal. Neither pilot had been anywhere near Tweedledum—or Taqaddum, the actual name of the Iraqi installation. They didn't know anything about a lake, but they had seen plenty of things on fire.

Military intelligence at its finest, the lieutenant thought as he returned to the intel Humvee.

Bauer didn't seem all that broken up about the lack of information. He sent Dixon to debrief a pair of French pilots who had somehow wandered up to Al Jouf in their Jaguars.

Unfortunately, Dixon didn't speak French. And though the other pilots spoke English, it rolled off their tongues the way a Mark 82 would fall down a flight of stairs at Versailles.

Like the A-10, the aging Jaguar was primarily designed to support front-line troops, but it represented an entirely different philosophy, something more akin to the F-16's—get in and out as fast as possible. And that was about the only element of their mission Dixon could understand—the two pilots gestured freely as they described an attack on a target that for all the world sounded like a circus tent. Even more of a mystery was how the Frenchmen had managed to get way the hell out here. They were based at Al Ahsa, back near Riyadh. Dixon hadn't seen the entire ATO—the air order dictating the first day's game plan ran hundreds of pages—but he knew the Frenchies had started out from the eastern part of the theater.

Every time he asked how they got here, the two pilots began replaying what sounded like a seriously awesome, close-in furball gun battle. Their desert-brown ships bore no evidence of a gunfight, however, and Dixon got a firm "no" whenever he used the word "damage."

Eventually, the lieutenant decided he had as much information as he was ever going to get. He thanked the men, who now began to pepper him with questions about how in God's name they could get home from here. Dixon nodded cheerfully, answered "yes" as much as possible, then turned and ran for Bauer.

At last he was getting the hang of this intelligence stuff.

The major reinterpreted the pilots' pigeon English and added a few notes to a thick stack of papers on the Humvee seat. Looking up, Bauer pointed to an F-14 that had swung its wings out wide to land and announced that it belonged to the *Saratoga*, a carrier in the Red Sea; it had been part of a Navy package striking deep into west Iraq and lost its INS, among other things.

"You want me to go debrief him?" Dixon asked.

"Nah. I'll get that one myself. Got a cousin on the ship I want to say hi to. Listen, the parts you were waiting for landed about ten minutes ago. Ought to be at the repair area by now. Why don't you go make sure they get to the right place? Thanks for helping. You're ever looking for a job in intelligence, come see me."

The Hog had been moved several times in the past few hours, and was now at the far edge of the maintenance area. A tubular steel ladder had been erected around part of the wing and fuselage, and a small figure was atop it, busily tossing pieces of the plane to the ground. As Dixon got closer, he realized a succession of curses was accompanying the work.

He also realized something else—the tech sergeant working on the plane was a woman.

Though he recognized her from his unit, Dixon didn't know Becky Rosen; in fact, he didn't know most of the maintenance people besides his own crew chief and one or two of the men who habitually worked on his plane. He'd heard a few things about her, though, none of them pleasant. Short, built more like a mud wrestler than a bikini babe, she had cat eyes and round, freckled cheeks.

She turned around and saw him staring at her from the ground. "Dixon, right? What the hell did you do to this Hog? Drive it through a wheat thresher?"

"I didn't do anything to it," he said, taken by surprise. "Captain Glenon was flying."

"Doberman, huh? I thought he knew better than this. Fuck, did he think we were bored or something?"

"Maybe," said the lieutenant, not really knowing what else to say.

She scowled. "What the hell happened to yours?"

"My plane? Nothing."

"Well, where is it? Did you walk back from Iraq?"

Dixon felt his entire body begin to burn. His temporary assignment as non-intelligence officer had taken his mind off his screwup, but now the guilt shot back in a heavy dose.

But damn it—when did a tech sergeant earn the right to grill an officer?

"Major Johnson bumped me," he said stiffly.

"Oh." She looked at him a moment, then turned back to the plane.

There was something in the look that pissed him off even more than her tart tone.

Pity?

He didn't need that from a stinking technician.

"Say, Lieutenant, you think you could hand me up that TACAN aerial cover?"

"What?"

"The big flat doohickey thing by your feet. The radio antenna? The fin?"

"I know what it is." Dixon was so flustered with anger he

couldn't say anything else. He reached over and picked up the thick blade. Rosen had returned to work on the Hog, and so he had to climb up onto the wing to hand it to her.

"Thanks. Looks like the IFF is fine, but these wires here are toast. You all right, Lieutenant?"

"Yeah, I'm fine."

"Get shot at?"

"I guess so."

He tried to make his voice sound hard, but Rosen laughed as if he were joking. "Hand me the screwdriver out of the bag over there, okay?"

"What, you think I'm your gofer?"

"No, sir, Lieutenant," she snapped. "But I was under the impression that you wanted to get this airplane back in the air as soon as possible, and helping me out a little will expedite matters."

"Expedite. Where'd you learn that word?"

"I have a master's degree in English lit," she said, holding out her hand for the tool.

Dixon couldn't tell if she was serious. He reached into the large bag Rosen used as a tool carrier and handed her the screwdriver. He noticed that the bag, though covered with grease and dirt, was made of leather.

"My dad gave it to me. Sentimental value," she said.

"The degree?"

"No, the bag, wise guy. I earned the degree myself. Romantic poetry." She took the tool and went back to work connecting the fin. Dixon couldn't see what she was doing beneath the access cover and fin, but there were loose parts everywhere. "What was it like?" she asked.

"What?"

"Jesus—bombing Saddam," she said. "Did you hit your target?"

"I guess."

"You guess?" Rosen turned so quickly her face almost smacked his. "No offense, Lieutenant, but we're busting our butts back here for you guys, and a straight answer wouldn't hurt now and then."

Dixon stepped back. "What's up your ass?"

"Lieutenant?"

"Why are you riding me?"

"I'm not, sir." Her eyes were all innocence. "I'm not. Come on, help me get these wires in here. Don't mind the sheet metal. I had to bend things a little. We'll straighten that out later. Not by the book, but you want to fly before tonight, right?"

She didn't mean anything, Dixon thought to himself. She's just blunt.

"Watch your hands. That end's sharp. Twenty-three millimeter went right through here, see? Doberman was flying?"

"Yeah."

"He's one lucky son of a bitch, I'll tell you that." She slapped the side of the plane as if she were smacking a favorite horse. "Of course, a Hog can take a lot of shit. But what I'd like to know is how he managed to take triple-A on the top of the plane. I can understand the holes in the belly and the back, but this?"

"Probably he had the Hog on its side, rolling out of the attack," said Dixon. He motioned with his hands. "The shells would have gotten him like this. There was a lot of triple-A."

"I thought you guys were supposed to stay above the flak."

"We were. But the cloud cover was kind of high. Have to see where we're bombing. And you know—"

"Anything over five hundred feet you want oxygen, right? That Hog macho anti-snob snobbery shit." She slammed an access panel closed, then scooped up her tools and slid down the ladder to the ground, half-running to work on another part of the jet. Dixon, still unsure what the hell to make of her, followed tentatively.

"By three. Four the latest," she said.

"Huh?"

"It's going to take me a little while to finish. I want to make sure it'll work the whole way home. The rest of this we can tidy up back at the aerodrome. The crew here did a kick-ass job. Looks like they stamped you out a new rear end. Honest. You'll be taking off for King Fahd in no time."

"Great."

"You sound disappointed. You looking to go back north?"

"Yeah," he said, his anger stoking up again.

"You're not scared?"

Scared?

She wasn't busting his chops. It was a real question.

"Yeah," admitted Dixon. "I was petrified."

Her eyes softened. They were pretty eyes, actually, when they looked at you like this.

"Takes balls to admit it," she said, dropping her stare to look back at her work. "Don't worry, you'll get another shot. Say, listen, Lieutenant, you think you can go steal a really big hammer off that crew over there? A really big one. I may have to do some serious banging if we're going to get you back to Fahd in time for dinner. And don't tell them what it's for. Somebody comes over here with a manual and we're going to bed without supper for three weeks."

22

The first refuel was a piece of cake.

It was on the second that Doberman lost control of the plane.

They grabbed a tanker and top priority about three seconds after crossing the Iraqi border. Doberman had a good feel for the plane by then; the damaged Hog didn't have the most desirable flying characteristics, but he could hold her reasonably steady at five thousand feet. The tanker, though, ordinarily did its business much higher than that. Apprised of the situation, the KC-135 pilot slid down to about ten thousand feet; Doberman coaxed the Hog toward her gently. Even under the best conditions, it took the underpowered plane an eternity to climb; now it seemed like he was climbing Mt. Everest in a wheelchair.

The director lights beneath the tanker normally provided a reference for approaching planes. They seemed only to throw him off, juggling back and forth as he eased in. Finally Doberman got close enough for the boom operator in the back of the tanker to hook his spike into the receptacle. The Hog snorted with pleasure as it sucked up the fuel.

That was the first time. Swinging southeast toward King Fahd, they had to be vectored out of the path of a large package of bombers headed north. Doberman's right hand started shaking uncontrollably as he brought the plane to the proper course heading. At first it was just a twitch in his thumb, and he laughed at it—compared to the immense knot in his back, this torture was amusing.

But as it spread from his thumb to his other fingers, he stopped thinking it was funny. He grabbed the stick with his left hand and shook his right in the air before him, as if he could shoo the problem away. When that didn't work, he tried stretching his hand out against the top of the instrument panel. Finally, he yelled at it to stop.

It stopped.

"Doberman, you okay in there?" Shotgun asked. Shotgun had slid behind him; Mongoose was in the lead.

"Yeah, I'm fine," said Doberman.

"You know you're down to three angels."

The pilot looked at the altimeter in shock. "Yeah," he said. "I know. I was just looking for a good draw. I got an ace in my hand."

"Huh? What the hell are you talking about?"

"I'm bringing it back up." He put his right hand back on the stick, holding the control with both hands for a few seconds, not sure he could trust it.

"How are you on fuel?"

"Fine," he barked.

"Just asking."

Mongoose called in with the time to tanker and the frequency, then double-checked the course headings with both pilots.

Doberman barely acknowledged. There was so much shit to do, so much blank sky to fly through.

Luckiest dead man, huh? What the hell were the odds of getting all shot to hell twice in one day?

Worse than pulling a full house on a four-card draw. Worse than hitting an inside straight.

Never in his life had he done that.

Nah, he must have. All the years he'd played cards, since his Uncle JR taught him at age seven, and he hadn't gotten one?

Didn't remember if he did. Shit, it was just that he'd never tried to do it. A sucker's move.

Good ol' JR. Taught him how to play poker, taught him how to smoke cigars, taught him just about everything important.

Ought to call him.

Jesus, that would be a good trick, Doberman realized. JR died two years ago.

Hell of a thing to forget. Son of a bitch got crunched so bad in a car accident they had to close the coffin.

"Doberman, you awake back there? The tanker is trying to reach you on their frequency."

The pilot gave the com panel a dirty look, as if it were responsible for JR's death.

"They're at twenty-four thousand feet," said Mongoose. "You're two cars back."

At 24,000 feet? No way he was getting that high. Hell, even a perfect Hog didn't like being that far off the ground.

"Devil Four?"

"Yeah, I'm switching to their frequency now," Doberman snapped. "I need them to come down. Way down."

The tanker was a KC-10A Extender, a military version of the three-engined McDonnell Douglas DC-10 adapted to a tanker role. Taking the boom from the jet was similar to grabbing a line from the older KC-135, and in fact Doberman had flown his Hog into the Gulf following a KC-10A. He could suck up to one blind, and had come close to doing so on several night flights.

But no way he was getting to 24,000 feet, not in this lifetime. He was at six thousand, and struggling as it was.

How high could you fly with a hole in your wing?

The tanker pilot brought the plane to about seven thousand feet, and threw his landing gear out to help slow himself down. Doberman huffed and puffed to hold the Hog relatively steady as he closed in. Everything was taking so damn long, but at least the A-10 was flying predictably: slow and perfect, considering the conditions.

Then, as the pilot pushed the Hog the last few feet toward the long pipe extending from the plane's rear end, Doberman felt his head starting to spin. His eyes seemed to slip back behind their sockets and down into his cheeks. When he got them back in place, he thought he was coming too close too fast and backed off the throttle; the next thing he knew, he was heading downward, the plane threatening to spin.

Shotgun, riding off Doberman's starboard wing, saw the Hog tilting to the left. Before he could key the mike to say anything, Doberman's plane had rolled toward the earth.

Shotgun tucked his wing and started to follow. There was no fresh sign of damage to the Hog, and the wing remained intact despite the stress of the dive. In fact, if Shotgun didn't know there was a hole in it, he would have sworn there was nothing wrong with the A-10A that was plummeting toward the earth at several hundred miles an hour.

Doberman didn't answer his hail. Shotgun tried choking back the metallic taste that crept into the corners of his mouth, but it kept coming.

Lines and circles. You could divide the world into lines and circles. Everything could be measured. In the physical world, at least. Measuring changed it—Heisenberg's uncertainty principle, right?—but it could always be counted off somehow.

Counting off. Ten, nine, eight—

Doberman's eyes found the altimeter clock as he pleaded with the stick to right the aircraft. He had a bum wing but he could do it. He'd been a check pilot, putting newly overhauled Hogs through their paces. This was a piece of cake.

Unlucky or not, he could do it.

His head was flooded with images that rolled and pitched much faster than the injured Hog. He was dizzy as hell, and the shake had returned, only it was hitting his chest. He reached for the throttle, discovering with a start that his hand was already on it.

What the fuck is going on with my brain!

Yo! Snap the hell out of it!

Something in his head hiccuped as the Hog fell from his hands. Now he felt a numb pain in his chest.

Maybe the damage this morning was supposed to take him

out. Maybe somebody somewhere was fixing the ledger. Luckiest dead man my ass.

JR was there, giving him advice. "Fold when you see the other guy's eyes twinkle."

What the hell was that supposed to mean?

Why'd you teach a little kid how to play poker for?

Because you're too young to parachute.

JR took him up in a Cessna for his thirteenth birthday, got him hooked on flying.

For his fourteenth birthday, JR got him a parachute ride, the damn coolest thing that had ever happened to him in his life.

Too cool to tell his mom, though, until after he landed intact.

Jump, JR was telling him. Just jump. Everything else is automatic.

Shotgun watched as Doberman's starboard wing began to edge upwards; the plane was heading into a spin.

"Eject!" he yelled over the radio. "Doberman, jump! Jump! Get the hell out of that plane!"

Doberman felt it getting further and further away from him. He couldn't get the nose pointed back upwards, and now the wing was sliding out from under him.

The air brakes weren't working. The right aileron and its companion deceleron had been hit, and probably the left ones were screwed up, too.

There was a simple formula in his head for fixing all of this. It was just a matter of finding it in the clutter.

Call with two pair. Fold on anything less.

Shotgun was yelling at him, but Doberman couldn't hear what he was saying.

He could hear his uncle, though. He was telling him to jump from the Cessna. Jump; everything else is automatic.

No, that was the problem; he was so tired he was trying to fly on instincts and the Hog didn't like that, not with a frazzled wing.

He wasn't compensating right. He was pretending he was

just out of the maintenance shop. Straighten up and fly right, he told himself.

The refrain danced in his brain. JR used to hum that song. Meant he had a good hand. Gave himself away. Made it easy to beat him.

The Hog snorted as Doberman's hands finally took hold of its sides. The metallic animal sniffed at the air, unsure where the hell it was. A small piece from its wing—part of the flap, damaged by debris when the missile hit—flew backwards like a Frisbee. Then the craft straightened herself out.

Doberman leveled out at one thousand feet, heart pumping, feet shaking, but head clear.

"Man, you got a one-track mind with this ejection thing," he told Shotgun. "I don't feel like jumping today. Maybe tomorrow."

23

Mongoose found the two Hogs flying together at about three thousand feet. They were climbing back toward the tanker like a pair of little old ladies walking up a staircase.

"What the hell happened?"

"I think the wash from the tanker knocked something loose in the wing," Doberman told him. "That and I had a touch of vertigo creeping in on the tanker."

"Definite on that first theory," said Shotgun. "Part of your flap is missing."

"Can you fly that thing?" Mongoose asked.

"Watch me."

"I don't know how that fuckin' wing is holding together," said Shotgun. "I say we head for the nearest set of sandbags and the hell with King Fahd."

"I can make it," said Doberman. "I just need some more gas, that's all."

"I think we've pushed it far enough," said Mongoose. He pulled his map open, double-checking their position. "Let Shotgun and me gas up, then call it a day. We'll hang with you until the chopper comes."

"Jesus, we've come this far," said Doberman. "I know I can do that tanker. Just get the guy to come down to me instead of the other way around."

"The tanker just bingo'd," said Mongoose. "A replacement is on the way."

"Fine. Have him meet us en route to Fahd. Hell, I got plenty of fuel. I can squeeze another hundred miles out of what I've got left. I'll back off power another ten percent."

"You're flying backwards as it is," said Shotgun. "No shit, Goose, I think we've pushed this as far as it can go."

"You can't order me to bail out. That's bullshit. I'm not losing this plane."

"You have to get a lot higher and faster to refuel," Mongoose told him. "I don't know if you'll hang together."

"Get me a divert field then."

"What if the gear doesn't come down?"

"Man, why are you giving up on me?"

"I'm not giving up on you, Doberman. I'm trying to keep you in one piece."

"Screw you."

Mongoose bit back an angry response, then looked at the list of fields. They were all pretty damn far from here; might just as well go on to King Fahd. He checked his map and the lat-long on the INS again. But it wasn't until he glanced at his own fuel stores that it all clicked.

"Devil Two, give me your fuel status."

Doberman reported the weight of the fuel in his tanks with a hair less belligerence than before. Mongoose worked out the math. He checked his altitude, then cut his own power to take the Hog down to about 185 knots. It was at or close to stall speed and the plane didn't like it; he dropped the nose and went down to five thousand, where her complaints weren't quite as vociferous.

"Were you serious that you could cut power ten percent and still fly that thing?" he asked.

"Shit, yeah."

"Try it."

"What's going on?" asked Shotgun.

"I may have to take it lower," said Doberman.

"Go where you feel comfortable," said Mongoose. He could tell Doberman had already figured out what he was thinking. "Just don't put it into the sand."

"We have to correct three degrees back north."

"Affirmative. I'll have the controller tell King Fahd we're on the way. Shotgun, go to the replacement tanker, top off, and come find us. There's a track ahead that I'll jump on as soon as you're back. Doberman, listen—let's talk it up the rest of the way back."

"You think I'm falling asleep?"

"Man, I'm tired," said Mongoose. "You got to be exhausted."

"Yeah, well, maybe I'm a little beat. What do you want to talk about?"

"Who's gonna win the Super Bowl?"

"Washington."

"They're not in it."

"They will be by the time I land this thing."

According to Doberman's calculations, the stricken Hog had precisely enough gas to fall one hundred feet short of King Fahd. And no amount of math could change that.

What he hoped for was a strategic gust of wind at the last moment. Or maybe the uncalculable effect of fumes and pilot willpower.

But even if he managed enough glide to make the strip, he needed several things to happen. First of all, he needed a clear runway. While the tower had relayed word that he would get it, things had a way of changing at the last minute.

Secondly, an A-10A's flaps were generally set at twenty degrees to land. Doing that on only one side would be like telling the plane to pretend it had been made by Black & Decker. He hoped he would be going so damn slow he might be able to fake it. There was enough runway to roll for quite a ways—unless the strip was cluttered with traffic. Then he'd have to stand on very thin brakes and pray.

Assuming the right-side landing gear worked, of course. There was no way of knowing until he was ready to land.

But aside from those minor considerations and the fact that for all he knew the wing could sheer off at any second, he was having a wonderful day.

• • •

The thing was, Shotgun had a double standard. If it had been him flying the Hog, sure as shit he'd have argued for King Fahd and told Mongoose not to sweat it.

But since he wasn't flying it, and no reflection on Doberman's flying abilities because the Dog Man was a hell of a balls-out driver—but damn it, he should have punched out as soon as they were over the border. True, they would have lost the A-10 in the process. But better safe than sorry. You just didn't fly a Hog with a hole in the wing.

Oh, sure, you could. Shotgun could. But he had a double standard.

"Doberman, you read that?" he asked when the pilot didn't immediately acknowledge the tower's instruction that he was cleared to take it in any way he could.

"I got it," snapped Doberman.

"You okay with this?"

"You're sounding like my fucking mother today, Shotgun. I don't know which one of you assholes is worse, you or Mongoose. Why don't you guys relax, huh?"

"Just making sure, prick-face. You ready to try your gear?"

"You gonna hold my dick for me while I pee too?"

"I might."

Shotgun slipped his Hog lower, trying to get a good look beneath Doberman's wings. The front wheel was down smooth, and so was the wheel beneath the damaged right wing.

But of all things, his left wheel was stuck.

"Uh, Doberman, you're not going to believe this."

"I'm already trying to get it down manually. It must have been hit when the missile struck."

"No, man, the left wheel. The right one looks fine."

"You sure you know your left from your right?"

"What's your indicator say?"

"Damn."

Doberman hit the handle to lower the gear twice more. He couldn't for the life of him figure what the hell the problem was. Just as on nearly all other aircraft flying, a hydraulic system automatically snapped the Warthog's landing gear in place. But the Hog also had a safety system; because of the way the wheels folded, they could be manually released and locked into place with help from the slipstream or wind beneath the plane. And that should have happened by now.

One good thing—dropping the right wheel hadn't snapped the wing in two. Not yet anyway. But it hadn't made it any easier to fly.

The runway was maybe a hundred feet away. And damned if the engines weren't starting to choke.

He reached for the handle and once again dropped it. Finally, he felt it move.

Or thought he did. Or hoped he did. There was no turning back now.

Mongoose felt a surge of relief as Doberman's Hog touched the tarmac, rolling smart and sharp as if she'd just been up for a quick qualifying spin. Right behind her came an HC-130 Spectre gunship, also low on fuel and just about trailing an engine.

The major gunned his engine. Looking for his place in the landing stack, he realized that he had to pee so bad he was going to have to duck under the wing once he touched down.

Assuming he could wait that long.

24

Technical Sergeant Rosen did a decent job with the Hog, good enough to get the radio and all of the instrumentation working. Between her and the scrub base's mechanics, the A-10 was patched and ready to go in what must have been world record time. In fact, for a few minutes it seemed like the base colonel was going to stick it into a four-ship element tasked to go north and bomb trucks.

Dixon felt a twinge of panic when he heard that. But he was also disappointed when the idea was dropped and he was told to go home instead.

The fuel queue was backed up worse than the entrance ramp to an LA freeway at rush hour. There was an HC-130 at the head of the line, and damned if the four-engined monster didn't look like she was going to drain the trucks dry.

Dixon tried to look disinterested as he sat in the cockpit, checking his way points and all of the marginalia critical for his return trip to King Fahd. He was nervous, and he wasn't nervous. He could do this in his sleep—it was an easy ferry trip home through friendly skies. With all the stops out he'd be able to do it in maybe two hours.

As long as he didn't come under fire. Then all bets were off.

No, they weren't, he told himself. He'd gotten spooked, sure, but that was because it was the first time and he didn't know what to expect. The next time would be better. The next time he'd nail the son of a bitch.

He hated the fact that he had lied to Mongoose about dropping the bombs. Not lied, but not given the whole story. Same thing.

But on the bottom line, it really didn't matter. He'd dropped them. He'd gotten his plane back in one piece. That was what was important.

He wondered if he shouldn't feel a little pissed off at being moved into Doberman's plane. Yeah, he was the lowest-ranking pilot on the mission, the least experienced by far, but damn—that was his plane.

And the son of a bitch had kept him from redeeming himself.

You fell off a horse, you got right back on.

He could. He knew he could.

Whether the Herc was finally topped off or had just exceeded the limit on its credit card, the gas line began to move. Dixon eased up, wondering at the succession of jets that kept straggling onto the desert strip. The end of the runway and the access ramp were crowded with planes. If Jouf was this packed, he wondered what the home 'drome, King Fahd, would look like. Though much further behind the lines, it housed a long list of units, including every A-10 in the theater. And its long, smooth runways would make it a convenient rest stop for battle-weary planes based further south or on one of the two carriers in the nearby Gulf.

"Hey, Yank! Yank!"

Dixon suddenly realized that a man in a green flight suit was doing jumping jacks in front of his right wing. His mouth seemed to be moving; in any event, it was obvious that he wanted to talk to him. Dixon waved the fellow around to the left side of the plane and popped down the cockpit ladder. He soon found a British pilot leaning over the side into his seat. And damned if, through the myriad of fuel and oil smells, the stink of exhaust, sweat, gunpowder, and metal, he didn't catch a strong whiff of Scotch off the man.

The Brit gestured for Dixon to take off his helmet so he

could hear better. Reluctantly, Dixon did so. It didn't help him hear any better, and now he was sure it was Scotch.

"I want to thank you for helping rescue me," said the visitor.

"When?"

"Just now. Up near Mudaysis."

"Wasn't me."

"What?"

"Wasn't me," shouted Dixon. He tried to explain that the Hog had been grounded for the entire afternoon, and had only just been repaired. The Brit nodded at about half of what he said.

"Some of your mates then," said the other pilot. "They were definitely A-10's."

"There's a bunch of us."

"Bloody good crew. They risked their lives. All kinds of radar operating there."

"Radar?"

The man nodded. "Got us coming in and out. My commander got a clear signal."

"Commander?"

"Lost, we think." The pilot's eyes edged downwards ever so slightly, then rose again, as if he had been watching a rowboat on a gently ebbing river. "Thank your friends."

"I will."

Dixon waited for the man to jump down and run off before obeying the ground crew's wild gestures to come the hell forward and take fuel. Cinching up to get ready for takeoff, he wondered if he had heard what the man said correctly.

The GCI site they were supposed to take out that morning was just south of Mudaysis.

His screwup had cost someone his life.

PART TWO

TENT CITY

25

When Michael Knowlington was young, the sky was a romantic place, full of possibilities and speed. Then it became a place for defying death; the rush-in-your-face seat-jolt he got nearly every time he went up was like an addict's fix. For a brief time it was an extension of his mind and body, reaching out into the future and the past in the same motion. Then it became an ugly place, a place that told him how old he was, how useless.

Now it was just the sky, empty and gray. Colonel Knowlington stared at it, alone at the edge of the runway, the only place he had to himself on the massive base.

The truth was, Knowlington had expected to lose at least one pilot, and probably more. They'd all survived, and the preliminary reports on their missions were glowing. Now as the last Hog straggled in, he felt himself overcome by emotion. He walked a few feet further along the runway, making damn sure no one else was around.

Tears dripped from his eyes. He bent his legs, lowering himself down in an Indian crouch as the flow became uncontrollable.

He couldn't have picked out a specific reason. He didn't know any of these men very well, with the exception of Mongoose, his operations officer. And yet he knew them all too well, as well as the Blazeman, Cat, and Clunker.

Each a wingman. Each dead.

An F-4 Wild Weasel Phantom, diverted to the base because of mechanical problems, squealed in behind a Hog. The familiar whine of its engines as it touched down, the squeal of its wheels, the heavy suck of oxygen through the pilot's mask snapped Skull's head straight up.

He was in the Philippines, months after his second Nam tour had ended with his splash in the Tonkin Gulf. Still younger than most of the men he trained, he'd already gotten the hotshot star tag and the medals to justify it.

Knowlington was standing at the edge of a strip like this one day when he saw a Phantom smack down, just implode right there on landing. No one really knew why it had happened; mechanical failure of some sort, since the landing itself had looked perfect.

He'd been due to take that plane up, but a hangover and a sympathetic duty officer had saved him. Only his second hangover in the service to that point, a true accomplishment.

It had taken forever to unlearn the lesson he thought he'd learned that day.

Knowlington pushed himself past the memories, past regrets, back to the present. A chill whipped across the back of his neck. It startled him; the chill was familiar, though he hadn't felt it now in a long, long time.

He had a job to do; it was time to stop wallowing and get it done right.

26

Captain Bristol Wong jumped from the chopper a good five feet before it hit the ground. He was higher than he thought—a lot—but he was so annoyed at being here he didn't let it bother him; his legs sprang a bit, absorbing the shock, then steadied as he half-walked, half-ran from the commandeered Army Huey. The exasperated Huey pilot mouthed a silent curse—Wong had been a less-than-ideal passenger, even for an Air Force officer—and skipped away without touching down.

It took Wong several minutes to get himself pointed in the direction of the 535th Tactical Fighter Squadron, and considerably more time for him to arrive at the ugly clump of trailers that served as its headquarters. Scowling at the hand-painted "Hog Heaven" sign nailed near the front door, he barged inside and strode down the hall, looking for Colonel Michael Knowlington, the unit commander. He was surprised to hear laughter coming from the squadron room, and even more surprised to find it dominated by several couches and a large-screen TV. The fact that none of the officers inside could tell him where Knowlington was stoked his anger higher. He stomped into the hallway, nearly running over an airman who volunteered that he had seen the colonel near the runway sometime before. The man was not otherwise helpful; it was only by sheer luck and some desperation that Wong managed to stumble across Knowlington inspecting several A-10A's in the squadron's maintenance area. The captain's ill humor had long since passed from impatience to irritation. By now he knew he would never keep his evening dinner date in the foreign section of Riyadh; the deprivation riled him because he had been unable to contact his friend, which would undoubtedly make future dinner dates a difficult proposition.

Still, this was his first encounter with Knowlington, though he had of course heard of him; Wong coaxed as much energy as he could into seeming polite, giving him a false smile and a smart salute, then asked if they could speak in private.

"Shoot," said Knowlington.

There were at least a dozen enlisted men, mechanical specialists and other grease monkeys from the look of them, within earshot. As far as Wong was concerned, any one of them could have a cell phone and Saddam's home number in his locker.

He shook his head, trying to retain the veneer of politeness. He did, after all, respect Knowlington's rank. "I'm afraid you don't understand, sir," he told him. "We need a secure room."

"A what?"

"I have code-word material to discuss."

"What the fuck does that mean?"

"Sir?"

"Where are you from, Captain?"

"The Pentagon."

"Don't bullshit me, son. Are you with CENTCOM? Or what?"

"I'm afraid it's 'or what,' sir, until we are in a secure facility."

"You think there's a spy crouching behind that A-10 over there?"

"I try to follow procedure, sir. I work for Admiral McConnell," added Wong. McConnell—the head of the Joint Chiefs of Staff's J-2—was a heavy, and mentioning his name always tended to soothe the waters.

Except now.

"So?"

"You do know who the admiral is, sir?"

Knowlington's expression left little doubt that he did—and couldn't care less. "You know what, Wong? I have about three thousand better things to do than stand here and be unimpressed by you. Either make me interested real fast, or disappear."

It's because I'm Oriental, Wong thought. The geezer scumbag flew in Vietnam, so he thinks I'm a gook.

He'd run into that before. Not a lot—most officers were extremely professional, especially when they saw his work product. But every so often there'd be an old-timer who wanted to tell him to go back to Commie Land.

"Sir, this has to do with one of your men," he said, feigning a note of concern. "Could we discuss it in your office?"

Knowlington looked as if he'd eaten a peach pit as he finally put his feet into motion.

The crisply pressed fatigues were what pissed Knowlington off.

He could deal with someone who went around with a stick up his ass—just nod and listen. Being uptight didn't necessarily make you a jerk; plenty of excellent pilots and commanders were by-the-book pricks.

But a fucking captain who ironed his slacks and spit-polished his boots in a war zone belonged to a special class of idiot.

Knowlington's office door wasn't locked. Not that Wong was surprised.

The colonel pulled out his simple metal chair from the desk and waved Wong into the other. "Shoot," he told him.

"Colonel, we have a report that one of your pilots was hit by an SA-16."

"Captain Glenon. That's right." Knowlington nodded. "Did a kick-ass job getting that plane back. Wait until you see it."

"I'd like that very much. I would also like to speak with him as soon as possible."

"Why?"

"I'm investigating the missile strike."

Knowlington's face screwed up. "That's what you wanted to talk to me about?"

"Colonel—"

"No, wait a second, Wong. This whole production is about a shoulder-fired missile? You marched me back here to find out who it was? Are you shitting me? We're fighting a war."

"Colonel, I've had a long day and—"

"*You've* had a long day?"

"Perhaps if we start from the beginning. I am Captain Bristol Wong; I'm from Joint Staff/J-2 intelligence, on loan to General Glossom in Riyadh. My area is weapons, Russian weapons in particular. One of your pilots reported being hit by an SA-16. Naturally, I'm here to check it out."

"What do you mean, naturally?"

"Saddam Hussein doesn't have SA-16's."

"Says you," sneered Knowlington.

"No, actually, sir, I don't say any fucking thing at all," snapped Wong, his patience finally gone. "As far as I know, Saddam shoots down planes by putting his head between his legs and farting."

Knowlington's angry expression evaporated with a sheet of laughter. "Jesus, Wong, you had me going there. I thought you were a real tight-ass. Your uniform threw me off."

"My uniform?"

The colonel shook his head. "You're a fuckin' funny guy. I didn't realize you were busting my chops back at the hangar. I'm sorry. I'm a little tense, I guess."

"But—"

"You have to be careful, though; a lot of people don't have our sense of humor. Not when they're tired, at least." Knowlington waved Wong's perplexed protests away. "What'd you do to get sentenced to J-2? Screw somebody's wife? I mean, you're on the level about that, right? That's for real, isn't it?"

The captain turned red—which made Knowlington laugh and clap him on the shoulder as he rose from his chair.

"Ah, the admiral isn't that bad," said the colonel. "I mean, for a Navy guy. Fucking sailors. Working for the Joint Chiefs'll help your career. No, really. Don't take it so hard. As long as you don't pull this kind of stuff on the wrong guy. Who put you up to it? Sandy?"

"I, uh——"

"Come on, let's go get you some coffee and find Glenon." He stopped short, suddenly serious. "Let me ask you, though: What do you know about Hog drivers?"

"Nothing."

"You're not shitting me this time?"

"No, sir. Not at all."

"Good men, all of them, but a breed apart. In a weird way. But good weird. They all have a little bit of a grudge because, hell, a lot of people put the plane down. And by extension, them. Shit, I'll tell you the truth," Knowlington added as he ushered Wong out of his office. "I thought the Hog was a piece of crap when I first saw it. Swear to God. You check the records. I was on an advisory board that said get rid of it ten years ago. No shit. But now, I have to tell you, I'm a believer. Damn converted. Every one of those suckers came back today. You should see Doberman's plane. Glenon. That's Doberman——the guy who took the SA-16."

"Colonel."

"Yeah, I know. Doesn't exist." Knowlington nearly doubled over with laughter. "Jesus, you're a ball buster. I have to tell you, though, you made my day. Broke me right up. You remind me of a couple of guys I knew in Vietnam. Your dad in the Air Force?"

"Navy, sir."

Knowlington laughed even louder. "Glenon's probably still around here in Hog Heaven somewhere. What a fucking ball-buster you are," he added, leading him down the hallway.

Wong decided it was best not to set the record straight on that particular point, and followed silently.

27

Even Clyston was amazed at the amount of damage on the A-10 Doberman brought in. While the structure of the wing was intact—a miracle in itself—a good hunk of the surface panel was gone or chewed up, with the nearby interior guts twisted beyond recognition. It looked nearly impossible to fix.

Which was why he'd called the Tinman in.

"I don't know, Sarge," said the Tinman. The ancient mechanic—rumor had it he had worked on Billy Mitchell's planes in World War II—shook his head. The Tinman had an odd accent, though no one could figure out where it came from. Besides dropping the occasional verb, he stretched out words in odd ways. "Sarge" sounded like "Sarr-chh."

"I don't know, Sarr-chh," said the mechanic. "You want a new wing."

Wing, in Tinman's mouth, sounded like "wink."

"Nah," said Clyston. "We don't need a whole wing. Come on, Tinman—you got spare parts. Use them."

"Sarr-chh. Demolition derby cars I've seen in better shape." Tinman shook his gray head. He stood about six and a half feet tall and weighed perhaps 160 pounds. "You could place new sheet metal on it, but Sarr-chh. I don't know."

"See, there we go. Now you're getting creative," said Clyston. "Georgie and his guys'll get the new motor up while you're taking care of the wing. What do you think, a couple of hours?"

"Days, Sarr-chh. Days. We could fly in a new wink."

"No time for that," said Clyston. "I need this plane tomorrow."

"I don't know, Sarr-chh."

"Just as a backup." Clyston turned his palms to heaven. "No big deal. Come on, Tinman—I'm counting on you here. I know you can do it. We're in a war."

The Tinman shook his head again, but then he put his bony fingers to his face and pinched his nostrils together—the sign Clyston had been looking for.

"Good man," the capo di capo told him. "Tell me what you'll need and it's yours."

"A new wink."

"Besides that. Ten extra guys?"

"Maybe some coffee."

"Good man."

28

Captain Glenon had long since left Hog Heaven. He would, in fact, have been celebrating his safe return home with a very sound sleep had it not been for Shotgun, who was standing over his bed, urging him to get up and party.

"Screw off," said Glenon. "Get out of my tent. I'm tired."

"Doberman, you are one lucky pup. You have to celebrate it."

"You don't know what you're talking about."

"Anybody else would have been shot down."

"I call that skill."

"You're on a roll, man. It's time to celebrate. Come on, let's hit the Depot before it wears off."

"I'm not going near the Depot for the rest of the war."

"Well, at least come and play cards. Shit, I want to sit next to you."

"Why, so you can look at my hand?"

"So your luck rubs off on me. Hell, man, today's the day you win the lottery."

"Damn it, Shotgun, leave me alone. I'm not lucky. I'm unlucky."

"How do you figure that?" asked Mongoose, coming into the room.

"Doesn't anybody knock anymore?" Doberman complained.

"I did. The canvas doesn't make much noise," said the major. "What are you doing in your underwear?"

"I was trying to jerk off until Shotgun got here."

"Aw, you always let me watch," said Shotgun.

"No shit, I got something serious to talk about," said Mongoose, pulling over a small camp chair.

The major amenity of Doberman's tent was its cement slab. He and the other Devil squadron pilots had arrived at King Fahd far too late to command any of the good berths. After a few days, the fact that they were living in tents had become a point of honor among them, and they voted to refuse the offer of better quarters—trailers being considered moderately better—when it was made.

Doberman hadn't been present for the vote. No one took his request for a recall seriously.

"What do you think I ought to do about Dixon?" Mongoose asked.

"What do you mean, do about him?" said Doberman.

"He screwed up."

"He lost me because my radio went dead," said Doberman. Mongoose shook his head. "No. It was more than that. He totally missed SierraMax, didn't call in, didn't answer the AWACS until he was halfway back to Al Jouf."

"Gees, Goose," said Shotgun. "Give the kid a break. None of that's worth hanging him on. He got turned around in all that flak. You know how garbled the radio transmissions were. All his Mavericks scored."

"He could have cost Doberman his life," said the major. "He should have been on his back when the Mirage jumped him."

"Aw, gees, give the kid a break," said Doberman. "Nobody expects him to be Superman. Besides, it was my fault."

"Your fault? How the hell do you figure that?"

"I should have looked for him after my bomb run. Things got busy. I didn't realize the radio was screwed up."

"I don't see how it was your fault," said Mongoose. "You're lucky you're alive."

"Stop calling it luck!" shouted Doberman.

• • •

Shotgun listened to the two pilots debate what had happened on the mission for a while longer. They were rehashing what they'd said at the debriefing without going anywhere, and finally he just left. Mongoose seemed bent on keelhauling Dixon—though he never specified how—and Doberman was determined to defend him. Both men were getting angrier by the minute.

Shotgun had little patience for formal debriefings, let alone this bullshit. He was just deciding whether to find the poker game or slip into the Depot when Colin Walker, one of the junior airmen assigned to squadron supply, ran up to him with a pair of envelopes.

"These just got here," said the clerk. "I didn't know they had Federal Express in Saudi Arabia."

Shotgun nodded solemnly as he took the packages.

"You gonna open it?" Colin asked.

"Can't out here, kid. Sorry."

Colin's eyes opened wider than the opening on a sewer pipe. "Classified?"

Shotgun leaned toward him. "I didn't say that, right?"

"No, sir. Never. Gees, what's in there?"

"Did you see the manifest?"

"No, sir. I mean, well, you mean the airbill? Says they're from D.C."

Shotgun winked, then turned quickly and walked to his tent.

Which quickly filled with the aroma of McDonald's as he ripped open the first envelope.

With the help of a few old friends, Shotgun had managed to have a happy meal overnighted to Saudi Arabia. Two Big Macs, extra large fries, and a strawberry shake.

Separate bags, of course. To keep the shake cool.

As he finished his first Big Mac, Shotgun wondered if there was some way to get his Harley over. Not by Fed Ex, of course. That was the sort of thing you left to UPS.

29

Dixon debriefed with one of the intelligence officers in the hangar area. He answered questions about the bomb damage and other questions about the mission succinctly, with as little detail as possible. It helped that the officer had already spoken with the others and written the report. Overburdened, the lieutenant was as anxious as Dixon to be done with the interview.

Dixon told him he'd fired the Mavericks very poorly, no matter what the tape showed. He told him about seeing the radar dish and then losing it; he admitted that his memory now was so hazy it might not even have been a dish—especially since they now were pretty sure Doberman's missile had blown it to pieces. As for the cluster bombs, he said he hadn't seen them hit, and frankly doubted they had done much damage, because he knew he had pickled them from too high an altitude. Their fuses had undoubtedly ignited too high, causing the bomb pattern to disperse too widely.

Leaving out the details about how he'd panicked and run away might not have been lying, but Dixon felt inside that he had committed high treason. The only thing worse was the cowardice that had led him to it.

The pilot slipped away, then wandered aimlessly through Tent City, working off the raw anxiety churning in his stomach. When anyone greeted him, he either shrugged or looked beyond them, continuing on.

Dixon did this for more than an hour. Finally realizing he was hungry, he started in search of food, then lost interest. Somehow, he found himself in the canvas GP or general-purpose tent he shared with two other lieutenants.

It was empty. Erected on a concrete pad, the tent and its furnishings were an odd mix of monkish austerity and modern luxuries. His pillow was a scavenged sack filled with T-shirts; one of his "bunkies" had shipped in a stereo setup worth several thousand dollars. The stereo nightly accounted for half of the unit's theoretical power allotment.

Dixon sat on the edge of his cot, the mission replaying over and over in his head. He'd been fine, cocky even, until Doberman pushed ahead to start his Maverick run.

He followed. They started taking flak very, very high—unaimed triple-A, much thicker than had been predicted.

The next thing he knew, he was in a cloud, a few feet from making a permanent impression on Iraqi real estate. Everything streaked together in a nightmare blur.

He was such a goddamn great pilot—how could he panic like that? How could he screw up? That wasn't him.

William James Dixon never ever screwed up. He had an A average through high school, and was summa cum laude in college, even with a heavy athletic schedule. Aced every test from grade school to flight school.

And failed the only one that counted.

How many linebackers had tried to shake him up on the gridiron, to get him to lose his cool? Couldn't happen.

But it had.

Dixon took his silver Cross pen from his pocket and stared at it, working the point up and down with his hands by slowly revolving the casings. His mother and father—his mom, really, since Dad was pretty much shot by then—had given him the pen for his high school graduation.

She was an odd woman, his mom. Hardworking and loving, but the kind of person who kept her only son at arm's length. She'd never been too crazy about his joining the Air Force, even though he'd talked about flying jets since he was nine or ten. It was the only way he could afford college, one of the rock-bottom goals she'd given him; still, there was a certain look on her face whenever he wore his uniform.

What the hell was he going to do? Ask to be grounded?

Maybe Major Johnson had already done that.

What sense would being in the Air Force make if he couldn't fly?

He wasn't scheduled for another mission until Saturday. Johnson would undoubtedly be on his back before then. He didn't buy what Dixon had told him. Who could blame him?

And Colonel Knowlington. A no-bullshit bona-fide war hero, with two Flying Crosses and a piece of shrapnel in his back for good measure. A couple of guys whispered that he was a washed-out drunk, and everybody knew he had been assigned to command the Hogs more or less by accident— but hell, he'd earned those medals.

Sitting on his bunk, Dixon fought the bile that kept creeping up his throat. He'd never been much of a drinker, but he considered it now, only to decide it would depress him more. Sleep was impossible. He'd read nearly everything in the tent, including the mattress labels, at least twice. Finally his eyes fell on the pile of "Any Servicemen Letters" on a nearby footlocker. The CO had suggested that squadron members take a few at random and respond; good for morale at home. A clerk had delivered the lieutenants' modest allotment of two letters apiece the other day; since then, the six letters had been moved only to get to the gear stored in the footlocker.

Dixon picked up the top two and took them to his bed. He fished out a yellow pad, and began reading.

The first letter was from a fifth grader in Florida.

Dear Sir or Madam:

Thank you for taking the time to fight for our country. My classmates and I want you to know that we apreciate it. Thank you for losing your blood.

James Riding

An easy one, Dixon thought, beginning to write:

Dear James:

Thanks for your letter. I'm real proud of being here to serve you.

His pen stopped; he considered for a second being completely honest with the kid—telling him how badly he'd choked.

As if he didn't have enough trouble.

Myself and my buddies are thankful for your support. Believe me, I'm trying not to spill any blood. My own, especially.

Lt. BJ Dixon

The second writer had enclosed a photograph of herself; she was nineteen, attractive, and Dixon suspected she was looking for a husband. She wrote in frank terms about how lonely she was back home and how happy she was to have this chance to cheer someone up. The photo would undoubtedly supply someone with several weeks worth of fantasies; Dixon slipped the letter and snapshot back into the envelope.

In its place, he found one written in a shaky hand on unlined white paper, obviously labored over, with cross-outs and corrections.

Dear Serviceman:

I know what you're going through. I served in the Second Marine Division on Okinawa. I won't bore you with the details; you've probably read in your history books enough already. There isn't anything that words can do about it anyway. Things are always more important than you can say.

I hope that you will remember two things while you are over in Saudi Arabia.

Number one is, your family and your country love you. No matter what you hear. We had our Tokyo Roses too.

Number two is, you will survive. No matter what happens. You will see a great many things. You will be changed. Some of the things that you find out about yourself, you will not like. Believe me, I know. When you see a buddy get shot and have to leave him there, screaming, etc., because if you moved, then you would be the next to die—that is the most horrible experience of all. But somehow, you get through it.

Remember that. Remember to keep your head up and moving toward the next battle.

I wish you the best. I know you will do very well. I know all of the men, and now I guess women too, will. Make us proud.

Sincerely yours,
Lance Corporal
Frank L. Simmons (ret.)

Finished reading, Dixon stared at the letter a while, the shaky blue letters blurring into a haze. Finally he folded it into its envelope. He started to put it back in the pile, then stopped; he slid it into his pocket. Getting up from the cot, he told himself maybe having a drink wasn't all that horrible an idea.

30

Colonel Knowlington decided to help Wong find Doberman himself. Ordinarily, he didn't like guys who worked in intelligence or for the Joint Chiefs, but this one had a quirky sense of humor that made it impossible not to.

"I have to confess that I don't know Captain Glenon all that well," Knowlington told Wong as they wove their way toward the pilot's quarters. "This unit has only been together a few weeks. But he's a short guy, really short, and I'd be careful about his temper. Short guys always have quick fuses. Plus, he's going to be tired."

"I try to be professional at all times," pronounced Wong.

Knowlington smirked. "See, Captain, that's what I'm talking about. You and I get the joke, but he might be a little sensitive, you know? Tread lightly."

Now he got it—Knowlington realized that Wong reminded him of his first Phantom backseater, Mark Dalton, a snide-talking, sharp-eyed prankster whom he'd first met in the Philippines. Mark—a major at the time—was only so-so as an RIO, but a world-class cutup. And he'd made general before he retired.

"This is his tent," he announced. The lights were on, but he held Wong back. "Have to knock first."

"Colonel?"

"Knock, knock," Knowlington announced in a loud voice. "Hey, Doberman, you decent?"

"Go away," growled a voice inside.

Knowlington winked, then led the way. Major Johnson was sitting on a camp chair across from Glenon, who had his arms over his eyes, trying to block out the light.

"Tommy, I got somebody here from Black Hole who wants to talk to you about the missile you took in the wing."

"Aw, fuck," growled Glenon. "Can't anybody see I'm sleeping?"

"Wong's a good guy," said Knowlington. "He won't take long."

"Why are you here?" asked Johnson.

"Who are you?" said Wong.

"Oh, excuse me. Major Johnson, Captain Wong," said the colonel, making the introductions. "Mongoose is the squadron's director of operations. He led the flight."

"I'll want to talk to you too," said Wong. "But I would prefer to do this one at a time to avoid interview contamination."

Knowlington started to laugh. "Come on, Goose. I want to talk to you about something. We'll be outside," he told Wong, adding, to no one in particular, "He's a pisser, isn't he? Interview contamination. Shit."

"Don't get up," Wong told the prone figure on the cot.

"I wasn't planning on it."

"Your name is Doberman or Glenon?"

"It's Glenon. Doberman's what they call me. After the attack dog?"

"Oh." Wong sighed. He had never understood what the deal was on pilot's nicknames. "Okay, now tell me what happened."

"When?"

"When the alleged missile hit you."

"Go take a look at my plane if you don't believe me."

"Please, Captain, I have a job to do. From the point you were fired on."

"You going to take notes?"

Wong shook his head. "I don't think it will be necessary."

The pilot described a low-level cannon attack, pretty much as the weapons expert expected. It sounded to him particularly careless, especially in light of the declaration that low-threat tactics—medium-altitude bombing—were to prevail in theater. But he wasn't here to offer a critique.

"Okay, Captain," he said when the pilot began describing his egress toward Saudi Arabia. "Now, why are you calling the missile an SA-16?"

"Because that's what hit me."

"With all due respect," Wong said, "you've just described an SA-7. Think about it. You were below a thousand feet, you—"

"I know where the fuck I was. And I know what hit me."

"There's no need to use profanity, Captain. Did you see the missile actually go through the wing?"

"Now how the hell would I do that?"

"Did you see the missile at all?"

"Of course not. But it had to be an SA-16. There's no way in the world an SA-7 is going to survive all that jinking. No way."

"Are you sure there wasn't a second missile?"

"From where?"

"The ground."

"Give me a break, would you?"

"Are you sure you were able to perform the maneuvers precisely as you remember?"

"Hey screw you, okay?"

Wong sighed. Patiently, he began to explain how important his investigation was to the war effort, how critical it was for other pilots to know what sorts of defenses they were facing so they could adjust their tactics accordingly. Realizing he was dealing with someone who was tired, the captain consciously chose words with the least number of syllables possible to convey his meaning. He had gotten through the first half of his first sentence when the pilot interrupted him.

"What do you know about missiles?" demanded the pilot.

"I know a great deal about them," said Wong. "I've written three papers and—"

"Go write another one and let me sleep."

"What's that all about?" Mongoose asked Knowlington as soon as they were outside the tent.

"Some jerk in Riyadh doesn't think Saddam has SA-16's. Wong has to prove them wrong. We went through this shit in Vietnam," Knowlington added. He kicked himself as that slipped out, but was powerless to stop the words.

"Whatever hit him wasn't an SA-7. It stayed with him too long."

"Yeah, Wong's on it. Don't let his deadpan fool you."

Johnson frowned, giving off a hint of disapproval but saying nothing. Talking to him, Knowlington always felt as if he had to justify himself.

He felt that way with a lot of people, actually; it was just more acute with Johnson.

"You wanted to talk about something?" the major asked.

"Apparently our western GCI site is still on the air. Intelligence thinks they patched the dish and moved in a new trailer. Or that we missed."

"Yeah, I just heard." Johnson's voice had an edge to it, as if Knowlington was accusing him of screwing up. He wasn't.

"I'm wondering if you think the squadron should ask to take another shot at them," said Knowlington, trying to step lightly.

"I was thinking about it."

"We can swing Smith and—"

"I want to lead it myself."

"Okay." Knowlington nodded. "They may want it hit soon, though."

"So?"

In theory, pilots were supposed to have a decent rest between missions, but Knowlington didn't push the point. He would have felt the same way. Besides, it was all moot until he talked to Black Hole and the general.

"I don't think it was a screwup," added the colonel.

"Why not?"

Johnson's snap surprised him so much, Knowlington took a step backwards. "I'm just saying, this happens—"

"Dixon froze. I'm not blaming him for the station still being on the air. but he froze."

"What do you mean?"

"Dixon lost it. He panicked. I saw it in his eyes. He came back like a rabbit in shock. I found him puking out his guts beneath his plane."

"Glenon didn't say anything about that."

"Yeah, well, it's my responsibility."

And mine, Knowlington thought. "Is that why you had them switch planes?"

"I would've had them do that anyway."

Knowlington nodded. "First time in combat can be pretty tough."

"It was the first time for all of us."

"You're not blaming him for the station still being on the air?"

"No, of course not. But he lost Glenon. He should have been there when the Mirage jumped him. Hell, Doberman's lucky to be alive."

"You don't think the radio going out had something to do with that?"

"He still should have been on his butt."

Knowlington really couldn't argue with that. Except— well, shit happens. "What'd you have in mind?" he asked.

"I want him to sit down, for starters. Take him out of the cockpit."

"For how long?"

"I don't know."

"That's kind of harsh, don't you think? What did he tell you happened?"

"Nothing."

"Nothing at all?"

"He was very vague."

Knowlington began rocking gently on his feet, considering the situation. "Something bothering you, Goose?" he asked.

"No."

"You feel strongly about this?"

"Yes."

"Okay, let's take some time and think about it. Saturday he's flying?"

Mongoose shrugged. Knowlington saw Wong coming out of the tent. "He's all yours," the colonel said, leaving the major to be entertained by Wong while he went to find out how important the GCI site really was.

31

Shotgun nearly flattened Dixon as he stepped out of his tent.

"Whoa—what the hell are you doing out here, BJ?" he said to him, physically lifting him out of his path. "You trying to sniff Mickey D fumes?"

"Mickey D?"

"Got a shipment today. Big Macs, large fries. Should've gone for a double order, though. I'm still hungry."

"Oh."

"Hey, sorry, it's gone. Check with me tomorrow." Shotgun took a step away. Dixon followed.

Until now, they hadn't been particular friends. But Dixon wasn't particular friends with anyone, to be honest, not even the other lieutenants.

"Yo, kid, what's up?" Shotgun asked, realizing he was trailing him.

"Nothin'."

"You want something?"

"A drink."

Shotgun laughed. "I thought you didn't drink."

"I do. Sometimes."

"I'm on my way over to the Depot. Come on."

Dixon fell in alongside as Shotgun sauntered through the back alleys of Tent City. En route, he launched into an explanation of why the A-10A Thunderbolt II—also known as the Warthog, or Hog to those who knew her ugliness the best—was the finest warplane ever created, bar none.

"Maneuverability and toughness. That's what it comes down to," explained Shotgun, whose dissertation was more like a rant than a lecture. "Those are the only things that count. Speed? Hey, that's fine, if you want to run away. You know what I'm talking about?"

"Uh-huh."

"Turning radius. Get me into a one-on-one with a pointy-nose, okay? Let's call it a two-turn deal, all right? Hey, screw him, I'm inside, I'm on his tail, I'm signing my name with my cannon in two seconds, right? That's what I'm talking about. Pick your plane. What do you want? Hornet? Okay, good choice. But I'm on it. I don't care if there's a marine in the stinking cockpit and he's brought a Deuce with him. You know what a Deuce is, kid? It's a .50-caliber machine gun. Oldie but goodie. I'm going to get me one and strap it to my seat. Kind of thing that makes you want to eject just to use it. Anyway, I don't care who the hell is flying the damn plane, put Doolittle in the cockpit—hey, put Knowlington in there, okay? In his prime, that is. You know, back in the old days. I'll spot him a dozen rounds in my tail. Because as soon as I light up my gun, he's a dead man. No shit. You think a Hornet could last as long as a Hog?"

"No."

"Hell, no. That's what I'm talking about. Very nice airplane. Very nice electronics. But stick and rudder? No, no, no. You were supposed to be in F-15's, right?"

"Well, not supposed to be—"

"Yeah, I heard the deal. Too bad about your mom. But listen, let's say you have an Eagle and a Hog, okay? Now I got to grant you the magic missile bullshit, but I'm not talking missiles at a million miles. I'm talking up close and in your face, where it counts. You know what I'm talking about?"

There were, of course, logical arguments to counter Shotgun, but even if Dixon weren't a Hog driver he wouldn't have offered them. Shotgun's enthusiasm made it seem possible—

hell, likely—that he could take apart anything he came up against in a dogfight.

Maybe that's all I need, Dixon thought to himself. Enthusiasm.

But how do you get it? By eating Big Macs?

The older pilot seemed to know everyone he passed, no matter their rank or occupation. Occasionally he would stop and have a quick conversation. Dixon waited dutifully, nodding when introduced but inevitably saying nothing.

"Kinda quiet tonight, kid," Shotgun told him as they continued on. "Something eating you?"

"No," he said quickly. But then he grabbed the older pilot's arm. "Hey, let me ask you a question."

"Shoot," said Shotgun, still walking along. His gait had a hop to it, as if he had just won the lottery or planned to that evening.

"You ever get scared?"

"Shit, yeah. All the time. Why? You scared right now?"

"On the mission."

Shotgun snorted. "Only an asshole doesn't get scared." He slapped him on the back. "Come on. Let's find you that drink."

32

The GCI site turned out to be very important—it had to be taken out tomorrow.

And as a matter of fact, the mission planners at Black Hole were looking for someone to do it.

"We volunteer," Knowlington told Al Harris, a young captain on the staff who happened to be a friend.

Actually, his father had been a friend. But Harris was a lot like his dad. Knowlington had helped him in some minor ways during his first year or so in the service, and they got along well.

"I have to have the general get back to you on it," said Harris. "This is his call."

"My guys would really appreciate it," Knowlington told him. "And so would I."

Five minutes later, the sharp, direct voice of the general in charge of planning the air war came over the secure line. Besides being one of the brightest minds in the Air Force, the brigadier was a flexible if demanding officer who had been convinced early on that the Hogs had a place beside the glamour boys in waging the air war. He was also the kind of guy who got right to the point.

"Mike, you see your frag yet?"

"Just trying to make sure I have enough planes to fill it," said Knowlington.

"And?"

"More than enough, General."

"I hear your boys want to take a shot at that radar station."

"That's right."

"The dish itself isn't the major problem. They've only come up once since your boys hit it, and we'll have a Weasel in the area tomorrow. But their antiair guns are a problem."

"How's that?"

"We have to run a Special Forces unit through first thing in the morning. Looking for a downed Englishman. We've been scrambling to get everything together. We might make it without taking out the guns—there's a bit of a leeway. Still, I'd prefer not to cut it too close."

Knowlington sucked air. The turnaround was going to be a major problem—not only for Mongoose, who wanted to be part of the group hitting the site—but for the rest of the squadron, which was already fully committed to other tasks. But he wasn't backing out now.

"No sweat," he told the general. "We can take it."

"Short notice."

"Not for these guys."

There was silence on the other end of the line as the general conferred with one of his staff members. "You're going to have to hit the target around oh-six, six-ten, somewhere in there," he said finally. "Harris will get the details."

"Thanks."

"No problem." The general's voice relaxed a little. "How'd it go today, old-timer?"

"Damn good. One of my guys got a missile right through the wing. Made it back."

"Through the wing?"

"Blew a hole the size of a watermelon and the plane kept flying. Maintenance guys claim they'll have it patched and ready to go tomorrow. By the way, somebody from Joint Chiefs came over to check it out. Apparently the Pentagon doesn't think the Iraqis have the latest Russian missiles."

"Yeah, I know," grumped the general. "Wong, right? Sorry, but we had to give him something to do."

"Hell of a sense of humor."

"Captain Wong?"

"Yeah. He had me rolling on the floor."

"Really? Wong?"

"Reminds me of a guy I used to fly with. Very droll."

"Say listen, Mike, can you use him for anything? He knows a hell of a lot about Russian weapons. Supposed to be the world expert. Outside of Russia, that is. At least, he says he is."

"He's available?"

"Oh, yeah. A lot of people bruising elbows bumping into each other over here. Guy like Wong—well, let's call him a fish out of water over here."

"We can always use help," said Knowlington.

"Borrow him for as long as you want. The admiral won't mind."

"You sure?"

"Use him for something important—cleaning latrines, if you have to."

"Oh, we'll find something better than that."

The general's tone abruptly changed. "Say, Michael, you're not thinking of getting back in the air on this one, are you?"

Knowlington laughed, brushing aside the obvious concern in the general's voice, brushing aside a mountain of unspoken reservations. The question hurt more than he expected— more than it would have yesterday, certainly. But he buried the resentment. "Well, maybe a few months from now. I'm afraid I'm the least proficient pilot on the base."

"That's an exaggeration, I'm sure."

"These guys are good."

"I know they are. I'm counting on them."

33

It was Chief Master Sergeant Alan Clyston's everlasting regret that his assignment here had come at what amounted to the very last minute. By the time he'd gotten to King Fahd, all of the good quarters were long gone; he'd had to scrimp and practically beg for the bare necessities. Granted, he'd procured an oversized temper tent for his home, but really, it was only the metal equivalent to a canvas GP job. He felt limited by the fact that it was equipped with only three air conditioners, though they were oversized units. Since only one was actually necessary at any given moment, he alternated their use, but it was his firm belief that you could never have enough air conditioners in the middle of a desert.

The refrigerator was standard operating equipment, as was the freezer, though perhaps there had been a clerical misunderstanding about the nature of the medical supplies to be kept inside it. The sergeant had a prescription entitling him to a special, overstuffed mattress, though the particular unit in his tent had been intended for a staff officer until misdirected to Clyston; he deemed it wise to hold onto it until its proper owner could be located.

The large generator unit outside the tent was a squadron backup. Not the Devils' actually; it belonged to a Marine unit located at another base. One thing about the Corps—they always stowed their gear where it was safest.

The satellite dish had been rescued from a garbage heap and was currently undergoing "operational testing," thanks to some video and television equipment that bore a serial number identifying it as Navy property. Clyston realized that its delivery here had been a clerical error, and had assigned one of his best men to check into the matter.

Actually, there was one non-military, non-accounted-for item in his quarters—a Laz-E-Boy recliner. But as transporting it out of the premises and off base would require the requisition of resources critical for the war effort, the chief master sergeant thought it his duty as a senior noncommissioned officer to guard it until it could be disposed of.

He was headed for his tent and that very chair when two of his most trusted crew members—Kevin Karn and Bobby Marks—appeared from around the corner. He grunted in acknowledgment. They followed him inside, where they pulled up seats as he completed the chore he had put off all day—transporting the newest batch of C Brew to the fridge. When the twenty-four bottles of homemade porter were safely ensconced, he retrieved two bottles of his previous home-brewing effort—a passable pilsner, though perhaps too heavy on the hops—and handed them to his men.

"Thanks, Sarge," said Karn. "Not having one yourself?"

"I got some things to look after," said Clyston. He took a Coke from the refrigerator and sat in his easy chair, pushing it backwards. "Bobby, hit the go switch on the stereo, wouldja?"

The young airman complied, and the room exploded with a Mozart concerto. Clyston closed his eyes. The others, who knew better than to disturb him for the next five minutes, exchanged glances and sipped their beer. It was only when the capo di capo had reopened his eyes that Karn—about fourth down on the squadron's NCO pecking order and Clyston's personal work-it-out guy—ventured to remark that it had been a hell of a day.

"Sure has. Nobody broke my planes," said Clyston, taking a swig of the soda. "Though Captain Glenon took a good run at it. How's the one he tried to use as a missile-catcher coming?"

"Tinman is kicking butt getting it back together," said Karn. "Can't beat the old-timers, I'll tell you."

Clyston smiled wryly. "Cursing a lot?"

"Big time. Says we need a new 'wink.'"

The capo di capo laughed. "I wouldn't be surprised if he finds one."

"Some Pentagon jerk wanted to inspect the damage," added Karn. "Tinman gave him a slab of metal and chased him away."

"Yeah, I heard. He gives you trouble, send him to me. Say Bobby, who worked on Major Johnson's INS?"

Marks was only an E-3 and a bit undernourished, but Karn had taken him under his wing. The kid showed great promise in his chosen field, electronics, and had helped locate spare parts for a down television. He also prepared a frankly superb barbecue sauce that even now lingered on Clyston's lips. It was that sort of versatility that made him a comer.

"Gees, Sarge, I'm not sure. Would have been either of a half-dozen guys."

Clyston, who not only knew damn well that it had been Sanderson but knew that Bobby knew, nodded. The noncommittal answer combined tact with deference. The kid definitely had potential.

"Goose on the rag again?" Karn asked.

"Yeah," grunted Clyston.

"Poor Parker." Parker was Mongoose's crew chief.

"He'll leave Parker be," said Clyston, taking another sip of his soda. "For now anyway."

"They're all crap, but there's something really screwy with his," said Karn. "No matter what we replace or what we do, it gets whacked. Sometimes it's a gyro, sometimes it's a freaking contact, sometimes the whole thing is just, well, hexed. I'm thinking serious short somewhere, but damned if I can find it."

"You tried?" Clyston asked.

"Half the damn squadron tried. The thing is, it passes all the stinking tests. It's voodoo. Parker and Sanderson both went over it with him," added Karn. "You know, they told the major—"

"I know what they told him. And I know what he told them," said Clyston. "He's right—this is war. It may be one of the few things he and I agree on."

Clyston felt Johnson was a good pilot and a decent officer, but at times a bit too prissy. Plus, Johnson didn't like Knowlington all that much, a serious character flaw in the capo di capo's estimation.

"Good beer, Sarge," said Bobby.

Clyston frowned. One thing he still had to teach the kid was not to kiss ass.

"What the hell hit Captain Glenon's plane?" asked Bobby, realizing his error and trying to backtrack.

That earned a nod.

"Looks like he flew it under a drill press," said Karn with a laugh.

"Shoulder-fired missile. I've seen some strange ones," said Clyston. They looked at him, expecting him to elaborate, but he wasn't in the mood. "Glenon's got to be the F-ing luckiest pilot in the wing. Anybody else, that would have taken out the fuel tank."

"Couple inches further forward, it would have gotten the spar and snapped it in two," said Bobby. "I heard—"

He was interrupted by a knock on the door.

"Come!" Clyston commanded.

Technical Sergeant Rosen squeezed her head inside.

"Rosen, get your fanny in here before one of those P-heads outside spanks it and I have to file charges against them," said Clyston.

"Hell, just take them out by the hangar and let Rosen have five minutes with them," said Karn. "They'd wish they had a court-martial."

Rosen glared briefly at Karn before turning to the capo di capo.

"Help yourself," Clyston said, gesturing to the refrigerator.

"No, thank you, Sergeant."

"How'd it go?"

"I fixed it."

"Yeah, I noticed. Problems?"

"Not really."

Clyston nodded. "Freddy take care of you?" He was referring to a friend of his who had arranged transportation for her out of Al Jouf.

"More or less."

Clyston frowned. "All right. Tell me about it. You two shut your ears," he added.

"The copilot on the KC-130 coming back was a jerk. That's it."

"He's going to complain?"

"He might."

Clyston sighed. Hopefully, the man would be so pissed off he would go right to Knowlington. The colonel would nod seriously, scratch his chin, and promise to look into it. As soon as the door closed, he'd shake his head, roll his eyes, and do what he always did about insignificant bullshit—forget about it.

"You didn't break any bones, did you?" the capo di capo asked, trying to make light of the situation. But Rosen didn't take the hint.

"I shoulda," she said.

"Relax, Rosen. Come on, have a seat."

She glanced at the others, deepened her scowl. "I have work to do, Sergeant."

"The hell you do. Your shift ended hours ago. Hell, I didn't expect to see you back here tonight, let alone this early. You nearly beat Dixon back."

Rosen's face flushed momentarily—she seemed genuinely touched by his concern.

Must have been the light.

"I caught a Herc back," she told him. "Lucky timing."

"I guess."

"I heard Tinman needed help on Lieutenant Dixon's plane, the one Captain Glenon tried to break," she said.

Clyston nodded approvingly. One of these days he was going to file the papers to adopt her. "Tinman may not let you help," he warned her.

"We can get along if there's work to be done."

"Your call. Good work at Al Jouf."

She flushed again, but left before it was too noticeable.

"Lesbo, right?" said Bobby.

"Nah," said Clyston. "She just has trouble getting along with people. Officers especially. Takes them seriously. That's where the trouble starts, as a general rule."

34

Officially, the club didn't exist.

Unofficially, it didn't exist either.

But its thick, smoke-laden air was real enough. The bikini-clad Pakistani waitresses—with a few similarly dressed men thrown in to provide gender balance—were actual flesh and blood, mostly flesh. The dim lights, live music, and flowing booze had a hallucinatory quality at first, but soon proved as physical as anything else there.

"Never been in the Depot before, huh, kid?" Shotgun asked as he threaded his way through the crowd at the bottom of the entry stairs located just a few yards from the base property line.

"No," said Dixon. He looked a bit like a five-year-old taking his first trip to the circus.

Or a whorehouse.

"Used to be a bomb shelter. I think. People get kind of bristly when you ask. My idea is, enough guys had enough wet dreams and it sprang together out of thin air. Or sand. Whatever." He stomped Dixon's shoulder to show he was kidding. "Here come on, this is my spot."

Shotgun slid in behind a round cocktail table in a corner. From there, he had a perfect view of the small stage, in case one of the unscheduled floor shows stoked up.

"Shit-faced, kid, that's what we're getting," he told him. "And then, we're going to have to cook you up a nickname. BJ sounds a little too, you know, suburban. You need something new."

"Like what?"

"I don't know. You need something that fits you. Finding the right nickname is a delicate art. How long have you had BJ?"

"All my life."

"That's what I'm talking about. Time for a change." He motioned over a waitress whose black leather thong looked vaguely familiar. "Pair of Buds," said Shotgun. "And maybe later, talk to the kid a little."

"I'd love to," she purred, running her fingers lightly across his head before disappearing.

Shotgun laughed as the kid turned paler. "Lighten up, BJ. Hell, you were in combat today. You're a man from now on. Cherry broken."

"I don't know."

"Hey, relax. Uncle Shotgun isn't going to make you do anything you don't want to do." He leaned across the table. "And they all get shots once a week."

Doberman found them sitting in Shotgun's favorite corner.

"How much have you guys had to drink?" he asked.

"Hello to you too," said Shotgun.

The pilot pointed to the bottles. "How many?"

"Relax," said Shotgun. "We just got here. I've had a sip, and Junior's been too interested in the floor show. You'll catch up in no time."

"I'm not catching up. Knowlington's called a big meeting over at Cineplex."

"For when?"

"Now." Doberman glanced at Dixon. He'd expected to find Shotgun there, but the kid—hell, he went to church services, for crying out loud. Doberman glared at him; Dixon, who looked paler than the albino strip artist on stage, remained silent.

Obviously in shock.

"No shit," said Shotgun. "What's up?"

"The GCI site BJ and I hit this morning is still on the air. Apparently the stinking radar dish I hit didn't stay hit. There's a British flier on the ground somewhere near there that they want to rescue first thing in the morning, and the squadron's been tasked to shack the shit out of the dish and the guns on the southern side."

"Ouch. Who's going?"

"Believe it or not, Mongoose wants to."

"Figures." Shotgun pushed the beer away. "And here I thought I'd get some sleep. Oh, well—who needs sleep when you can fly?"

"You're going?"

"Aren't you?"

"Yeah," said Doberman. "But I ain't fucking happy about it."

"Who's happy?"

"You're crowing," said Doberman. "Like you're happy."

"Nah."

"I'm going because it was my job in the first place," said Doberman. "I screwed it up; I'll fix it. You stay home. You need sleep."

"Tie me to the fucking bed and I'll bring it along," said Shotgun. "No way I'm not going."

"*I* screwed it up," blurted Dixon.

"Relax, kid," said Doberman. "Drink your beer."

"I blew it. I saw the dish and then I lost it. I thought you took it out."

"Nobody blew it," said Shotgun. "You guys have to learn to deal with reality. Sometimes you miss."

"You're giving lessons on reality?" said Doberman.

Shotgun started to say something, but then just waved his hand. "Let's get back," he said, standing. "How'd you know we were here anyway?"

Doberman rolled his eyes, then stuck his finger into Dixon's chest. "Him, I'm surprised about."

"Hey, easy on the kid," said Shotgun. "BJ's okay. Hell, he's coming on the mission too. Right kid?"

"I—"

"Look at his face, Dog Man. Kid's a Hog driver. All we got to do is come up with a new nickname for him."

"Like?"

"I don't know. But BJ sounds like he ought to be on *Little House on the Prairie,* don't you think?"

Lieutenant Dixon followed along as they threaded out of the club, his heart pounding wildly. It had begun thumping as soon as he'd heard the words, "British pilot."

He was being handed a chance to redeem himself. He had to get back in the sky and grab it. Everything he had been wanted to make it right.

But another part of him said no. Another part said stay home. You'll never make it. You'll screw up again.

It wasn't that he was afraid of dying. He was afraid he'd be afraid—that he'd panic again. He felt his hands trembling as he gripped for the stair rail, climbing back toward the night air.

35

Rosen found Tinman grumbling as he leaned head-first into the wing of the damaged Hog. In her opinion, his curses had a Celtic-Scandinavian lilt to them, though she was as clueless as anyone about his background.

"Sergeant Clyston asked me to help you out," she called up.

Tinman grunted something in her general direction.

"What happened to the rest of your crew?" she asked.

"Go sleep. Tired."

"What about you?"

"Work. Work," he said, adding more unintelligible words.

Rosen surveyed the wing from the bottom. The hole had been squared off and the interior guts replaced—quick work, all things considered.

"Was the wing spar okay?" she asked.

"Checked out, yes," he answered. "Bones okay. New lines. Check, check. Lots of work."

I'll bet, she thought to herself. Lots of work for a lot of people. And it wasn't like this was the only A-10A that had been damaged—the plane Dixon had flown back was sitting not very far away, the last bullet hole being patched by an airman with a trusty drill set.

"Hey, Tinman, you got any electrical work that needs fixing?" she yelled up. "Otherwise, I'm going to bed."

"New wink, that's what we need," grumbled the mechanic, pulling himself up. "But Sarr-chh doesn't want to hear about it. Have to do this from scrat-chk."

"You put this aileron in by yourself?" she asked incredulously, looking at the large and obviously new wing section.

"No time to fool around," he said, hopping down the scaffold. "Sarr-chh wants it flying tomorrow."

"Sarr-chh is out of his mind."

"You tell him."

Not even Rosen would try that. "If there's anybody who can fix it by then, it's you," she said.

"Thank you. I'm your friend too," he said. "How was Al Jouf?"

"Not bad. I was talking to one of our pilots there. Lieutenant Dixon. He's actually kind of cute."

Tinman shook his head. "Bad idea, sergeants and pilots."

Rosen felt her face blush. "You need help or not?"

Something in the crusty old mechanic's eye twinkled. "You help me find patch metal?"

"Patch metal?"

Rosen started to protest, but Tinman blinked mischievously. "Sarr-chh said we could have anything we need. Come, you can work acetylene with me."

"Acetylene? Hold on a minute. Tinman? Where are you going?"

Rosen followed as the skinny old-timer walked briskly, not into the parts area, but back behind the hangar where a damaged C-130 had been stowed two days before, waiting for engine parts.

"Oh, Tinman," she moaned. "You're not thinking what I think you're thinking."

"Why not? Need new wink."

"Wing. You mean wing."

He shook his head up and down, opened his mouth in a shy smile, and pointed at the big general cargo plane.

"You mean the C-130? No, it doesn't need a wing," she protested.

"It will," he said. "Come on. Help me get torch. Then we need some paint."

36

Mongoose nearly fell over when he walked into Cineplex and found it filled not only with all of the squadron's pilots, but a good portion of the NCOs as well.

"There you are, Major," said Knowlington, standing at the front. He rocked a bit on his legs, smiling bashfully—as if Mongoose had caught him talking about him behind his back. A rough diagram of the GCI site Doberman and Dixon had hit had been sketched on the large easel behind him. "I was just bringing everyone up to speed."

Mongoose was so flustered he wasn't sure what to say. Until now, Knowlington had pretty much left him to run the squadron. He actually felt disoriented, slipping into a seat near the door as the colonel relayed a generalized version of his conversation with Black Hole.

"I'm not going to kid you guys," Knowlington concluded. "This isn't an easy mission. It's long and grueling, as the pilots who undertook it this morning can tell you. Cloud cover is going to be very low, which will make things a hell of a lot more dangerous. We have to hit the site at 0600. The helicopters will be coming through this way, close enough to get into trouble if something goes wrong. There'll be a Weasel in the area, but the odds are the dish itself will stay off; it'll be our job to make sure it sleeps permanently. Now, participation will be voluntary—"

"Hey, I'm leading the flight," said Mongoose.

Knowlington looked at him, nodding as if he had been going to suggest that.

"Shotgun and me are going too," said Doberman. The pilot was sitting in the back of the room, arms folded and frowning. "And BJ. We're the volunteers. We missed it and we're going back to nail the mother."

He was so emphatic that no one stated the obvious objection—the pilots would have no, or nearly no, sleep before the mission.

Not that Mongoose would have let that stop him. But he would have used it as an argument to keep Doberman and Shotgun home.

And as for Dixon, no way did he want him on the mission.

"That's great, guys," said Knowlington. "But slow down for a second. We only have two planes available. I think Johnson and Glenon, if they're up for it, get the first shot. Rank and time of service."

"I'm up for it," snapped Mongoose.

"Great."

Before he could say anything else, Knowlington swept the group into a discussion of tactics—as if they were all sitting around a bar discussing possible baseball trades. It wasn't that anyone was saying anything particularly stupid or wrong— there were only so many ways to go after the radar dish and guns. What Mongoose objected to was the discussion itself. Planning a raid wasn't a team sport.

And given the sudden change in Knowlington's behavior, it was impossible not to think he might have hit the bottle.

But he sure acted sober.

"Assuming we get these two guns here," said the colonel, pointing to the board, "we go for the dish next. The question I have is, what else is left up there that we have to make sure we get?"

"Damned if I know," said Doberman. "If the Maverick didn't hit the dish, who knows what else we missed? I don't understand how the missile could have screwed up."

"Maybe the guidance didn't," suggested Captain Blake, one of the pilots with extensive weapons training. "It might be that it flew right through, if the fuse screwed up. So you'd just have a hole."

"Could have just blown up part," said another pilot. "But left enough for it to work, or at least send out a signal."

"Maybe we should put the cannon on it," said Shotgun, talking like he was going to fly on the mission. "No way you miss with that."

"Way too dangerous," said Jimmy Corda, the squadron's intelligence officer. He had come back a few days ago from serving as a liaison with Black Hole, and had helped plan the original mission. "You'll be walking through a minefield."

"There's a hell of a lot of triple-A," said Doberman. "You go low enough to make sure you hit it, the plane'll get fried. And the cloud cover's supposed to be worse tomorrow than it was today."

"We have to make sure we get hits," said Shotgun. "Hell, if we can't trust the Mavericks, what can we trust?"

"There's another dish!" Dixon blurted out.

Everyone turned around to look at him. He'd been standing behind the couch, arms stiffly at his side.

"What do you mean, BJ?" asked Knowlington.

"I—when I came at it from the north, I saw a dish. It was strange, because I knew that Doberman had fired on it already. I didn't think he could miss. Then I lost it and got confused about where I was."

"A second dish?" asked Corda. "It didn't show on the photos. Hard to hide."

"Locate it for us," suggested Knowlington.

Dixon walked slowly to the front of the room. Mongoose saw that his hands were shaking.

Kid was fried. He felt sorry for him. He'd had a hell of a lot of promise, but not the stomach.

"I don't know," said Dixon. He took the target photos the squadron had received, and the map, trying to correlate them and put the spot on the diagram. "Maybe this shadow. I—I don't know. Maybe I'm wrong. If I could go back up there and see—"

"Let me see," said Corda. He took the photos in his chubby

fingers, examining them. "You know, if it is there," he told Knowlington, "the satellite angle might have obscured it."

"If there were two dishes instead of one," said Shotgun, "then it explains what the problem was. And it explains why the radar is still up when we know Doberman's Maverick hit."

"Yeah, okay," said Doberman. "I didn't see another one. But you know—the RWR got a bleep of something that I couldn't account for. Like a second dish being turned on for a quick second. I thought it was just a flakeout."

"There are definitely two," said Wong. He walked to the front of the room with the intel photos. "The layout of the trailers gives it away."

"In case you haven't met him, this is Captain Wong, the newest member of the squadron," Knowlington explained. "The captain came over working on a little intelligence project, and now he's going to hang out with us a while."

Wong's head practically snapped off its neck in surprise.

"I talked to the general and it's all set," Knowlington told him. He turned back to the group, ignoring Wong's expression—which was somewhere between confused and ballistic. "The captain knows more about Russian weapon systems than the goddamn Commies. Or ex-Commies, excuse me. Come on, Captain, give us the spit."

Wong stifled his objections and began explaining how Soviet intercept radars were configured; a few paragraphs into his lecture, one of the pilots cut him off. "So why didn't Black Hole catch it?"

"It is camouflaged, as you noted. Still, some things even I cannot answer."

"It's not their job. They only get the sites and then dish them out in the frag," said Corda. "They don't usually get so specific, like trailer A, not B. Besides, there's a real disconnect between the planners and the intel people. Hell, I'm surprised we got this much data to begin with. Pictures—shit, anybody here ever see photos in an A-10 strike folder?"

"Only of Goose's wife," said Shotgun.

He was about the only one in the squadron who could make that crack and not get his butt kicked.

"You can target both dishes to make sure," said Wong. "Let me make another suggestion," he added, walking to the dry-erase board and its layout of the target area. Taking a black felt marker from his pocket, he pointed to two Xs in the lower left-hand corner, sites where 23mm guns had been located earlier in the day. He added two more Xs, then moved his pen across the board and added several more.

"If I can see those photos again, please." He waited while they were passed up, then once more began drawing on the board. "There are more guns here than you have diagrammed. And they are not merely the 23mm weapons, though of course those can be quite effective at low altitude, even if you jam the radars and they use optical aiming. Of greater importance for your strategy are these 57mm S-6 cannons. Very significant weapons. We can quibble about the guidance systems, but that is academic if you are hit, I assure you."

He scratched his cheek. "These four at the south are all big ones. There are considerably more large-caliber weapons here than the Iraqis typically employ. So they have you high and low. By high I mean, for you; these guns are not very effective above, oh, we should say thirty-five hundred meters. This is an interesting deployment, incidentally. The Russians use this pattern themselves every so often for a number of reasons."

He was about to list them, but changed gears at a glance from the colonel.

"The thing that is important is that they are effective at a much higher altitude and longer range than you have calculated," he said. "If you are protecting your helicopters, you must consider that."

"No shit," muttered Shotgun, just loud enough to provoke a nervous laugh from half the room.

Wong ignored it. "The configuration gives them very potent killing cones through eleven thousand feet. Even when optically aimed, they are bound to hit anything passing through these arcs."

He drew a pair of thick cones that included the flight pattern Doberman had taken on his bombing run that morning.

"Those Xs at the bottom aren't 23mm?" asked Corda.

Wong shook his head. "This barrel configuration, did you notice it in the picture?"

"Looks like a cat's whisker to me."

"A very deadly meow. So you make your attack at six thousand feet, thinking you are safe, but you are not. Your plane had that problem today. They will be difficult to spot until they begin firing; you see how concealed they are. Most experts would miss it, though of course not someone like me. Now, this camouflaging I have seen only in a few other places. I think that the idea came from a Major Andre Kar—"

"Yeah, okay," said Doberman. "So what do you suggest?"

Wong smiled. "If you know where they are, you can attack them safely from a distance. For that, you must use their tactics to your advantage. If they acquire you here first," said Wong, pointing at his Xs on the bottom, "and think you are attacking from this direction, all of the guns will be aimed in this arc. Let the radars think they have you. They all fire. Then you come quickly from the rear. You will have no less than ten seconds to make your attack."

Somebody in the back whistled.

Wong shrugged. "Of course, sooner or later, they run out of ammunition. The Iraqis' supply—"

"Thanks," said Knowlington. "Okay, so we have four guns down here that have to go, plus the dishes. How do we get close enough to see them?"

"What if we tickle them at twelve thousand, look for the sparks, and then hit them?" suggested Corda.

"Then we need more than two planes," said Doberman. "The first two come in on the south, turn around, and the others nail the bastards."

"You're going to need four planes just to make sure you hit everything," said Corda. "Can we take them off another mission?"

"This is more complicated than a stinking ballet," said Shotgun. "I say just pour on the gas and take out the mothers. Hogs weren't made to bomb from twelve thousand feet. We got to get in the mud, man. That's our job."

"Our job is to take out those guns and the dish," said Knowlington. "And to come back in one piece. Everyone.

Wong's idea makes a hell of a lot of sense. The problem is, we need four planes. Every Hog we have capable of flying is allotted."

"We have two more," said Clyston. "We've been holding back the two Hogs Captain Glenon tried to crash. We'll just have to get them ready by 0400."

There were a few worried looks on the faces of Clyston's sergeants, but none of them said a word.

"Not enough time," said Knowlington.

Even pushing as fast as they could go, the Hogs would take close to an hour to get to King Khalid Military City; gassing up there would cost at least thirty minutes. Add an hour to Al Jouf, another pit, and then thirty to find the target—all of the times were optimistic, in everyone's opinion—and you were talking at least three and a half hours, with no margin for error and a hell of a lot of luck riding along as your wingman.

"You just know Al Jouf is going to be a madhouse," said Shotgun. "Ask Dixon what it was like this afternoon."

"Why stop at Al Jouf?" said Doberman. "If we refuel by air, we can cut some time off."

"And if we miss the tanker?"

"We won't miss the tanker."

"It's dark outside, Shotgun, or haven't you noticed?"

"What if you went straight to the target from KKMC?" suggested Clyston. "You can make it if we lighten your load and cheat a bit on the time over target."

Mongoose rose and got a calculator from the desk, working the numbers. He hated to admit it, but having the entire squadron involved in planning the mission generated an energy that wouldn't have been there if just a few of the pilots worked it out alone.

"What do you leave behind?" asked Doberman.

Clyston poked one of the sergeants sitting next to him. "You go with only four Mavs apiece, no iron," said the man. "That gets us to two and a half hours, pushing the speed north a bit. Even with a good time over target, you can make it with about ten minutes of reserves to spare, assuming you refuel just over the border."

It took Mongoose, pressing the calculator buttons madly, several minutes to discover the sergeant was correct.

"Ten minutes is tight," said Knowlington. "And four Mavericks doesn't give us much backup."

"The sergeant's right about the time," said Mongoose, looking up from the calculator. "But the planes have to go like hell to KKMC."

"Four o'clock is still a half hour short," said Knowlington.

"We'll make it by 0300," said Clyston. He caught a glance from one of his men, and amended his prediction to 0330. "And what if we put six Mavericks on two of the planes? Just load up the triple rails."

Clyston held up his hand as one of his weapons specialists leaned over and whispered in his ear. They talked back and forth a second; then the capo di capo announced that they could work it out. Though designed as a triple-rail, the launchers ordinarily carried only two Mavericks.

"Fuelwise, it'll work," said Mongoose. "The tank on the way out has to be a quickie, though, or the fourth plane drops into the sand."

"Very risky," said Corda. "I almost ran dry waiting on line this afternoon."

"Me too," said Hobbes. "All these stinking Navy guys cut in front."

"Go to separate tanker tracks after the attack," Wong suggested.

It was one of those solutions so obvious everyone had missed it.

"You sure you're from the Pentagon?" asked Clyston.

"Sure he is," said Corda. "The pen he used on the dry-erase board is a permanent marker."

As the meeting was starting to run out of steam, Mongoose leaned toward Knowlington and said, "I'd like to have a word."

There was no mistaking the tone, but Knowlington took it mildly. He nodded, and gestured toward his office.

"You've got a beef," the colonel said when they got there.

"Several."

"Shoot."

"Number one—why the round robin discussion?"

"I thought getting everybody involved would be good," said Knowlington. "And not just for morale."

"Having all the techs in—"

"You don't think they contributed?"

"I didn't say that," sputtered the pilot.

"I don't think anyone abused the privilege. This was a special situation. What were the other things you wanted to say?"

"Dixon."

"What about him?"

"I don't trust him on the mission."

Knowlington had expected to be questioned on the meeting, which had been a spur-of-the-moment decision. He knew that Johnson's real problem with it was that it signaled he was taking a much more aggressive role directing the squadron than he had until now—not that he wasn't doing his job, just that he hadn't really done it until now.

He'd felt tentative, out of his element with the unfamiliar planes, an old pilot good for nothing more than initialing requisitions. Watching the Hogs land had somehow changed that.

It was natural that the major, who'd more or less been filling the void, would have his nose slightly out of joint. But that didn't account for his feelings about Dixon.

"Why don't you trust him?" the colonel asked.

"I think he's a liability."

"Because he lost Doberman?"

"No. It's more than that. Think about it, Colonel. Doberman's plane comes back like Swiss cheese and his is clean."

"There's no question he was over the target," said Knowlington. "His Mavericks locked."

"I'm not saying that."

"Well, what then? Are you saying he was too lucky?"

"No." Mongoose sighed. "He flew today. He's tired as hell."

"I have to tell you, Goose, I think you need a pretty specific reason to hold him back. He knows the site, and if he's tired,

what about you?" Knowlington paused, scanning the major's
face for fatigue. It had to be there, but it didn't show. "Is there
something else? I mean, obviously Dixon screwed up with his
cluster bombs and he's taking it hard, but I don't think that's
a reason to ground him."

"I'm not grounding him," snapped the major. "I just don't
want him on this mission."

Knowlington again studied Johnson's face, but he was
really trying to sort out his own thoughts. On the one hand,
the major ought to have the right to choose who went on this
mission. On the other, keeping Dixon back without a solid
reason wasn't fair to the lieutenant, and would probably affect
him for weeks if not forever. Knowlington had seen more
than one pilot completely tank after being treated unfairly;
he'd had a buddy who'd been shot down because he did
stupid things after losing his self-confidence.

There were other considerations. The way they had it
drawn up, Dixon would have to be replaced with a pilot from
another mission. Sure, Knowlington could get plenty of
volunteers, but how did they then fill *his* slot? And if there
were doubts about Dixon's abilities, wouldn't it be better to
fly him in a place he already knew—and had volunteered
for?

It seemed to Knowlington better all around to keep Dixon
on the mission. But he decided he had to defer to Johnson, if
he felt strongly about it.

"Let me tell you a story," the colonel started.

"I don't want to hear another of your goddamn stories. This
is our war we're fighting," said Mongoose, storming away.

37

Dixon curled on his cot, trying to calm his stomach and slice away maybe half of what was in his head.

He was getting his chance to redeem himself.

What had the old guy said in the letter? He thought about pulling it out and reading it again, but the words came back without effort.

Keep your head up and moving toward the next battle.

Not particularly profound, but the best advice never was.

What if he screwed up again? What if this time they lost someone in the squadron because of him?

Should he go to Major Johnson right now and tell him he wasn't up to it?

And be forever branded a coward?

Was that better than screwing up again?

Maybe it was better to go, get shot down, and die a hero.

No—someone people *thought* was a hero. There was a difference.

A voice cut through the tangle of contradictions racing in his brain. Dixon turned over toward the door, startled.

"Excuse me for barging in like this, guys," said Colonel Knowlington. "If you're up."

Dixon bolted upright. His feet found the floor as he jumped up and started to salute.

The colonel laughed softly, glancing at the tent's other two cots. One was empty; on the other, Lieutenant Phaze snored peacefully, deep in oblivion.

"Gees, BJ, relax. What do you think, we're in the Army? I don't think even GIs salute in tents. Besides, relax." Knowlington took a chair and pulled it close to the cot. "Phazer asleep?"

"Bomb wouldn't wake him," said Dixon.

"You tired?" the colonel asked, keeping his voice soft.

"No."

Knowlington smiled. His grayish-white hair seemed like a halo of light around his balding skull. The colonel had the subdued air of a college professor nearing retirement, not the gung-ho, in-your-face attitude of a television war hero. But that only awed Dixon all the more.

"I want you to know, there's no problem deciding to sit down. According to regulations, you shouldn't be flying. You're supposed to get a good long break. Even in war. Especially then."

Dixon started to mumble something, but felt his throat choke off.

"You can stay home," repeated the colonel. "No problem."

He knows I'm a coward, Dixon thought. He's giving me an out. "I, uh—I want to fly, sir. Really."

Knowlington nodded. He was silent for a moment, considering what to say next. "Anything happen up there you want to tell me about?"

Dixon considered telling him he'd dropped the CBUs blind. But if he did that—if he admitted how badly he'd panicked—wouldn't Knowlington take him off the mission?

He couldn't chance that.

"Nothing much," said the pilot. "I screwed up."

Knowlington squinted, but said nothing.

"I was too high with the CBUs," said Dixon weakly.

The colonel was silent for a while longer. Dixon stifled an urge to blubber out the whole truth.

It wouldn't help, he told himself. It's too late. Keep your trap zipped.

"On my first combat mission, God, I was petrified," Knowlington said finally. "I think I took twelve dumps in the hour before I got dressed. Ten at least. Hell, I think I wore out two dozen pair of underwear my first week."

"You were scared?"

"Shitless. Literally." Knowlington seemed far away, reliving the flight. "You get used to it. Part of you does. You learn how to deal with everything coming at you. You get pretty good at that actually. That's when you have your real problems. That's when you start taking things for granted."

Dixon nodded.

"I remember the first time I ever flew an F-4," continued the colonel. "I'd kicked some butt in a Thud—I already had two air-to-air shootdowns. You didn't get too many of those on the missions we were flying, believe me. So the first time I checked out a Phantom, boy, I thought I was something. Then I nearly ran the plane through the concrete on takeoff. Seems I set the flaps wrong. Tried turning it into a tank instead of an airplane."

Knowlington's head snapped up quickly, his soft laugh choked off. His eyes swept around and grabbed Dixon's.

"You up for this?"

The pilot nodded.

"Good." The colonel slapped him loudly on the back, then realized someone else was sleeping nearby. "Break things into pieces if you feel it starting to get away from you," he whispered. "Step by step. Shit's coming at you, the world's going crazy, look down and check your belt."

"My belt?"

"That or your throttle." Knowlington winked. "Do something that makes you start all over from scratch. If you feel like you're losing it, take a breath, come back fresh like a new man. Step by step."

"My throttle?"

"Anything that will get your brain to hiccup back into gear. Breath's important too. Hyperventilating will kill you. Look away, take a breath, then go back. Just slow down. If you feel yourself losing it, that's what you have to do."

"Yes, sir. Thank you," mumbled Dixon as the colonel left.

38

When you were in war, the night was never a friend. You could learn to fight in it, learn to exploit it, but it was never truly on your side. Technology could help you see through it, sheer guts could make you survive it, but the darkness remained forever foreign.

It enveloped Mongoose now, standing at the edge of the hangar area, watching the crews bust their butts trying to get the planes ready in time. His eyes swung around, fixing on the vanishing flare of a jet exhaust, shrinking and shrinking into a small dot. He guessed it was an F/A-18, diverted here from one of the carriers because it was low on fuel, but its actual identity was irrelevant; he watched it only to watch something.

He should be taking a nap. He'd have to preflight in another two hours. But there was no way he could rest, and he doubted the others could either.

Well, no. Shotgun definitely would be sleeping. He could sleep through anything.

Mongoose was mad at himself for snapping at the colonel. The guy deserved a little bit of respect.

He hadn't been drinking, at least not that Mongoose could tell. To be honest, he seemed more sober than anybody on the base.

No matter what, you had to give the guy one thing—he'd been there and done that until the cows came home.

Mongoose blamed himself for the kid's getting lost. He should have put him on his wing, not Doberman's. Granted, intelligence had tagged their site as the more difficult one, but he should have had the kid with him no matter what. He could have put Doberman and Shotgun on the tougher target.

Then what would have happened? Would his radio have gone out?

Would he have been as lucky as Doberman?

That was his fuckup, and he wasn't about to sit down for it. He was being hard on Dixon because they were in war, and one little screwup could kill you. But wasn't part of it that the kid reminded him of himself? Starting out, at least? Dixon had that cocky kid thing about him that made you want to like him, made you want to think he was you before you got a bit wiser.

And slower. Just a little.

Jesus, he was a natural stick and rudder man. He'd hit his targets with his AGMs, even though he had said he'd missed. He deserved another chance.

Bottom line—Mongoose had to go with Knowlington on this.

In the darkness of the night, the canvas enclosure Mongoose called home seemed like a safe haven, a small cave against the harshness all around. It was lit by a small "mood" lamp his wife had given him as a joke; the sixties relic had some sort of moving liquid inside that was supposed to reflect his changing moods.

It was green purple tonight. Hard to tell what mood that was supposed to be.

Mongoose lifted his mattress off the cot and pulled out a battered manila folder. As he opened it, his wife's last letter slipped onto the bedding. He considered rereading it, but thought it might slip him into terminal homesickness; he simply slipped the letter back inside and sat down to write her instead.

Every night, he wrote two letters. The first usually flowed quickly, even though the emotions were carefully guarded:

> *Hey:*
>
> *Thanks for your letter and keep them coming. Big morale boost.*
> *Fun and games today. All went well.*
> *I can't tell you how much I miss you and Robby. In my head, he's up to my chest now. Though of course I know it's only been three weeks and that makes him—two months old!*
> *Send me a new picture of him as soon as you can. Send a picture of you too.*
> *Don't let my mom drive you crazy. She does mean well.*
> *I'm sorry this is so short. I confess to being tired. But happy with a job well done—I have to get some sleep now, not overworking myself, I promise.*
> *I'll write tomorrow.*
>
> *Love*
> *Jimmy*
>
> *kisses and hugs*
> *kiss Robby for me*

He drew a succession of small hearts with arrows through them, then folded the paper. Impulsively, he wrote "I love you" on the back; before stuffing it into the envelope, he wondered if it was too much—too sappy, or maybe too depressing. Too late, it was done—he sealed and addressed the envelope.

The second letter took much longer. It was similar to a letter he had written the day before, but it felt important to take a new shot every day.

Dear Kathy:

I know, hon, how terrible it will feel to read this.

Seeing you in my mind at the kitchen table, unfolding the paper—I'm shaking. I think of poor Robby, crying, though he doesn't know why.

I want you to remarry. Things are tough now, but I know you'll pick up and go on; you've always been a survivor—you said that the first night we met.

Well, the second really.

See, even now you can smile. I don't want you to feel guilty about it. I trust that you'll do the best thing for our little sweet potato sonny boy.

I love you. I love you. I love you.

That's why I want you to be happy.

The mission that I went on today, the reason you're reading this, was an important one. The Iraqi radar site we bombed was in a location that made it difficult if not impossible for our special ops units to get deep into Iraq undetected. If it had been allowed to stay operating, pilots who were shot down would have no chance of being rescued. I'm sure that they gave you the old cliché about, "He died so others could live, etc., etc.," but in this case it was true.

I know, that's really not much comfort.

The guys I flew with, no exception, are great pilots and good men. They did their best.

I'm sitting here thinking of the night in the hospital. God, I was scared. Rob, you looked like a Martian coming out of your mom, you really did. And when that nurse took you and everything started flying, it was crazy. But they pulled together and you pulled out and are fine. There were a few seconds there where I was holding your little hand, and I had Mom's hand, and I didn't know what was going to happen to you both. And I prayed in that instant, if you could both make it, I'd take anything else that came. God could have anything, me included, as long as he saved you both.

So I have no regrets.

I love you, Kath. I wish I could hold you and Robby one more time.

Think of me doing that, and I will.

Jim

PART THREE

FIRE FOX HOG

39

"Here's my point," said Shotgun, trying to pinch his belly back far enough to pull the stiff charcoal flight suit over it. "What are the odds of getting Scudded in a Hog? You think Saddam's going to waste his chemicals on me?"

"Hell, no," said Doberman, already dressed in the protective undergear. "He'll just poison your coffee."

"That's what I'm talking about," said the pilot, struggling with the suit. He momentarily lost his balance and fell back against his locker. The rebound helped loosen the zipper. "Goddamn carpet makes it tough to take a leak."

"I thought you never had to pee," countered Doberman.

"Never say never." Shotgun paused in his struggle to get dressed, reaching over to his extra-large coffee sitting on the table. Steam poured from the Styrofoam cup, which had a large Dunkin' Donuts logo on the side. "The secret to flying is to be prepared for any contingency. First flight instructor told me that."

"Did he tell you to drink a gallon of coffee before you took off?"

"Shit, you wouldn't believe what he drank before he took off." Shotgun took a slurp from the cup and went back to suiting up. "Guy was a barnstormer, that's what I'm talking about. But man, he knew his shit."

Dixon kept to himself as he put on his G suit across the room. With nearly everyone else in the squadron either sleeping or scrambling to get the Hogs ready for their mission, the three pilots had the shop completely to themselves.

The G suit wasn't just an overtailored air hose, designed to counter the effects of high-speed maneuvers. Its pockets were a pilot's suitcase, stuffed with maps, survival gear, extra water and candy bars for energy. Dixon ran his fingers over the breast pocket where he'd stuffed Lance Corporal Simmons's letter. Sitting next to it was a set of rosary beads his mother had given him years before as good luck.

Not that he—or she, for that matter—was Catholic, but some things went beyond religious beliefs.

Dixon next pulled on his nylon mesh survival vest. This was more an excuse for pockets than a garment. It held his survival radio, compass, flares, and a first-aid kit, not to mention one of the sharpest knives he'd ever owned.

And ammo for his gun. Dixon had a standard-issue, old-style .38 caliber revolver that he had fired exactly once.

Over the vest came a parachute harness. This would be attached to the chute in the plane, where it was housed in the ejection seat.

"Gun, is that really Dunkin' Donuts coffee?" asked Doberman.

Shotgun just smiled.

"Let me smell it."

"Hey, get your own," said Shotgun, grabbing the cup away. "Next you're gonna be stealing my Tootsie Roll Pops."

"You're awful quiet this morning, Dixon," said Doberman, looking over at him. "You awake?"

"Yeah," he said, trying to force some of the adrenaline rampaging in his stomach up into his voice.

"What do you think, real Dunkin' Donuts or what?"

"Probably real," Dixon told Doberman. "He had a Big Mac last night."

"Jesus, kid, thanks a lot," Shotgun barked in mock anger. "Why don't you just tell the whole base? Dog Man here would kill his own mother for Mickey D fries."

"They weren't real," said Doberman.

"The hell they weren't," said Shotgun. He had finally managed to get his protective suit on and was pulling on his custom-designed G suit. It was the envy of the squadron, if not the entire Air Force. Shotgun's bulk made it possible to cram an incredible number of compartments into it, and every inch of real estate was packed with extra equipment—though a high proportion might be considered extra-military, if not downright bizarre. A lot of guys carried a Walkman with them on routine flights; Shotgun had wired his suit for sound, with a CD changer somehow stored in one of the crannies. And he habitually carried more candy with him than a well-stocked vending machine.

"What's today's music?" Doberman asked.

"The Boss. 'Darkness on the Edge of Town.'"

"Appropriate."

"Plus Pearl Jam. Ever hear of them?"

"Rap?"

Shotgun spat derisively. "Yeah, that'll be the day. I also have Guns 'n' Roses. You really don't want to fly without them."

"Yeah, how could you?"

"Only question is, what do I listen to on the bomb run?" said Shotgun, dead serious. "I'm kind of leaning toward Springsteen and 'Candy's Room,' because of the beat and all, but there's a certain ontological dissonance with the words."

Doberman rolled his eyes nearly out of his head.

"How can you concentrate?" Dixon asked. "I mean, seriously, doesn't it throw you off?"

"Nah. It's kind of like having a sound track. Theme music, you know. Kind of like *Apocalypse Now,* where the helicopters attack to the Ride of the Valkyries."

"Next you'll want to mount speakers on the wings," sneered Doberman.

"I've thought about it." Shotgun took his helmet and adjusted it over his ears—checking not the fit but the volume control on his stereo.

"You're one of a kind, Shotgun," said Doberman. "Thank God."

"How's that?" said the pilot, removing his helmet.

"Never mind. Come on, kid, you ready?"

"Uh-huh," said Dixon, waddling over toward them. The chem suit tended to cut into his crotch, and walking could be a little tough at first.

"We got to come up with a better name for him," said Shotgun. "BJ's too tame."

"BJ's fine," said Doberman.

"Nah. He needs something with balls."

"Like what?"

"I don't know. I've been trying to come up with something all night. Everything I think of is obscene or taken," said Shotgun. "We could call him Balls. What do you think?"

"Nah," said Doberman. "Then you'd have these radio transmissions—where are your Balls?"

Shotgun began laughing uncontrollably, as if it were the funniest joke in the world.

Mongoose nearly ran Dixon down outside the hangar where the last Hog was being readied.

"Sorry, Major," said the pilot. "I didn't see you."

"I wasn't watching where I was going," Mongoose told him, determined to be as conciliatory and upbeat as possible. "Here, come with me just a second."

Dixon followed him around a corner. The reflected light threw odd shadows on the ground, and made the young pilot, dressed in his survival gear and ready for flight, look like Frosty the Snowman on safari.

"Look, we're going to do things a bit differently than we choreographed before. Same plan, just different people—you and me are going to tease the defenses, instead of you and Shotgun."

"Okay."

"It makes sense to pair the most experienced guy with the least," he explained. "I should have done that yesterday. I'm sorry I didn't."

Dixon didn't say anything.

"You okay, kid? I have to go tell the others."

"I'll be fine," sputtered Dixon.

"I know you will. Otherwise I wouldn't have you covering my ass, right?"

Dixon nodded. Mongoose was grateful he didn't ask why the switch hadn't gone the other way, with him in Doberman's place bombing the dishes. He had a namby-pamby answer—too many people changing position, with Doberman moving up into Shotgun's slot because of rank and experience. But that was so obviously bullshit that the kid would instantly realize he didn't trust him to make the bomb run right.

He might already. But at least he didn't say it.

"Clyston rolled up Tommy Corda's Hog for you," he told the young pilot. "We're running a little tight on time, so we figured we'd shuffle around the planes."

"If it's all the same to you, sir, I'd rather have the Hog I flew yesterday morning. If it's back together. I know its personality."

"It's already armed."

Dixon's disappointment was obvious.

Mongoose glanced at his watch. "Hey, look, if they get your plane up in time, you can take it. But we're tight—you got that?"

"Yes, sir, I do. Thank you."

"Sure." Mongoose took a quick look into the kid's eyes. They told him exactly what he'd expected—nothing.

He chucked Dixon on the shoulder and went to find Shotgun and Dixon.

Did the kid just use the word "personality," he wondered to himself as he walked away. Goddamn Shotgun was infecting everybody.

Finished dressing, Doberman took a step in the direction of the door, and a shiny piece of copper caught his eye. It was a penny, right side up.

Hadn't seen one of those in a while.

He scooped down and snapped it up.

"Whatcha got?" asked Shotgun.

"Penny," he said sheepishly. "See a penny, pick it up, all the day you'll have good luck."

"Aw, you don't believe in that crap, do you?"

"Couldn't hurt," said Doberman, looking at the coin. It was from 1981. Had that been a good year?

"You going to step on all the cracks out to the runway?" Shotgun asked.

"Hey, you're the guy who said I was lucky."

The other pilot snorted. "Want a Tootsie Roll Pop?"

"You're out of your mind," said Doberman, sliding the penny into his glove.

40

Dixon had never seen anything like it. What seemed to be an entire squadron of maintenance experts were working on the plane, slapping parts in and out, checking and rechecking equipment, fueling, arming, and maybe even buff-waxing. The lieutenant had always heard that the Air Force technical experts, the people who handled the planes, were without peer in the world, but this was unbelievable. They were going at the plane like a team of surgeons doing a heart transplant. Not only had the wing been completely repaired, but it looked as if it had been repainted. It was hard to imagine this was the plane that had barely made it back to the base less than twelve hours before, a basketball-sized hole in its wing.

Someone stuck a cup of coffee—black—in Dixon's hand. It was far too hot to drink, even if he had wanted to, but it somehow seemed wrong to refuse it.

Sergeant Clyston materialized in front of him. "Yeah, I know, Lieutenant—you want your Hog, right? I don't blame you. We're kicking ass, but no guarantees, okay?" He pointed at the coffee. "You're not going to drink that, are you? You'll be peeing all the way to Baghdad."

Dixon shook his head. He started to pour it out, then felt a powerful hand grab the cup.

"No sense letting it go to waste," said the sergeant with a grin. Clyston took a slug, winked, then turned back to his crew. "Pull that F-ing dragon back up here and get the damn Hog loaded while Rosen finishes up," he shouted. "Come on, come on. Let's look alive. What the hell, you guys looking to join the Navy? Get moo-ving!"

The dragon was pushed into place beneath the Hog's throat. A small flatbed with a special treadmill, it loaded the A-10A's cannon with bullets.

Things looked chaotic, but Dixon could tell that even with the rush, the crew was still dotting the i's and crossing the t's. "Rosen, kick butt up there," Clyston called. "I need you done in five minutes. Got that? Five! No, that's too long. Make it three. Hey, Larry—what the hell are you doing up there, sawing fucking wood? Let's go, people—we have some Iraqis to bomb! This ain't a goddamn high school play we're putting on!"

Suddenly, all of the techs were doing rolls off the plane. Equipment was trundled away and the crew fell silent.

"Lieutenant, let's preflight," barked Clyston—more an order than a request. The gray bear loomed in front of the pilot. A smile broke on his grizzled lips. "Now you take your time, sir. Anything you want fixed, it gets fixed. You just go at this like you have all day, you hear? Don't let us rush you."

Dixon nodded and started toward the nose of the craft. He liked to touch the very tip of the Gatling gun before he began his walk around—it was a superstitious thing, and he sure as hell didn't want to miss it this morning.

As he leaned forward to touch the weapon, he realized he had an audience. The squadron's entire mechanical crew was looking over his shoulder, worried that he had found a problem.

"It's okay," he explained sheepishly. "I just like to touch it. For good luck."

A murmur of approval passed through the techies.

The crew members followed him around the plane, silently shuffling along as he examined the belly, the weapons, the flaps. Clyston hovered at his shoulder, silent, nodding, sometimes frowning, once or twice ducking in to take a look at something himself. Dixon moved deliberately, trying not to rush things and yet be as thorough as possible given the time limits.

The bottom line was that he had to trust the people who had just given over the plane to him. But it seemed somewhat disrespectful not to look closely at their work, not to nod or pat the part and move on. Once or twice he thought he saw something; each time, three or four crew members lept to the plane and helped make sure there wasn't a problem.

Dixon had done many preflights; certainly he had done more thorough examinations of the airplanes he was to fly. But he had never felt so confident climbing into the cockpit.

"Kick-ass job, Sergeant," he said, swinging onto the ladder. "I'll say hello to Saddam for you."

"You beat the living shit out of them, you hear me?" said Clyston, slapping the pilot on the rear.

From the crowd, Dixon heard a throaty female voice yell out, "Hey, Lieutenant. Break a leg up there, huh? Just make sure it ain't yours."

He turned down and saw Rosen, gave her, gave everybody, a salute.

"Yeah, yeah, yeah, get going. And don't break my god-damn plane," snapped Clyston. "All right, everybody, party's over—we got eight more planes to work on. Get your F-ing butts moo-ving!"

41

For a long, long second, Doberman thought he'd lost the plane fifty feet off the runway. It was still dark, and as the Hog roared off the concrete he felt a touch of weightlessness. He started to bank as planned—they had choreographed just about every foot of this mission—and felt his right wing coming up too fast. He began to correct, then felt he was overdoing it, then felt a queasy hole in his stomach.

He wasn't sure where the hell he was. The dark night loomed out in front of him, vast and empty; clouds covered the stars. The wind rushed around his head, spinning it, confusing him. He saw the earth, an old mistress, trying to lure him back to her bed.

Doberman's head swam. He was back under the tanker, trying to connect. He was playing cards, getting creamed again.

Lucky my stinking ass, he told himself. I got the luck of Job.

Somehow his eyes found the artificial horizon in the center of his dash. Somehow his brain managed to tell him he was precisely at the proper angle. Somehow his hand held the stick steady, calming the rest of his body.

I'm okay, he told himself. It's vertigo because of the dark. Fly your instruments, not your eyes.

He flexed his fingers inside their Nomex gloves, felt the

lucky penny in the palm of his hand, frowned at himself for being superstitious, and put the Hog on course.

Mongoose could feel the fatigue riding behind his eyes. He hadn't gotten any real sleep—undisturbed, head sinking below-the-horizon sleep—for nearly a week now. He promised himself he would have a full eight, ten, twelve hours, at the end of this mission.

But none until then.

The pilot had a small pill box in a pocket on his leg; he hoped not to have to use any of the pills inside, but would if absolutely necessary.

He envied Shotgun. The guy could fall asleep anytime, anywhere, doze ten minutes, and then go twenty-four hours. Not only that, but he could then go party his butt off, snooze twenty minutes on a pile of bombs, and come back fresher than a flower the next morning. Truly amazing.

Of course, he drank coffee like it was water. But damn if he never had to pee.

Inhuman. No wonder he'd become a Hog driver.

Mongoose checked the INS, hoping to hell it would work more accurately than usual.

KKMC was now just under an hour away. The crews there had been alerted to perform the fastest hot pit they had ever attempted.

They'd be over their target fifty-five minutes after taking off from KKMC. Assuming the planes cruised well, didn't run into an unexpected head wind, and didn't suddenly run low on fuel.

It was all doable. Mongoose had worked the calculations himself. But that was on paper. This was for real.

On paper, everything always went precisely according to plan. Everyone followed the dotted lines. The Iraqis swallowed the bait and Doberman and Shotgun went in unscathed. Dixon didn't get lost on the quick jink toward the guns, then followed him out to safety and the tanker.

In real life, Mongoose hoped like all hell the kid hung in there. He'd never forgive himself if he lost him.

• • •

Shotgun rocked off the strip, feeling a little like he was straddling his first Harley, unwinding the big old bastard up the Pennsylvania mountains on I-81, wind cutting into his face as the road narrowed for a bridge through the fog.

The crew had done something special to the Hog tonight, goosed her engines or something—maybe even juiced the plane with super-unleaded. She was cranked and she was cranking.

"There's a darkness on the edge of town," wailed Bruce Springsteen in his ears.

The man knew what he was talking about.

The plane wrapped itself around him like a familiar coat, taking him in its arms as it leapt into the Saudi sky. It was as if it had been waiting for him, counting the hours until Lieutenant Billy James Dixon would return to the cockpit and push its nose toward the dark shadows of Iraq. There was no logic to it, but this A-10A felt very different from the one he'd ferried back from Al Jouf only a few hours before. It felt different from the others he'd flown, more familiar than any plane, even the old T-38 he'd spent so much time in. There was definitely something particular, something personal about this particular arrangement of sheet metal.

Everything was going to be perfect on this flight. He had Mongoose's butt pasted to his windshield and wasn't going to lose him.

Step by step by step.

Screw the major if he didn't think he could handle it. Everybody else did. Everybody in the squadron was cheering him on.

Dixon walked his eyes through the cockpit, triple-checking the gidgets and gadgets. Fuel was good, airspeed was fine. The weapons hung low and ready on his wings, each one signed and sealed with a personal kiss for Saddam.

I'm going to make it, Dixon told himself. I'm going to help rescue the pilot and make up for my fuckup. I'm going to be brave this time.

I'm going to redeem myself.

42

The first hop went smoothly enough. Mongoose led the group off from King Fahd and headed north to King Khalid Military City, changing course only once, and even that was minor—they lowered their altitude to accommodate a pair of transports heading across their flight path. The KKMC ground crew did the hot pit with engines idling on the tarmac; the four Hogs cranked it up and headed into the night sky ten minutes ahead of schedule.

Five minutes out of KKMC, running parallel to the Saudi-Iraqi border, Mongoose spun his eyes around the cockpit on a routine instrument check. At first glance, everything seemed to be fine—temperature, fuel, everything was exactly where it was supposed to be. But when he returned his eyes to the large navigational display in the center of the front panel, he realized something was wrong— way wrong. The numbers marking his exact location hadn't changed since he lifted off from KKMC.

That shouldn't have been possible. It was like a car odometer not moving while the car was doing sixty on the highway.

Mongoose gave it the old car mechanic's fix—he pounded it with his fist.

Didn't move. He quickly double-checked the compass

heading against the dial that sat at the top of his windshield. They agreed—until he tilted the Hog a few degrees north.

The internal navigational system was whacked beyond belief; no amount of fiddling with the control display unit on the right cockpit console had any effect.

Big problem.

The game plan called for Devil Flight to fly parallel to the Saudi-Iraqi border until they were almost due south of their target. They would then angle hard north, flying nearly in a straight line to their target. The one serious jog was an angling maneuver around the edges of the radar belonging to a suspected SAM site.

Making the turns without a reliable INS wasn't particularly advisable. Especially since the rest of the group would be keying off him.

Mongoose blinked at the display a few times, hoping he'd made a mistake. When he finally admitted he hadn't, he felt as if he'd taken a shot directly in the stomach.

There were exactly two options—abort the mission, or have someone else take his slot as pathfinder.

And the most logical person to do that was Dixon.

Back in his plane, Dixon concentrated on not screwing up.

It was easy really. All he had to do was keep the dim glow of exhaust from Mongoose's plane in his eyeballs. Every so often he marched his attention around the cockpit, making sure the Hog was running normally. Flying at night, especially on silent com, had a special loneliness to it, all glow and hum. The plane hulked around you; depending on your particular mood, it could feel tremendously huge or tremendously small and fragile.

Dixon didn't want it to feel anything. He cleared his mind of all emotion and extraneous thought. He focused entirely on where he was.

All he had to do was follow Mongoose and he'd be fine.

Mongoose hesitated before hitting the speak button.

It came down to trust.

He'd chosen the kid to go on the first day's mission

because he had seen something in him. A lot of people had.

And Knowlington believed in him. That meant something.

Did *he* believe in him? Or had he only said he deserved a second shot?

The major keyed the mike. "Dixon, you awake back there?"

"Devil One?" The startled voice sounded as if it had just been awakened from a deep sleep.

"Look, kid, I've got a situation here with my navigational system. I'm thinking we're better off trading places. What do you say?"

The static that followed his transmission seemed to last forever. Finally, the voice came back.

"No problem."

There was no time to analyze if the words sounded confident or worried. Mongoose told the rest of the flight that they'd close up the trail a bit, but otherwise would proceed as planned.

With Dixon leading them to the target.

43

As he made the turn to head over the border, Doberman took a careful break from flying, flexing each arm and then each leg methodically, hoping to ward off cramps. The Hog didn't have an automatic pilot, so he couldn't exactly do a yoga routine. Still, he liked to stretch to keep the kinks away.

According to his watch, they'd fallen three minutes behind schedule. Doberman felt his face harden into a frown as he rechecked his instruments. The one interesting obstacle in their course lay ten minutes ahead, and he wanted to be ready.

With no time or fuel to get fancy, the line to and from the target had been drawn as straight as possible. Unfortunately, the straight line went almost directly over an SA-6 site. The mobile missile launchers were fairly impressive pieces of machinery, with radar the Hog's primitive electronic counter-measures pod couldn't hope to jam. Once a plane had been acquired by a ground battery's Straight Flush radar, the missile was difficult to lose; it could mid-course-correct and used its own semiactive system to score a kill. It loved high-G maneuvers, moved faster than greased lightning, and had a much more potent warhead than the puny shoulder-launched weapon that had given Doberman so much grief yesterday. With a range of about ten miles and an effective altitude above twenty thousand feet, it could barbecue a Hog any day of the week.

They had planned three tight course corrections to skim around the outer edges of the missiles' radar coverage while maintaining as direct a course to the target as possible. Doberman visualized the Iraqi radar groping through the early morning sky with long, slender fingers. It reached desperately, a blind man in a cluttered room, trying to find the doorway.

Not the doorway exactly. Just his plane.

Doberman laughed at his fears. It was a nervous laugh all the same. He longed to key his mike and ask Shotgun what music he was listening to.

This was the worst part of a mission, knocking down the miles until things got hairy.

Finally, the INS and his math told him it was time to turn. But Mongoose, flying dead ahead, didn't make the angle.

Had he lost Dixon? Or was the kid's INS also screwed up?

Every second would take them closer to getting nailed.

The RWR might at least warn him of the launch. But it couldn't save him.

He'd never see the missile coming for him in the dark. It would be worse than yesterday. He'd writhe violently, ducking and weaving, thinking at last he had escaped. Then he would hear a last-second hush, a vacuum of noise just before the wallop.

Bail out in the dark, deep in Indian country. Now that was where luck was involved.

But hell, nobody could be as unlucky as he had been yesterday. Getting banged around twice? What were the odds?

The small circles of blue exhaust dead ahead smeared into oblong cylinders and disappeared. Doberman took the cut, checked his watch, realized his heart was starting to race.

The next angle was the hairy one. Because of the configuration of the enemy radar, they would be turning and flying directly toward the missile site. In theory, there was a hole in the coverage there, allowing the Hogs to slingshot towards their target with their final cut.

In theory. Reality was never as neat as the carefully

calculated clouds showing optimum radar-detection envelopes.

Doberman held his breath. His INS said it was past time to
cut back, but once more Mongoose was lagging.

Jesus, he thought, a tiny mistake here is going to take me
right over the stinking goddamn site. Let's go.

Hell, maybe the missiles are destined to hit me. Maybe my
card's overdue.

The pilot saw the SAMs in his mind's eye, wheeling
around on their truck. Their noses swung upward, hit the stop,
came back.

Something creaked in the cockpit. It was nothing—a strap
on his seat maybe, shifting with his weight. But Doberman
jumped, nearly bringing the stick with him. If he hadn't been
belted in, he might have gone through the glass.

Mongoose was gone. Doberman yanked his stick hard,
taking the turn, correcting to bring it back to the proper
heading. His heart became a race car, surging in his chest.

Settle down, he told it, settle down.

He checked the INS. They weren't where they were
supposed to be, but now he wasn't sure about the coordinates.
Was the difference the same as when Dixon made the first
turn?

There was only blank sky in front of him. Blank darkness,
and a trio of missiles waiting dead ahead.

Shotgun reached to his chest and poked the CD player.
Springsteen's "Candy's Room" kicked back to the beginning.

"Driving deep into the night," Shotgun sang, echoing the
Boss.

He glanced at the compass and INS. If the instruments
were to be believed, they were tracking a bit north, flying
closer to the missile site and its radar than planned.

What the hell; stinking Iraqis couldn't hit the broadside of
a barn.

Besides, he was flying behind the luckiest SOB in the Air
Force. Some amount of that luck had to wash off on him.

Time for a Tootsie Roll, thought the pilot, slipping his

fingers into his vest. They were hell to chew, especially with the mask on, but worth every sticky moment.

Sweat funneled behind Doberman's ears and down his neck, tingling as it ran across his shoulders. He saw the missiles clearly now, saw the cluster of them turning on their rail as the radar waited for the optimum moment to fire.

The RWR was clear. But their ECMs were worthless against the advanced missiles.

The AWACS would warn them if the radar came on. But by then it would probably be too late.

Relax, Doberman told himself. There's a good cushion around the site. And hell, the damn SAMs were probably moved during the night.

You're running scared. Not like yesterday. Luck wasn't involved—you are a kick-ass pilot. Nothing is going to touch you. Nothing.

But his heart kept pounding despite the pep talk. He couldn't see Mongoose. His eyes flailed through the sky.

Nowhere.

This close to the missile site, he didn't dare use the radio. He was completely on his own, not just now but for the rest of the flight. He couldn't even be sure Shotgun was where he was supposed to be.

Doberman squinted at the compass heading. The bearing was right. By his watch, he had another thirty seconds on this course.

But the navigational system disagreed. It was telling him to stay on course ten seconds beyond that. He ran the equations back and forth through his head. That translated into about a tenth of a mile, which would be compounded by the angle of the turn into roughly a fifteen-to-forty-eight-second error, south or north or God knows what of the target.

What will it feel like to die?

Goddamn hell, he shouted at himself. Screw the math, screw the numbers—forty-five seconds isn't going to make one bit of stink-ass difference.

See the raise and get on with the game.

Doberman took the Hog in toward the SA-6 site the extra

ten seconds to prove to himself that, despite the water pouring down his back and chest, he wasn't scared. Even so, he gulped air as he yanked onto the new course.

And then he saw the soft blue glow of Mongoose's rear end dead ahead, right where it was supposed to be.

44

The helicopter's heavy whomp rattled Captain Hawkins's teeth as it took off, making it difficult for the Special Forces officer to sip from the canteen of tea. Fortunately, the Earl Grey had cooled somewhat; it didn't burn as it sloshed around his mouth and dribbled onto his chin. You could say a lot of things about the MH-53J Pave Low IIIE helicopter, but smooth wasn't one of them.

Not that he necessarily wanted it to be. The craft's hulking presence was somehow reassuring. Though it was officially an Air Force helicopter, the Special Forces troops considered that a mere technicality, and looked on the nimble linebacker as a flying version of the Bradley fighting vehicle.

Only not quite as pretty.

The captain capped the canteen and glanced over the gunner's shoulder into the dark morning, low clouds mixing with a dusty haze. The basic reality here was desert, unending and unrelenting.

Approximately ninety miles ahead, an RAF pilot was staring up at the sky, freezing his butt off, waiting for this helicopter to materialize and pick him up.

Assuming no one had found him during the night.

"Iraqi border coming up in two," said Sergeant Winston, a wiry young noncom from the South Bronx. Looking at Winston, you wouldn't think he was Special Forces material, but he was pound for pound one of the toughest soldiers Hawkins had ever come across. Yesterday, Hawkins had seen him pick up a 250-pound Special Forces corporal—not exactly a wimp himself—and lug him back to the helicopter after he'd been hit and knocked unconscious.

"What do you think? They hit those guns yet or not?"

Hawkins shrugged. "Not supposed to for a half hour yet."

"Going to cut it close."

The captain nodded. If the site wasn't taken out, the mission would be even more difficult than planned. Their helicopter and the one following right behind as a backup would be sitting ducks not only for the guns, but for anybody the Iraqis scrambled into the area. The British major had had the bad luck to go down not only near Iraqi air defenses, but near an airfield and army barracks as well.

Hawkins had the option of turning back if the base hadn't been hit at five minutes past six.

He didn't plan on doing that. But he didn't plan on getting shot down either.

The captain opened the canteen for another swig of the Earl Grey. "From what I hear, those A-10 pilots like to play it close to the vest," he told Winston. "Otherwise they don't look like heroes."

The sergeant scoffed. "As long as they show up."

"Oh, they'll show up. Planes that ugly can't afford to miss a date."

45

The clouds were incredible. Dixon stared down at them from fifteen thousand feet. They seemed as thick and endless as an overloaded chocolate shake. The lieutenant leaned forward against his shoulder harness, urging the Hog forward. They had a little less than two minutes worth of flying time before their stubby wings and dolphin noses would kick off the ground radars.

A little less than two minutes before the most important part of their job, and the most dangerous, was done.

The radar warning system would alert him that the radar had snapped on and the guns had found him. Then he'd be able to breathe again.

He couldn't breathe now. Dixon felt his throat tightening, pulling back into his chest. Don't wimp, he told himself, pushing the plane downwards.

Eighty seconds. Maybe less. But the radar detector still hadn't tripped off.

Come on, come on. Wake up down there. Just shoot at us already.

What a thing to wish for.

He heard something that very second. It was faint, delicate almost; he thought it had come over the radio, but the sound itself was nothing he had ever heard on a Hog communications set; nothing he'd ever heard in an airplane before, period.

It was a bell, a vague tinkle of a ring, as if the clapper of a small hand chime had gently kissed its metal mouth.

Silence followed in the next second and the next.

Then another.

He glanced at the RWR. Nothing.

He glanced at the other indicators. All were at spec. Nothing wrong, no alarms.

Time was moving in ultra-slow motion. He heard the sound again—gentle, almost quiet.

It was nothing like an alarm, or anything else in the A-10A cockpit.

A muffled church bell?

Except that it wasn't muffled, exactly, nor distant—it was as if a small bell were whispering.

And again and again and again.

As soon as Mongoose followed Dixon into the cloud bank, he realized they were already being fired at—shells were popping all around him.

Doberman yelped on the radio that they had their targets, bright and shiny.

"Go, BJ. Break," Mongoose barked. "Good show. Turn off."

He put the Hog in a hard pull over his right shoulder, wrestling the spitting airplane away as he realized they had flown in a little closer to the guns than originally planned. Otherwise, the kid had done perfectly.

The Iraqis hadn't bothered to turn the big radar dish on, or at least if they did, it hadn't activated the RWR. A thousand thoughts shot through his mind, propelled by the onrush of images and the plane's momentum. He held the Hog steady, kinetic energy devoted entirely to gaining speed, altitude still dropping. He set a spot where he would start recovering, orbiting back to wait for word from the other element. He felt the Hog shake in the air, buffeted by the violence the guns were wrecking on the atmosphere below. He pulled back, rolling and yanking and turning, zipping off the chaff, bundles of the metallic, radar-confusing tinsel spreading out from his wings just in case Saddam had some surprise down there he didn't know about. He pressed the Hog into retreat, diversion accomplished.

The sounds grew closer together, as if they belonged to a song he could not hear, a triangle twanging on a solitary track as the orchestra wailed away on the main line. Dixon held his plane steady; he knew he had only to fly this straight line and no matter what else happened today, no matter what Major Johnson might say, he would have done his job. That was all he was interested in, all he had to prove—that he belonged.

Each second of his life equaled about five hundred feet. So why was he still in the clouds? He had been diving through them for whole minutes, not seconds. How thick could a cloud bank be anyway? A few thousand feet max?

But there were still clouds all around him, and the light tinkle of the bell, a church bell.

Johnson's voice chased them away.

Break off, he was saying. Break off. They're shooting at us.

I'm not running away, Dixon thought to himself. Not this time. I'd rather get shot down.

He held the stick steady, descending through the angry gray chocolate. The damn clouds couldn't last forever.

46

As Doberman pushed toward the clouds, he felt something in his eyes tighten. He took a quick breath and glanced at the Maverick television screen over his right knee. Until the guns started firing, he couldn't be quite sure of his target. His fingers felt as if they were on fire.

There was plenty of time for this. Still, he wanted it to start already.

Done with waiting, Shotgun lined himself up off Doberman's wing and went for it. He had one eye on the screen, one eye on the HUD, and one eye on his stinking CD cartridge, which had managed to leap out of his flight-suit stereo as he took the Gs pitching toward the target.

The cartridge smashed into at least three pieces. And he just knew the CDs were going to be trashed by the time he got home.

Son of a bitch. That was his only copy of "Darkness at the Edge of Town."

Fucking Saddam. Now he was really mad.

The Maverick targeting screen suddenly lit up like a video game.

"Hot shit!" Doberman said—or thought he said. He was so busy guiding his hands that he couldn't pay attention to his mouth. Nearly instantaneously, two Mavericks shot out from his wings, gunning for the two gun emplacements furthest south. In nearly the same motion, he pushed his right wing down and started looking for the radar dish he'd missed yesterday morning.

Shotgun had to wait until Doberman fired and cleared his path before he could launch his own Mavericks. It seemed to take his flight leader all day. Finally, the second missile kicked off Doberman's plane, bucking like a wild bronco before putting its nose down and getting to work. Doberman cranked right, clearing his path. Shotgun had already locked on a target; he squeezed off the Maverick and dialed up a second, pushing the crosshairs fat into the last of the truly dangerous big caliber guns they had targeted.

"Nothing like a high-explosive enema to start your day, eh, boys?" he shouted as the missile winged toward the ground.

Doberman scanned the ground through the windscreen.

Nothing. Was that because he was confused about where he was, or because the dish didn't exist?

The Hog was screaming toward the earth. Sitting in his office, Doberman worked his head around the problem, checking the front corner of his screen for a large concrete building they'd picked as a good landmark. Sure enough, that was missing too. He realized his mistake—he'd flown further north than he thought—then slammed the Hog nearly upside down in a twist back in the other direction, gravity sharpening its claws as he accelerated in a violent plunge.

Suddenly, the RWR screeched—the Iraqi operator had snapped on the dish to see what was coming for them.

And damn if that big, ugly catcher's mitt didn't smile for Poppa, front and center in the Maverick's TV screen. The phosphorus glow warmed his belly as Doberman got a lock and slammed the missile out. He let off another for good luck, then took the stick hard left for his second priority targets.

He'd been so focused on finding the dish in the small television screen that he hadn't quite been aware how low he was. The pilot reacted with shock as the rapidly approaching earth caught his full attention. Two thousand feet lay between him and the roof of the building he was auguring toward.

Shotgun lost sight of Doberman through the clouds. He was at ten thousand feet, just barely in range of any of the heavy stuff the Iraqis had left, but they could have fired bulldozers at him at this point and Shotgun wouldn't have noticed. He put the A-10A on its wing, winced as a piece of a CD flew by him, then got a lock on his next target, one of the trailers housing the GCI equipment. He fired; as the missile left the plane, he realized there was only half a trailer there. No matter; he was already lined up perfectly on a microwave transmitter, and that sucker was intact.

Not for long.

47

The powerful sensors in the Pave Low caught the Iraqi ground intercept radar as it snapped on.

Captain Hawkins glanced back at his squad members, then up toward the cockpit. Concerned, he looked at his watch for the thousandth time in the last five minutes. His eyes followed the second hand as it crept across the dark face. He hated digital watches, even if they were considerably more accurate and disposable. Digital watches didn't bring you luck, though at the moment he didn't need luck, he needed the damn Hog drivers to do their job, wherever they were.

He glanced over at Sergeant Winston. Winston, wearing a headset, had one hand on his gun.

"Sun's up," muttered Winston.

Hawkins nodded. His eyes remained pasted on his watch.

"Think the radar means they're hitting it?" Winston asked.

Hawkins shrugged.

"Can't afford to wait much longer," said Winston. "Sooner or later, someone's going to find our British friend."

"How's our Sandy doing?" Hawkins asked. "Sandy" was an A-10A assigned to maintain contact with the downed flier and chase away any bad guys on the ground.

"Still hanging in there. Gas is getting tight, though," said Winston.

"As soon as our boys take out the radar site, send him

home," said Hawkins. "I don't want to have to pick him up too."

"Yes, sir."

If he needed it, Hawkins could get a flight of Eagles for CAP and a pair of Spectre gunships up in about ten minutes. The Eagles would take care of enemy fighters. The Spectres were specially designed Hercules C-130's equipped with cannons; they could eliminate a battalion of ground troops in three minutes flat. But they weren't supposed to come north if the dish was still operating.

"He hasn't come up on the radio yet, has he?" the captain asked. The last thing he wanted to do was disobey orders for someone who'd already been captured.

"He's not supposed to for another five minutes. Sandy last talked to him an hour ago," said the sergeant. "Said he felt chipper, whatever that means."

"All hell's breaking lose at that GCI site," the chopper copilot yelled. He continued talking over the crew's com set as Winston jumped up to find out what was going on. The quiet but tense boredom was replaced by a cacophony of voices, everyone talking at once.

"Three, four aircraft—Hogs—northeast," reported one of the crew members, relaying the radar information.

"Right on schedule," shouted Winston. "Hot damn—radar is fried! AWACS says go."

"Go, go, go," Hawkins yelled.

"AWACS is reporting contact to our northwest, too low for a clear read."

"Ignore it. Go!"

48

They were like sleigh bells now, shaking in a steady, rhythmic beat. Dixon was entranced by the beauty of the sound, as if he were listening to some heavenly concert.

He wondered where the sound was coming from. His eyes flew over the control panels, but could find no indication of a problem. The airplane vibrated steadily around him in a reassuring hum.

So what the hell was it? Some angel whispering in his ear? An undocumented G effect?

He glanced at his oxygen hose. It seemed unobstructed.

And still the bells rang, growing louder now, slightly more urgent, yet losing none of their beauty.

The nose of the A-10A broke through the last tuft of clouds into the clear air at approximately 5500 feet. Only then did Lieutenant Dixon realize what he was hearing.

Shells. Exploding all around him.

The concert turned into a sinister screech. The Hog's grunts were drowned out by the reverberation of proximity fuses and high explosives. The pilot could see a gun emplacement directly below, centered precisely in his screen. He watched as a black puff erupted from it, then saw the shell rise, coming for him like a messenger from Hell itself. It grew larger as it neared him, so large that it seemed bigger than the airplane. Suddenly it opened its mouth, and its jaws exploded in a profusion of red and yellow, petals of a spring poppy bursting in the warm sun.

In the next millisecond, Dixon snapped out of his daze. Time began moving at its proper pace as his body reconnected to his brain. He pulled the stick and pumped the rudder pedals, jerking the Hog away from the gunfire, recovering from the dive in time to skim away from the antiaircraft shells. Here was a real G effect—he could feel the bladders in his suit erupting as the plane came around to his eyes, its forked tail bending to his will, the two turbofans pushing themselves to keep up with the pilot's hands. Dixon jerked to the left, kept accelerating. He nailed his eyes to the horizon bar, making sure he was upright as he ran south as planned, away from the guns.

Mission accomplished. At least the most critical part of it.

He took a breath and made sure he had a good memory of it—coming through the clouds in ultra-slow motion, the light sound of bells, breaking the clouds, realizing it was flak. What part was hallucination and what part was real, he couldn't say, but he remembered it all.

He hadn't chickened out.

Where was Mongoose? He did a quick scan and couldn't find the other silhouette. He could feel the first twinge of panic starting in his throat—he'd lost his leader again.

But no—Mongoose had been behind him. He'd called him off. By now he ought to be somewhere ahead, to the south, as planned.

The dark green shadow of an A-10A Warthog appeared in the upper left quadrant of his windscreen. Its forked tail was like something you'd see at a barbecue, not on an airplane; the round power plants glopped onto the fuselage seemed to have been stolen from a 707.

Dixon had never seen anything so damn beautiful in his life.

"Hey, kid, I thought I lost you there for a second," said Mongoose, his transmission fuzzed with static. "We're a little closer than we planned. Hang loose until Doberman gives us the word."

"Gotcha."

"You got your Mavericks ready?"

"Copy, uh, affirmative. Yeah."

"Easy. You're looking good."

Dixon's radio lost half the transmission. He pounded the com panel, but that only made the answering static worse.

"Okay, the big guns are gone and the dish is out," said Mongoose. "There's a ZSU-23 off your right wing. You see it winking at you?"

"Got it," said Dixon, already lining up the Maverick shot.

"All yours. Stay in the orbit after you fire."

Dixon pushed his lungs slowly empty, then fired the Maverick. It was easy now, easier than in training—Mongoose was floating off his left wing, lining up and firing on his own target. They planned to hold one Maverick back apiece, just in case Doberman and Shotgun missed the radar dishes.

"How'd you do back there?" said Mongoose as the two planes swung back around to take a look at the damage.

"Okay."

"Hot shit—look at the ground."

Dixon stared through the canopy. The Mavericks had hit, all right. There was smoke all over the place.

And no more winking. Or flak.

The pilot followed the flight leader into a wide, orbiting turn to the east, still climbing. He checked the fuel stores—a good ten minutes of loiter time left at least.

How'd he do back there?

Not horribly. Pretty good actually.

But he wondered about the bell thing. Some sort of weird trick with his mind, or maybe the radio.

Mongoose said something, but it was completely lost in static.

"I'm losing your transmission," he told the major.

There was no response. He saw Mongoose tucking back toward the GCI site, and pushed the Hog to follow.

49

OVER IRAQ
0555

Doberman screamed a pair of curses—one at himself, the other at Saddam—as he pulled the stick back with every ounce of strength in his body. The Hog coughed before finally agreeing to change direction, her nose nudging away from the yellow-gray splotch of earth very reluctantly. Sky edged into the top of Doberman's windshield as the HUD ladder told him he was at five hundred feet.

He eased off on the stick, back in control of his muscles as well as the plane. All hell was exploding around him as he struggled to orient himself. A fresh string of curses tumbled from his mouth when, for a quick second, he thought the engines had stalled because of the sharp pullback. Realizing they were still cooking—his fatigue was playing tricks with his senses—he began to bank toward his right, which ought to be north and therefore out of most of the heavy triple-A.

I did this yesterday, he thought to himself. I can do it again. I got the lucky penny.

The Hog began bucking as a solid wall of flak appeared right in front of him. Doberman jinked back to his left, unsure now what to do next. He was surrounded by bursts.

He asked himself which way he should go. Left? Right? Forwards? Back? The possibilities froze him.

Maybe it was luck, going one way or the other.

Good luck? Or bad luck?

Damn it to hell, he told himself. Luck has nothing to do with it.

He decided left, but as he began to pull the plane in that direction, he saw that his maneuvering had put his nose nearly head-on with a trailer.

"Here's some good luck for you, Saddam!" he screamed, bringing his cannon to bear. The trailer disintegrated in a haze of smoke that seemed to magically part as he flew into a patch of sky completely clear of flak. He brought the Hog around quickly and served up another Maverick to the dish he had hit the day before.

By the time Doberman called the shot on the infamous first dish, Shotgun had seen the explosion. He was at eight thousand feet and hadn't seen any flak yet. Suddenly, Tower Two and its Tonka Toy-like trailer appeared smack in the middle of the Maverick targeting tube.

Tower Two was supposed to be Doberman's—and even for him it was a low-priority, secondary, hit-it-if-you-got-it, left-at-the-end-of-the-war, what-the-hell-we're-going-home-anyway shot. But this was way too good to miss. Shotgun pressed the trigger to kick out the Maverick.

The exact second the Maverick fell off his wing, the damn tower went boom.

"Damn it, Dog Man," he yelled, dipping his wing back to look over the remains of the GCI site. "You're taking all my shots."

"Stop screwing around then."

There was a pile of rubble where the hidden dish had been; the one Doberman had gotten yesterday, further south, was now twice-fried metal. Running out of real estate—and feeling more than a little frustrated—Shotgun pushed off his last Mav at a trailer and began climbing back into the clouds to get into position for a cannon run. Doberman was already overhead, reorienting himself for a fresh attack.

"What do we have left down there?" he asked the element leader.

"There ought to be a couple of trailers back near that second dish," said Doberman.

"Negative," said Shotgun. "They're crispy critters. I just passed that way."

"Uh, copy, uh, how about that microwave transmitter out near two?"

"You got it and I got it. That's two gots."

"The bunker then. How's the flak?"

"They still have some peashooters, but nothing too serious that I saw."

"Follow me in."

Shotgun had only a vague notion of where the target was, but how hard could it be to find a bunker? Besides, Doberman had a sixth sense about these things. Shotgun followed him around, dipping his wing into the plunge.

The busted CD cartridge slid across the floor as he poked the A-10A back toward the target. Doberman screamed something along the lines of "got it," only with a lot more curses. Shotgun followed into a thunder-burst of flak, the plane bucking like an out-of-balance washing machine. Doberman was gone and the bunker had disappeared in a cloud of cement dust.

Shifting slightly to the south for a fresh target, Shotgun found a huge gun battery almost smack dab in the middle of his HUD aiming cue. He started to pull the Hog onto it, but miscalculated somehow; it slipped out of the crosshair and then fell totally out of view. There wasn't time to screw around—flak was flying all around him. Shotgun pulled left, found a truck in his screen, and pushed the trigger. The two-second burst hit; as he continued through his banking turn he saw another gun emplacement, and fired but missed badly. There was so much antiair now he looked like he was dodging through a snowstorm.

The Hog was in exactly the kind of environment it had been designed for—hot and dirty. The pilot hulked down in his seat, cradled by the plane's titanium plates, and wheeled toward a row of antiair guns on tank-type chassis. He was so low now that had he hopped out of the plane he could have hit the ground and bounced over the cockpit.

"Turkey shoot!" Shotgun shouted, the airplane's Gatling exploding with so much energy he felt the Hog move backwards in the air. His first two shells missed low, but the rest drew a thick line through the guns, metal evaporating as the pilot worked his rudder to literally dance sideways through the sky, erasing the Russian-made weapons in one violent smear. Barrels, turrets, trucks erupted as he whipped by.

"You do not shoot at Hogs, no, sir," Shotgun told them, pulling that A-10 into a bank to come back for anything he'd missed. As he turned, the Springsteen CD tumbled from behind his seat, cracking into pieces as it flew through the cockpit.

I really ought to make those bastards pay for that, he thought to himself. But there didn't appear to be anything left to hit. Most of the ground fire had stopped, and the radar intercept complex was now a former radar intercept complex, with emphasis on "former."

Damn, Shotgun thought to himself. I was just getting going.

Out of the corner of his eye as he turned he saw a small building with a gun emplacement on its roof just to the south. The glimpse was so fleeting he couldn't tell exactly what it was, but he knew he hadn't hit it before.

What the fuck, the pilot said to himself as he pushed the Hog's nose back. I still have bullets.

This one's for the Boss.

Doberman, back on top of the clouds, took stock of his airplane as he looked for his wingman. As far as he could tell, the plane was running Dash-1, exactly according to spec. He practically bumped his helmet on the canopy glass craning back to make sure his wings and fuselage were still there.

The attack had taken a bit longer than they'd planned, but they'd taken out everything they'd come for and more. The problem now was getting home—or rather, to the tanker that would give them enough fuel to make it home.

"Devil One, we're done," he told Mongoose. "Dishes are down, we've blown up every trailer we could find, and I think Shotgun got a hot-dog wagon on the last run. Time to go home now. Copy?"

He scanned the sky as he waited for an answer, still looking for the black shadow of Shotgun's Warthog. But his wingman was still somewhere below the ever-thickening clouds.

"Devil One, do you copy?" he asked Mongoose, wondering where the flight leader was.

"Affirmative. Saddle up. We'll meet you at BakerCharles after the refuel."

"Gotcha," snapped Mongoose. He put his eyes out of the plane again, craning his neck for a sign of Shotgun. "Devil Three, this is Two. We are out of loiter time. Guns, what you doin', boy?"

The thing was, the ZSU-23-4 was a very good gun. While its radar could be distracted, even by eye the cannon threw serious lead at you. The stripped-down version had done in quite a number of pilots, dating back to Vietnam. You had to give it to the gun's Russian manufacturers—once they got something right, it stayed right.

A bit of Shotgun's bravado, though not his courage, began leaking away as the shells whipped past. He realized that the Iraqi gunner was shooting high, and that this particular set of buzzing bees were probably not going to strike him. But he guessed smaller-caliber weapons nearby would be firing any second now, and given the general hail of bullets, one or two had no choice but to hit his plane. Titanium hull or not, the Warthog was not invincible.

Still, you couldn't, on general principles, break off an attack this easily. An American taxpayer back home in Duluth had just written his congressman asking for some bang for the buck. It was Shotgun's job to deliver.

The building jumped into his gun sight. Square and squat, the cement structure was just the sort of thing that could be used as a command and control center.

Or an outhouse.

Shotgun pushed the magic button. The GAU barrels rattled around, spitting 1.6-pound shells of spent uranium—augmented by the occasional round of high explosive—from the plane's nose. The ground in front of his target opened; a trench seemed to consume the building and its gun, It was as if the Devil had decided to reach up and pull it down to Hell where it belonged.

Springsteen properly avenged, Shotgun decided discretion was the better part of valor—or however the saying went—and kicked butt in the opposite direction.

"Lost airman, Shotgun," Doberman was saying on the radio. "Yo—acknowledge me, asshole. Where the fuck are you?"

"Who are you calling lost?" Shotgun answered.

"What the hell are you firing at down there?"

"A cement outhouse."

"Yo, we're bingo."

"Damn, and I just bought this card. How come I never win?"

Winging southeast of the site, out of range of the antiair weapons, Shotgun pointed the Hog's nose upwards. He found Doberman skimming the cloud ceiling, heading back in his direction.

"Are you out of your mind?" Doberman yapped, twisting his Hog due south for the tanker.

"You have to ask?"

"Didn't you hear me calling you? Why the hell didn't you acknowledge?"

"I just did."

"We should be halfway to the refuel by now. Sometimes I think that candy goes to your brain."

"Man, you are a boring date."

Starting to feel the fatigue of the mission and the long day before, Shotgun dug into his vest for a Three Musketeers Bar. The A-10A accelerated as it hunted for its companion's wing and the route back to the tanker.

50

The clouds suddenly broke. Mongoose turned and looked through the canopy, out across the clear sky toward Dixon's plane. The second Hog was still climbing to take its position on his wing, its black-green body none the worse for its dash at the ground cannons.

From what Doberman had just told him, there was nothing left to fire the Mavericks at. Mongoose decided to hold them back, either for targets of opportunity on the way home or for a future mission. It was time to go home.

The kid had done okay, no doubt about it. Mongoose told himself he'd overreacted yesterday; he owed the kid one. He keyed the mike and gave Dixon an attaboy.

"Repeat, Devil One, you're scratchy," answered Dixon over the Fox Mike radio.

"Good work," he repeated. "Now get up front and dial us a course for that tanker."

Mongoose eased the Warthog toward the south, waiting for the younger pilot to overtake him. He couldn't help but glance at the INS, which was still stuck back in Saudi Arabia somewhere.

How hard could it be, he wondered, to stick a state-of-the-art geo-positioner in the plane? More to the point, how much could it possibly cost? Bureaucrats and congressmen were screwing with defense appropriations and contract bids and all that crap while people's butts were on the line.

But then, the Warthog had always been the Air Force's forgotten stepchild. Low, slow, and ugly, the A-10A Thunderbolt II was supposed to be a limited plane with a limited mission, a throwback unsuited to modern warfare.

This group of Hogs—and the hundred or so that had flown during Desert Storm's first hours—had proved that was all bullshit. The naysayers were wronger than wrong.

Check that. They were right about one thing. The A-10A Thunderbolt II was a kind of a throwback, a blue-collar toughguy with an old-fashioned work ethic who could get all hell pounded out of him and still come at you. Maybe the Thunderbolt moniker the brass had stuck it with—a nickname no one used—was right after all. The P-47 Thunderbolt was a kick-your-butt fighter in World War II, a hell of a ground-attack machine.

But maybe the B-17 was a better parallel. Now there was a plane that could get sawed in half and still make it back to the airfield. The comparison seemed silly until you considered that a Hog could carry twice the bomb load as the World War II bomber. The Flying Fortress was damn ugly too. But ugly pretty.

Like the Hog.

Mongoose checked over his instruments, looked carefully at the artificial horizon in front of him, and made sure his fuel was okay. They had a very good margin for error to the tanker, at least ten more minutes than he'd planned.

Dixon gave his wings a gentle wag as he set his course. At least, Mongoose assumed he did that on purpose—because of the Hog's trim controls, you never could be sure. The old joke was that if you took your hand off the stick when you were under fire, the plane would jink and jive for you.

"I got your wing," Mongoose told him. "Let's get some breakfast."

Dixon blew a wad of air out of his lungs. His heartbeat was back to normal, his adrenaline already drained. His body felt as if it were covered with cement. A hundred different muscles ached, and his eyeballs were squeezed dry.

But he'd done it. He'd fought through the panic and made it.

He was who he'd hoped to be.

Except. Except he'd lied to Major Johnson, to everybody, about what had happened yesterday.

That was the part he hadn't made up for.

Mongoose had just stretched a cramp out of his legs when the long-range radio crackled.

"Devil Flight, this is Cougar," said the AWACS controller. "Devil One, acknowledge."

"This is Devil One. Go ahead."

"Devil One, we have a situation."

The calm voice ignited a fire in Mongoose's chest. Every part of him snapped back to attention. He leaned forward unconsciously as he told the E-3 Sentry crew to fill him in.

"We have two low-level contacts on an intercept to Buddy Boy," said the controller. "We believe they are helicopters, possibly transports, possibly Mi-8's."

"Copy. You want them driven off," said Mongoose, completing the controller's thought.

"Affirmative. Sandy bingo'd a few minutes ago. First Team CAP was diverted and the backup is five minutes off."

"Give me a heading," snapped the pilot.

51

Like most of his peers, Captain Feroz Vali hated his country's president and family, blaming them for the ruinous war with Iran and the difficult situation they now found themselves in with America. And like most of his peers, Captain Vali left his politics and preferences outside the cockpit.

A good thing, since the cockpit was cramped as it was. Vali's helicopter swarmed around him, a massive flying tank. Propelled by oversized TV3-117A engines, the Mi-24D Hind could dart through the sky like an avenging angel. With four ground-attack-rocket packs mounted on its planelike wings and a four-barrel 12.7mm machine gun under its chin, the Hind was as deadly an attack helicopter as any in the world.

The problem was, the helicopter was considered so valuable by the regime that Vali had been instructed to avoid combat. And to underline that instruction, he and the Hind following behind him had been posted here, far behind the lines in western Iraq.

Vali cursed his coward's role. Yesterday, the Americans had begun their long-awaited air offensive. The official news reports said that it had been a glorious victory for Iraq, with hundreds of American planes downed. Even as he doubted the details, Vali wished for a part of the glory. Heading out on his routine training mission, he toyed with the notion of taking the chopper south toward the Saudi border, well within its range. The only thing that stopped him was the realization that the desert there was most likely empty.

Captain Vali studied the gray overcast as he steadied the helicopter toward its patrol point on the Amman-Baghdad Highway. A trainee could accomplish this make-work mission.

The voice of his weapons operator snapped in his ear.

"Captain, I have two helicopter contacts directly ahead."

Vali glanced forward toward the operator's cockpit, directly below him in the Hind's nose.

Two helicopters? As far as he knew, his two-chopper flight should be the only one in the sky for at least fifty miles.

Before he could key his mike to acknowledge, the operator added, "Captain, I believe the Intercept Station G-5 is under attack."

Vali threw his hand to the throttle, nudging the big warship toward its 180-mile-an-hour maximum speed.

God had smiled upon him.

52

Smoke furled from the GCI site, now fifteen miles away. Captain Hawkins steadied himself near the door of the big Pave Low, his teeth rattling with the whomp from the Super Jolly Green Giant's rotor. Somewhere beyond the smoke, British RAF Major Clinton Rhodes was hunkered on the ground, waiting for the big green rescue choppers to appear.

"Says he could do with a spot of tea," Sergeant Winston announced, mocking the pilot's accent. He had the British major on the UHF rescue band.

"Tell him to keep transmissions to a minimum," said the captain, just barely loud enough to be heard. "We still got a ways to go."

If you stared at it long enough, the desert sand revealed endless varieties of shades, everything from yellow to gray to black and even green. Roads blurred; buildings and vegetation merged into the terrain. You lost a sense of where you were, forgot how much danger you were really in.

Someone yelled up front. A crew member barked in reply.

"He's waving—yeah, we got him. It's him, it's him," shouted Winston, talking to the pilot and his captain simultaneously. "He sees us. Damn—we got real contacts on the radar."

Hawkins folded his fingers around the metal bar he had

steadied himself on. The Sikorsky angled herself for the approach, skimming even lower.

"Enemy helicopters are coming right for us," Winston told him. "They're moving pretty fast."

"Let's hope we move faster." Hawkins cinched his helmet and checked his rifle, narrowing his eyes for the job at hand.

53

Dixon snapped the mike button angrily. "No way I'm backing off, Major. You can't go home blind."

"I can make it back. Besides, these are just transport helicopters."

"Let me do my goddamn job."

There was no answer for a second. Mongoose really had the lead out, pushing his Hog as fast as it could go along the heading Cougar had broadcast. Dixon did a quick check of his six, his hands glued to the stick and throttle.

"Stay with me," barked the lead pilot.

Mongoose dipped his wing toward the thick overcast between them and the ground. Dixon followed, his Hog plunging through the curtain of tufts and wind drafts. The plane bucked, then shrugged it off, slipping toward the earth like an Olympic-class diver, smooth and poised. Breaking into the clear, Dixon realized for the first time that their path was dangerously close to the GCI site. Though at the moment he was out of range of any antiair left down there, he had to keep it in mind if things got complicated.

Hell, he'd have to keep a lot of things in mind. Like the fact that they would almost surely end up with less than enough jet fuel in the tanks to get home.

• • •

It took a second for Mongoose's brain to register the helicopters, and another long second after that for it to realize they were the Pave Lows.

"Those are our friendlies," he told Dixon, just in the case the kid had the same trouble.

"Roger that," squeaked the kid.

"We want positive visual IDs before we take the bogies out," Mongoose told him. The rules of engagement issued for the start of the air war were not quite that stringent, but the major didn't want to take any chances, even though the AWACS had already identified the contacts as Iraqi. "Make sure the bastard's Iraqi before you blow him away."

"Roger that."

Three or four other voices overran the rest of the transmission. Mongoose pushed the confusing babble to the side of his brain and steadied the Hog, giving the MH-53's as wide a berth as possible. If they were talking to their downed flier he didn't hear it; at this point, the only voice that was going to make it through the filter of his brain was Dixon's.

And God's. In that order.

Air-to-air tactics weren't exactly his forte. The truth was, you practiced getting away from things in a Hog, not shooting them down. But Mongoose had a rough plan mapped out in his head. Once he had the enemy choppers in his face, he'd swing around to make a rear attack with the Sidewinders; the helicopters' exhaust would give the heat-seekers a good target to aim at. Even though the AIM-9Ms were all-aspect, the old-fashioned get-him-from-behind tactics were the surest.

And hell, how hard could it be to get behind a helicopter?

He double-checked the armament panel, making sure the Sidewinders on the double-rail at station one on the left wing were armed and ready. The missiles needed to cool their noses a bit, so their heat-seeking gear would work right. Once ready and in the thick of things, the missiles would cue the pilot for launch with an audible growl that meant "shoot me, shoot me."

Assuming he could find the enemy birds. The blank sky wasn't giving them up easily.

Finally, he spotted a black furball about seven o'clock off

his left shoulder. He had just pitched his stick slightly, willing the Hog toward it, when he saw a much larger black shadow considerably higher and directly in line with the bearing the AWACS had given.

"We got one high, we got one low," he barked over the radio. "Follow me through. We want to get them from behind their three-nine."

"Roger that."

Dixon stared at the immense black beetle growing in the bottom left corner of his windscreen. That was no utility chopper out on a picnic run. It was immense, with stubby wings projecting toward the ground like muscled shoulders. And the damn thing was moving.

Big-time Hind, he thought; he wasn't sure what model. It would—or at least could—have air-to-air.

Dixon's Sidewinders had been on long enough for the heat-seeking gear in their noses to cool down, and they were just approaching their maximum range. But the major was right—attacking from behind was the best strategy. The missiles would home in on the heat signature from the engine exhaust like a magnet seeking true north.

The helicopters weren't going to make it easy. Something sparked from the wing of the angry bug as it suddenly whipped out of Dixon's view.

54

Doberman didn't need a calculator to know they didn't have anywhere near enough jet fuel to double back and help Mongoose and Dixon. In fact, he suspected Mongoose and Dixon would run themselves dry even if they found the Iraqis and crashed them in record time.

Which made it all the harder to leave them. But it was the only thing to do.

Shotgun concurred. "I say we kick butt on the refuel, then go find them."

"You read my mind."

"Damn, I'd like a piece of that," moaned Shotgun. "Air-to-air Hog action. It's what I'm talking about."

Doberman decided to make absolutely certain the AWACS people knew how low Mongoose and Dixon were going to be when they finished their job.

"Cougar, this is Devil Two. Request that you expedite a tanker contact for Devil One and Devil Four. They're beyond bingo."

It took a while for the E-3 Sentry to respond.

"Affirmative. We will try to assist any way we can." The controller paused, then added, "How's your fuel situation?"

"We should be at Texaco in ten," Doberman said. Even with all the stops out, the estimate of the time it would take to reach the tanker was wildly optimistic.

"Affirmative. Don't worry about your buddies; we have some CAP coming up from the south to assist. Should arrive in three or four minutes."

"Appreciate that," he answered.

"Hey," barked Shotgun after the transmission with the AWACS was complete. "How come it's Texaco? Why not Sunoco? My cousin works for Sunoco."

"I didn't know you were related to a suit."

"What suit? He makes change in a little booth on the Jersey shore. You're ever around Cape May, tell him I sent you. He'll give you some free window-wash."

"Can't wait."

55

"They're firing at the choppers, not us."

Dixon had already pulled the Hog down and hit the chaff and flares before Mongoose's words sank in. Gravity and momentum whacked him broadside as he tried to yank the plane back onto the intercept course. The leading-edge wing slats groaned as the Hog literally slid sideways, engines whining. The pilot felt as if he were being stabbed in the chest as he worked the stick and rudders a hundred feet off the ground. Something—the missile that had been launched, one of the helicopters, maybe even an angel—whizzed by the canopy.

"You go high, I'll go low," said Mongoose, unaware that Dixon's position had changed so radically.

Mongoose didn't wait for the kid to acknowledge as he angled after the darting grasshopper. He knew now that his opponent was hardly a utility chopper. Iraq had something like forty of the Mil M-24 Hind helicopter gunships, extremely potent warbirds that combined the best features of the American Apache with the Blackhawk. Like the Apache, it was primarily a ground-attack weapon, but its nose-mounted Gatling cannon was not to be taken lightly by anybody, Warthog included.

Mongoose angled upwards, taking the Hog into a banking

turn toward the helicopter's vulnerable rear as he approached. But the chopper had been waiting for his move, and pushed to get inside him. He realized it too late to spin back sharply enough to get a firing solution. That left him further away as the chopper broke for all it was worth, running about two inches off the ground.

He lost it in the confusion. Mongoose went into a wide bank and started sweating—maybe it was only a helicopter, but that didn't mean it couldn't shoot him down if it was in the right position.

The pilot whirled his head around, eyes flailing the empty sky. Cursing, he yanked back in the other direction, then saw the black cricket kicking dust north. It fluttered through the diamond aiming cue on his HUD screen as he worked to bring his adrenaline—and the plane—back under control.

The AIM-9 growled gently at him, telling him it thought it could make the shot from here. He hesitated a second, then pushed the button.

Dixon found himself swimming in the cockpit, as if trying to get up from the bottom of a very deep lake. His head pressed back against the seat so hard it felt as if it would break through.

Oxygen gulped down his throat, his heart galloped. He was losing it again.

Look at the throttle, Knowlington had told him.

It was stupid advice. Take your eyes off the windscreen where they belonged, and look at the throttle? Maybe back in Vietnam they did that kind of thing, but not here. He might just as well get out of the plane and kick the tires.

Gravity was an immense piano, smashing down from twenty stories. His maneuvers robbed his brain cells of oxygen, robbed him of sensation. He couldn't think, couldn't see, couldn't fly.

Look at the goddamn throttle, he told himself.

What the hell.

Dixon wrenched his head to the left, forced his eyes downward, forced a slower breath into his lungs, saw the handle pushed all the way to max.

Okay, okay, okay, he said, pulling his head back to the front of the plane, focusing on the HUD. Start from scratch. Slow down.

Altitude 1250 feet, climbing.

Okay, okay, okay, he told himself, forcing an excruciatingly long exhale from his lungs. You don't have to be calm, just in control.

Okay, okay, okay, he told himself. Level off. Check your heading. Find the bastard.

Okay, okay, okay—the Hind darted across the upper right quadrant of his screen, gun flailing at the Pave Lows and the pilot they'd come to save.

"Fire Fox Two," said Mongoose, announcing the heat-seeking missile shot as the Sidewinder slipped off his wingtip. But even as the unfamiliar words left his mouth, the pilot realized that no matter what the missile thought, he'd fired from too great a range and angle to guarantee a hit. The helicopter was already whipping hard to the east, letting off a succession of flares to confuse the heat-seeker.

It didn't matter now. His job was to protect the Pave Lows, not collect a kill. Whether the missile got it or not, that Hind was no longer a treat. Mongoose swung back to help Dixon crash the other bird.

He saw the rescue helicopters first; both were on the desert floor dead ahead. The Hind materialized on his left, cannon smoking as it roared into the middle of his screen.

The Sidewinder growled. Mongoose punched the button, felt it kick off, and in the same instant saw Dixon cut across from the right toward the Iraqi, crossing directly for the path the AIM-9 would take.

56

The Iraqi pilot cursed as the cannon beneath the helicopter's nose began to rumble. His gunner had begun firing much too soon.

No matter. The distance between himself and the two American helicopters was closing rapidly. It was only a matter of ten or fifteen seconds.

The appearance of the American planes had caused him only a second's hesitation. He couldn't blame his companion in the second Hind for turning off; those were, after all, their orders.

But it was something Captain Vali would never do. The two American planes had flown past, obviously trying for a better position for attack. They were odd planes, nearly black with forked tails and strangely placed engines. He guessed that they had decided to concentrate on the other helicopter first, and would soon be coming for him.

He had several evasive maneuvers planned. But he would wait until he had accomplished his first mission—the enemy helicopters. Galloping forward, he heard his gunner shouting something in his com set, and realized the cannon was whirling around on its axis toward another target.

57

The helicopter's slow speed crossed him up. Dixon misjudged his approach and lost any possibility of a shot, not even with his cannon. As he pulled off he saw Mongoose coming out of the northwest; some inexplicable pilot's sense made him roll the Hog hard to the right even as the launch warning sparked the radio.

The indium-antimonide in the guidance section of the AIM-9M Mongoose had fired had its heart set on the Hind. Even so, the proximity of Dixon's exhaust was so tempting that for a half second the little brain couldn't decide what to do.

In that half second, two things happened: The targeted Hind shot off flares and changed course momentarily, away from the Pave Lows. And Dixon rolled the Hog and his IR signature away from the missile.

The Sidewinder's proximity fuse circuitry got so confused that it decided it had missed its target and therefore ought to detonate anyway.

Had they been close enough, the fragments would have done serious damage to a typical, unarmored airframe. In this case, however, they were just so much more shrapnel littering the air as Dixon recovered from his swooping roll and swung for the chopper. The Hind splashed out some bullets in his direction, then cranked back toward the Pave Lows, guns blazing.

Throttle to the firewall, the Hog moved nearly twice as fast as the Hind; the pilot was nearly in front of the helicopter before realizing where the hell he was. He pulled hard left, knocking the Iraqi off his course but taking a wing's worth of 12.7mm shells for his persistence.

Orbiting quickly, Dixon took as slow a breath as he dared, steadying his hand on the stick, glancing at the weapons panel though he knew the cannon was ready. This time he didn't need Knowlington's advice—he felt the stick in his grip, felt the plane around him, saw the Hind flashing to the right, and knew that it would fall into the Hog's crosshairs in a half second.

There is no precise formula for becoming a combat pilot, no clear line to be crossed. A green newbie passes a series of initiations that guarantee nothing and yet are more critical than oxygen. It happens in various ways at various times, sometimes noticeably, most often not.

For Lieutenant William James "BJ" Dixon, it happened the second he pressed his finger on the red trigger, lighting the A-10A's GAU-8/A Avenger cannon, and watched as the stream of 30mm slugs tore the helicopter in front of him to pieces.

58

Captain Hawkins shoved the British pilot to the ground as the fireball erupted less than a hundred yards from them. Oil, metal, and blood rained through the air, the Hind spewing its guts as it tumbled into the desert, the biggest chunk of the wreck just clearing the second Pave Low, squatting on the ground thirty yards beyond Hawkins's craft.

"Go, let's go!" he screamed, spitting sand from his mouth. He clawed the back of the pilot's flight suit, lifting and dragging him to the door of the waiting chopper. A crewman helped him pitch the major in head-first.

Sergeant Winston and one of the other squad members crawled over him. The inside of the giant chopper echoed with shouts. Hawkins felt the floor move beneath his stomach. He rolled, smacking his arm against something very hard as the MH-53 lifted off.

"Rhodes, you okay?" he asked the British pilot as he got to his knees.

"Bloody hell," said the pilot, looking up from the floor. "I do believe I've lost my lucky pen."

The Special Forces squad and nearby crew members exploded with laughter. Hawkins was practically blinking away tears as he scanned the compartment, making sure everyone had gotten back safely.

"We're all here, sir," Winston said with a smirk. "Cut it a

bit close, though. Good thing the Iraqi was off with that first round of missiles or we'd be walking."

While RAF Major Rhodes searched his various pockets for the pen, Hawkins patted his own uniform down—he wasn't entirely convinced he'd made it back intact.

He had. As had the rest of his team.

"Kind of close, huh, Captain?" Winston asked. "Our friends took their time," he added, jerking his finger toward the window. The two A-10As were disappearing in the distance.

"Were those Thunderbolts?" Rhodes asked.

"Warthogs," said Winston. "Nasty mothers."

"Quite," said the Brit approvingly. "But bloody ugly."

"I don't know," said Hawkins. "They looked kind of pretty to me. Welcome aboard, Major. You want some tea? It'll be cold by now, but it is Earl Grey."

PART FOUR

NO PLACE LIKE HOME 'DROME

59

Even though congratulations were still crackling across the radio, the euphoria of the battle faded as Mongoose took stock of their fuel situation. He unfolded his map across his lap, plotting how far they could nurse the fumes they had left. It wasn't pretty—even flying directly south, on minimal power and at dangerously low altitude, they would miss the border by a good five miles.

"Cougar, this is Devil One. Have to advise you of a fuel emergency," he told the AWACS, unsure of how precise to be—there was always a possibility the Iraqis could be listening and decide to send a welcoming committee.

"Affirmative," said the E-3 controller. "We're aware of your situation. We need you to fly to new coordinates—hold on just a second while we fix the math. My buddy here can't count higher than ten."

The joke sounded more than a bit hollow. Before Mongoose could ask what was going on, the controller shot them a heading that took them nearly as far east as south—further inside Iraq.

"Dixon, did you copy that?" Mongoose asked.

"Yeah, I don't get it either," said the kid.

Mongoose could feel a bubble of anger starting to rise in his chest. He told himself to calm down—the last thing he needed was to go ballistic right now. But it was a hell of a time for a screwup.

"Cougar, this is Devil One. Please recheck your numbers."

"Our math's fine," snapped the controller. "Just proceed."

"You're sending me to a tanker?"

"That's affirmative."

"You're aware where that takes me?"

"Better than you."

He got Dixon on the squadron's private—or semiprivate, as experience had shown—frequency, and asked his opinion.

"You got me, Major," said the pilot. "They repeated the numbers twice."

"Okay. Let's give it a shot. If we dump the Mavericks we'll give ourselves a bit more leeway."

"You read my mind."

Mongoose half-believed they had stumbled into an elaborate Iraqi plot until a dozen planes—all friendlies—appeared in the sky directly in front of them. A motley assortment of allied craft—a flight of F-15 interceptors, at least three F-16 Vipers, a British Tornado, and a Phantom Wild Weasel—had been rounded up to provide a posse for a KC-135, lumbering deep into Iraqi territory for the emergency refueling. There was a high CAP and a low CAP and a mid CAP, a pair of close escorts and a chase plane and an AH-130 Spectre gunship tagging along for good measure.

"Hey, you the guys that crashed the chopper?" asked one of the Eagle pilots.

"My partner got the kill," said Mongoose. As the words came out of his mouth, he realized he felt a bit like a proud papa. "Mine got away."

"Shit, you're gonna put us out of work," joked the F-15 pilot.

"You sure you shot him down, or did you just scare the hell out of him with that plane?" said another.

"Devil One, this is your milk cow speaking. How bad is your fuel situation?"

Mongoose glanced at the fuel gauge. "I got seven minutes. Devil Four's got eleven and a half. That right, BJ?"

"Make it twelve."

Mongoose could almost hear the tanker pilot whistling to himself. The lumbering jet—outwardly similar to a civilian 707—swung into an orbit toward them, still struggling to get low and slow. The pilots quickly decided Mongoose would grab a few pounds of fuel, then back off and let the kid tank before topping off.

In theory, it was a piece of cake. But both men were tired as hell, Mongoose especially. His arms and legs dragged at the controls as he pushed the Hog toward the director lights on the tanker belly. He'd probably done a thousand refuels over the years, but none this tight.

It wasn't his fuel he was worried about, it was Dixon's. If he took too long, his wingman's plane would turn into a titanium-hulled glider.

Mongoose nudged everything out of his mind as he pushed his fighter toward the wing-tipped nozzle protruding from the tanker's rear end. The line between his body and the plane blurred; he saw the boom and willed it into the port on his nose, nostrils flaring as the precious fuel began spitting into the thirsty Hog.

"I want high-test," he told the boom operator.

The crew member gave him a thumbs-up through the rear window.

Mongoose took a few hundred pounds—the Hog held ten thousand—before abruptly pulling downward to break the connection. Fuel sprayed over his fuselage, as if he were flying beneath Niagara Falls.

"All yours, BJ," he said, careful to keep his voice cold and calm, as if the two Hogs were out on a training mission.

Dixon had maybe three minutes of fuel left. Mongoose thought he was moving in tentatively, and had to fight the temptation to tell him to kick butt. At this point, there was nothing he could say that would help.

As it slid in under the tanker's tail, the nose of the hungry Hog suddenly bucked downward. The plane fluttered in the air, wings trembling. Finally, the front end lifted back toward the refueling boom.

The straw rammed home. Dixon looked over at Mongoose and gave him a wave and a thumbs-up.

Mongoose waved back, then snapped a salute as sharp and crisp as possible in the cramped office of a Hog.

60

The adrenaline from the helicopter tangle and refuel kept Dixon's heart pounding until they had King Fahd's long, gorgeous runway in sight. It was only as he took his place in the landing queue that Dixon's brain began reprocessing what had happened—not only this morning, but yesterday.

He had vindicated his flying by shooting down the helicopter; he'd overcome his fear—it was best to admit what it was, use the F word—and hung tough under fire. If a pilot had been shot down because of his screwup, at least he had helped rescue him. He'd made it right.

But something else remained to be done. Something scarier, and more important.

He had to admit he'd lied about what had happened, and face the consequences.

And so when they finished debriefing the flight in Cineplex, Dixon walked over to Mongoose and asked to talk to him alone.

The major got a funny look on his face. "Listen, kid, I know I was hard on you yesterday," he said. "Maybe too hard. Don't take it personally, okay? We're all feeling our way a bit, even me. All right?"

"Yeah, but, um, I really have to talk to you about something. Maybe the colonel too."

"Knowlington?"

Dixon nodded. Mongoose, confused, led him down the hall to the colonel's office, where Knowlington was talking to Captain Wong loudly enough to be heard in the hallway.

It wasn't an entirely pleasant conversation.

"You can pull whatever strings you think you have, you're here for the duration," Knowlington was saying. "Frankly, we can use a guy like you. You aren't just yanking my chain here, are you, Wong? I can never tell when you're bullshitting me."

"I assure you, Colonel, this is very serious."

Knowlington started laughing. "You son of a bitch. You son of a bitch. You're just busting my balls, aren't you? You bastard you. You had me going. Goddamn."

Mongoose glanced over at Dixon with a confused smile, then knocked on the door.

"Come," said Knowlington, still laughing.

The colonel got up as soon as he saw Dixon. "Kick-ass work, BJ. Kick-ass. We heard about two seconds after the Iraqi crashed. Three generals have called to tell me the media is on its way. You're a goddamn hero, kid." He pounded his shoulder. "Feels weird, huh?"

"I was just, uh, the helicopter was in my sights and I fired, sir."

"Yeah, believe me, I know. You just did what came natural, right? Don't worry about it. People want to make you a hero, don't argue with them. Relax and enjoy it. I'll tell you something, BJ, we need good stories like this. Believe me, you're doing everybody a favor, even if it hurts. I want you to head over to the host squadron commander's office. Couple of people from CNN and some lady from PBS waiting for you. Word travels fast."

Dixon nodded and glanced at Wong, who was still sitting in the chair.

"One thing I want to set straight," added the colonel. "That pilot you guys helped rescue says he had engine trouble up near Musail. Plane wasn't hit, at least not that he could tell. So your raid on the GCI site the day before had no bearing on him. We didn't cause him to get shot down."

"Really?" For just an instant, Dixon considered not telling them at all.

"Colonel, do you mind if the lieutenant and I had a private conversation with you?" said Mongoose. There was a certain official twist to the inflection of the words that Knowlington noted with his eyes.

"Excuse us, will you, Wong?"

"But—"

"Seriously, I have a lot of work to do this morning. You finish your report on the missile?"

"Well, I—it does appear to have been an SA-16, though we know that's impossible."

Knowlington laughed as if Wong had made the joke of the year. "You crack me up. Go on, get out of here. Tell me if you need me to sign anything. Impossible, Jesus."

"What was that all about?" Mongoose asked as he closed the door behind the perplexed Wong. There were only two chairs in the small office; all three men remained standing.

"Oh, nothing. He's just a world-class ball-buster," explained Knowlington.

"Seemed serious to me."

"Yeah, better watch out—he's exactly the kind of guy who kills you with practical jokes when things get too tense. I knew a guy like that, somehow convinced half the squadron to show up naked for a visiting general." Knowlington's expression grew more serious. "So what's up, guys?"

"I lied, sir."

The two men stared at him as the words gushed from his mouth. "I dropped my CBUs blind yesterday, without a target."

Mongoose's face turned ashen. Knowlington's looked grim, but he nodded. "What happened exactly?"

"I was so confused after I fired the last Maverick—well, confused isn't the word. I got panicked. With the flak, and with everything going crazy, I froze. I flew away from the site in a daze. Finally I pickled the cluster bombs and got the hell out of there. I just ran away."

Dixon made it clear that he had dropped the bombs over what he knew now was empty desert—and that he had then lied about it. Mongoose slipped back into the nearby chair as the story finally ran out.

"Okay," said Knowlington somberly. "Go on over and see those media people. Tell them about the helicopter."

Dixon nodded. His confession had been cathartic, but he wasn't necessarily looking forward to what would happen next.

"Goddamn," said Mongoose as soon as the lieutenant had left. "Goddamn. He fucking lied to me."

Knowlington nodded. It was one thing for the kid to chicken out—he'd guessed something close to that had happened, after all. But not giving up the entire story when he'd had the chance—when Knowlington had asked him point-blank—was unforgivable.

"What are we going to do?" Mongoose asked.

"Good question. CNN started talking about the helicopter shootdown ten minutes after it happened."

"What difference does that make?"

Knowlington smirked. Sometimes his DO could be very naive. "Brass is in serious search of heroes. Not that I blame them. They don't want this to be Vietnam. The media will eat it up. And there are plenty of A-10ers floating around who'll use this to defend the plane against the pointy-nose mafia. Not that I blame them."

"What kind of story is it going to be when they find out the hero's a coward?"

Knowlington shook his head.

"Yeah," said Mongoose. "What the hell do we do?"

"I'm going to have to think about it. When's he supposed to fly again?"

"Saturday, I think. I'd have to check at this point. I'm a little tired." The major tightened his hand into a fist. "I'll tell you, my first instinct—"

"That isn't going to get us anywhere, Goose," said Knowlington.

The colonel closed the door behind Mongoose. He sat at his desk, staring at the blank wall for a minute. Finally his rage exploded, and he smashed his arm down against the desktop so hard it stung.

In the kid's defense, he had come to them and told them what happened. If he hadn't, it was doubtful they would ever have found out.

Dropping the CBUs blind—not good, but not the worst thing he could have done.

Getting lost? Less than optimum, but again, it wasn't as if he had flown to Jordan and sat out the war.

Quite frankly, Knowlington couldn't hold any of what happened over the site the first day against him; the colonel understood fear quite well. And the kid had gotten through it. Knowlington knew enough about people to realize it wasn't going to happen again, not now.

But the issue was trust. Willfully misleading a superior officer. Lying. Even Knowlington, as far from a by-the-book guy as there was, couldn't allow that to slip by.

In his opinion, it deserved serious disciplinary action.

Which would piss a hell of a lot of people off. And with the media hanging around, someone was going to get a very black eye.

Knowlington didn't care how he would look. But he couldn't, wouldn't, let the Air Force look bad. Not in this war. Never again.

But how would the Air Force survive if pilots lied about what happened during their missions?

He slammed his fist down on the desk again, this time so hard it felt as if he broke it.

61

"I say we call him Blaze, because he blazed the chopper."

"How about Chopper? That's different."

"Blaze is better," insisted Shotgun. He and Doberman were sitting in Shotgun's tent, alternately teasing Dixon and congratulating him. Shotgun had broken open his daily Fed Ex Happy Meal, and Doberman had brought along a bottle of shampoo, which had proven to contain Jack Daniels bourbon.

The older pilots had napped after their flight and were raring to party. Dixon, on the other hand, had spent the past eight or nine hours telling camera crews and reporters— along with several dozen Air Force officers and enlisted personnel—how the Iraqi helicopter had gone bye-bye. His eyelids felt heavier than a pair of BLU-109B 2,250-pound bombs.

"Air War God, that's it," snorted Doberman, sipping the whiskey.

"Just God," said Shotgun. "How's that for a call sign? This is God talking."

The two men laughed like schoolkids watching a Three Stooges movie.

Since telling Knowlington and Johnson what had happened on the first mission, Dixon hadn't said anything to anyone else. He wasn't keeping it a secret necessarily; everybody would know sooner or later anyway. But he just didn't want to deal with telling people on top of everything else.

Except for Doberman. He'd been his wingmate, his flight leader, and he owed him an apology. His screwup could have killed him.

It was better to do that sooner rather than later. That was why he was here, rather than sleeping; he'd spent the last ten minutes or so getting ribbed, hoping eventually to get Doberman alone so he could apologize. He wanted to tell the captain himself before he heard about it from anyone else.

"What do you think, kid?" Shotgun asked. "You want God or Blaze?"

"What's wrong with BJ?" asked Dixon.

Shotgun laughed. "Too suburban. Preppy, you know. Fuckin' Hog pilot's got to have a good name, that's what I'm talking about."

"My mom used to call me BJ."

Doberman and Shotgun burst out laughing.

"I'm serious."

"We know you're serious, kid," said Doberman. "Have a drink."

"I'm afraid I'm going to fall asleep."

"So?" asked Doberman.

"How about Grunt?" said Shotgun. "Now there is a Hog name. Grunt. Yeah, I like that."

"BJ."

"Hey, okay," said Doberman, holding up his glass in a toast. "BJ it is. For your mom."

"It's not a joke."

"I'm serious. BJ."

"Nah. That ain't gonna do it." Shotgun got up. "I got to take a leak. Hold my place."

Finally alone with Glenon, Dixon exhaled deeply and turned to him. "Captain, I got to tell you something. You're gonna hate me, but I got to tell you something."

The word "Captain" struck Doberman like an iceball in the back of the head. He'd had just enough of the bourbon to feel comfortably mellow, but the next words from the pilot sobered him immediately.

"I lied to you about yesterday," said Dixon. "I lied to everybody."

Doberman poured himself another shot as Dixon slowly detailed what had happened. He sipped this one, not so much listening to the younger man's words as absorbing them.

It was a damn hard thing to admit you had been a coward, Doberman thought. Damn hard.

Then again, the kid had redeemed himself today. Shit, not too many guys got that chance, not with so much style.

Now that was luck, wasn't it?

Doberman curled his toe in his boot, feeling the penny. He'd plopped it into his sock for his nap, then decided to keep it there.

Luck, skill—who knew what part either played in the equation? One thing he did know, though—he was holding on to the damn penny. You couldn't be too certain of anything.

"You're being pretty hard on yourself. It wasn't your fault I got hit with the triple-A," Doberman told Dixon when the pilot stopped talking. "They aimed at me because I was the first one through, and I just happened to hit the route where all the guns were. You were lucky they didn't nail you too."

"I was scared. Nothing like that's ever happened to me. Not like that."

Doberman nodded. "You got through it. And you're past it. Hell, you're a hero now."

"But I lied to the colonel. I just ditched the bombs and ran."

Doberman scratched his chin. True enough, the kid did remind him of his younger brother. There was a physical resemblance, and hell if he didn't have the same sincere crap in his voice. Not made up either.

"Sooner or later, we all do things we're ashamed of," said Doberman. "It's what happens next that matters." He got up from the chair. "Hey, let's go get something to eat. I never really liked Big Macs, to tell you the truth."

62

Forty-five minutes later, Colonel Knowlington found Dixon walking toward his tent. He had just finished eating with Shotgun and Doberman.

"Come with me, Lieutenant," he snapped, leading him down a short alleyway not far from the hangars where they could be alone. The light cast a yellow pall over the lieutenant's face; he was struggling to keep his eyes open, and his cheeks sagged with fatigue.

"I've read through the reports on your mission, and talked to Major Johnson. There doesn't seem to be any basis for bringing formal charges against you, at least none that are likely to be upheld," said Knowlington. "The major concurs."

The words about formal charges sparked Dixon's eyes, as Knowlington knew they would.

"That doesn't mean I condone what you did. You can't leave things out, not like that. Not when people's lives are depending on you. It may seem trivial, but everything is connected, usually in ways we don't know about until it's too late."

The young man nodded.

"When I ask a question, I expect a full and complete answer. No bullshit. That's the bottom line with me. You understand?"

"I fucked up, sir. I know you gave me the chance and I blew it."

"Understand me, it's not about getting scared. Everybody gets scared. But we can't afford people lying about it."

"I know."

"Excuse me, not lying, just not filling in the blanks."

"Same thing."

"You're damn lucky it's not," said Knowlington. He blew air through his teeth.

The reality was, you could interpret what the kid said during the debrief as a pretty full and accurate account; he said he had lost track of where he was and that he did not think the bombs had hit their targets. Technically, that agreed with what Dixon had said later, though the colonel wasn't particularly fond of technicalities.

But Dixon had also said he had screwed up the Mavericks; the evidence showed he did not. It was still possible that he was just being harder than hell on himself because he'd been afraid.

"You're going to be on administrative duty for a while," said the colonel. "You'll rotate into Riyadh as an assistant to the fighter operations officer."

"Assistant?"

"It's a new position. Very temporary."

"Yes, sir."

"The matter is closed."

"Yes, sir."

Knowlington hesitated. They'd all seen something in this kid during his first days training. And they'd been right too—his tangle with the chopper proved it.

And maybe his coming clean about panicking proved it too. Really, it was more than you could expect from most men, facing up to the worst about yourself.

How long had it taken Knowlington to do that? Even now he felt the familiar ache in his throat, the incessant urge for just one tiny, meaningless drink.

"Mongoose told me he ordered you to return home when he went back for the chopper," added the colonel.

"I was his wingman," said Dixon. "I couldn't desert him. Besides, I felt like I had to make things right."

"Well, for what it's worth, I'm proud of you for hanging in there." Knowlington managed a smile. "You came around and did the right thing. You're a good pilot, BJ. You have talent. When you get back in the cockpit, don't blow it."

"I won't, sir."

"Good work on the Hind. Fire Fox Hog, huh?"

"Actually, sir, I used my cannon."

Knowlington's smile came easier this time. Probably for the rest of his life, the kid would be accurate to a fault—not a horrible character flaw to have, all things considered. "You have to be at Riyadh at 0800," he told him. "Don't be late."

Dixon cupped his face in his hands as Knowlington walked away.

Skull Knowlington was proud of him. Vietnam war ace Colonel Michael Knowlington, with more medals than a museum, had just called him a good pilot.

Bailed his fanny out of the fire too, something he didn't deserve.

But damn. Skull Knowlington had said he was proud of him.

Dixon made a fist and swirled his body around in celebration—nearly smashing Tech Sergeant Rosen as she walked by.

"Lieutenant?"

"I just—wow, I'm sorry," said Dixon.

"Congratulations on shooting down that helicopter." Rosen put her hands on her hips and cocked her head to one side. "We're all proud of you."

"I couldn't have done it without you. All of you, I mean," he managed, still flustered. "You guys, I mean, you all did a hell of a job on that plane."

"What'd you expect?"

A pause followed that was more awkward than the one after his punch.

"Maybe, uh, maybe I'll be seeing you around," said the pilot.

Rosen laughed, but there was a twinge of nervousness in her voice. "Probably."

"I got to go to Riyadh tomorrow."

"More hero stuff, huh? Well, don't let it go to your head."

"I won't. I mean—wait!" he shouted as she started to walk away.

Surprised, she turned back.

"Thanks, really," he told her, stepping forward to kiss her on the cheek.

At least, he aimed for the cheek. She turned and met him with her lips.

"You're welcome," she said, slipping away.

A few minutes later, back in his tent, Dixon took out Lance Corporal Simmons's letter and read it again. Then he fished out his pad and a pen. He wanted to tell the old Marine how right he was.

But he couldn't. He tried a few times, starting sentences only to stop and rip up the page.

He wanted the corporal to know that he'd inspired him, that his lesson had maybe helped save his life, or at least his career. But it was too hard to put into words. Finally, he read the letter one more time, then slipped it back into its envelope and returned it to the pile for someone else to answer.

63

Exhausted even though he'd had a nap earlier, Mongoose sat back on his cot, one more duty to perform before calling it a day. For maybe the first time in his career, he was actually glad he wasn't flying tomorrow. He felt old and achy, his legs especially. Even the plastic fountain pen in his hand felt heavy, though that was somehow reassuring.

Dear Kathy:

> *Hell of a day today. My wingman shot down a helicopter. I nearly waxed him by mistake. But it turned out all right.*

He paused, unsure whether to keep those last two sentences or not. His wife might misinterpret them, think he was in danger.

It wasn't a misinterpretation. But he didn't want to reinforce it.

He'd told Knowlington to go easy on the kid. In fact, he'd told the colonel to forget it. He'd had to argue actually.

Knowlington was a funny guy. He could make you think he didn't give a shit about a lot of things, starting with military protocol, but when it came to flying and fighting, he was hard-line. He didn't like anything less than one-hundred-percent verifiable truth. He hadn't really wanted to cut Dixon any slack, despite all of Mongoose's arguments.

Until yesterday, Mongoose had resented Knowlington, figuring he was a washed-up drunk. But he knew now he was wrong about that. His interminable stories were a pain in the ass, but they did have a point. And in the end, he too had decided the kid deserved a break.

They both knew Dixon was going to be all right. That was the one thing the colonel couldn't argue with. The kid had had to get through that first mission, the first real gut-check under fire.

Everybody had to.

Hell, he wasn't even mad at Dixon anymore. Mongoose had thought about it a lot. When Knowlington finally hauled the kid's butt back from Riyadh—he figured it would take a few days, a week at most—Mongoose would stick his finger in the lieutenant's chest and tell him how bad he would pound the shit out of him if he ever lied to him again. Never mind that he was giving up about half a foot and thirty pounds of what looked to be sheer muscle.

Then he'd slap the kid on the back and buy him a near-beer.

Mongoose ripped the page out of the pad and started again.

Dear Kathy:

Hell of a day today. Wingman shot down a helicopter. You probably saw it on the news. He's just a kid, at least he was until this morning.

I keep looking for camels, but I don't see any. Other guys tell me they're all over the place. Maybe they're hiding from me. I guarantee I'm going to get a ride on one before long. I promise to wear my helmet.

Miss you and Robby a lot. Give him a kiss for me.

I'll write tomorrow.

Love
Jimmy

kisses and hugs
kiss Robby for me

He went wild with his x's and o's, then tore off the sheet and folded it carefully, placing it in its envelope. He thought maybe he'd gotten too sentimental, decided what the hell. Then Major James Johnson drew a long breath, and began to write his second letter home, the one he hoped his wife would never get.

An Historical Note

The destruction of the Iraqi ground intercept stations on the first day of the Gulf air war by the A-10As was one of many great achievements of Desert Storm. As indicated here, the missions were far beyond the Warthogs' paper specs, but not the planes' or pilots' capabilities. All planes returned unharmed.

A-10A pilots are credited with shooting down two helicopters during the war, an Mi-8 Hip and what is believed to have been a Bo 105, a light multi-role helicopter. The second helicopter was so badly damaged that it couldn't be positively identified.

While this book was inspired by actual events in the Gulf War, it should be emphasized that none of the people are based in any way on real people. A great deal of what might be termed poetic license has been employed, starting with the creation of the Devils Squadron and Hog Heaven. In addition, locations such as the Depot and Cineplex are entirely fictional, as are any actions contrary to proper Air Force procedure and military law and/or regulations.

The Hog, of course, is real. If anything, actual A-10A Thunderbolt II Warthogs—and their pilots and crews—are tougher and more capable than fiction can depict.